Brunch with Bob and Mario was great, as always. As a bar owner and bar manager, respectively, they always have an endless string of stories and we all laughed a lot—something I, for one, definitely needed.

But eventually, as all conversations at the time tended to do, talk turned to AIDS and the countless rumors and speculations circulating through the bars.

"There's a new one going around that's really unbelievable," Mario said. "I don't know if Bob's heard it, but I'd guess so."

"What's that?" I asked.

"That someone is going around deliberately spreading AIDS."

Bob nodded.

"Yeah, I've heard it, too."

I shook my head. "How can people believe that shit?"

Mario looked at me. "I thought that, too, until I was talking with one of my regulars who had just lost his best friend. The friend had told him he got it from a really butch guy who refused to use a condom, and after they'd finished and the guy was leaving, he stopped at the door and casually said, 'Oh, and I've got gay cancer. Welcome to the club.' And he left. The friend thought it was just a really cruel joke, but then he got sick."

THE DICK HARDESTY MYSTERY SERIES

The Ninth Man, 2001, GLB Publishers
The Butcher's Son, 2001, GLB Publishers
The Bar Watcher, 2002, GLB Publishers
The Hired Man, 2002, GLB Publishers
The Good Cop, 2002, GLB Publishers
The Bottle Ghosts, 2003, GLB Publishers.
The Dirt Peddler, 2003, GLB Publishers.
The Role Players, 2004, GLB Publishers.
The Popsicle Tree, 2005. GLB Publishers
The Paper Mirror, 2005, GLB Publishers

THE DREAM ENDER

A Dick Hardesty Mystery

To Betty —
For her unflagging support
+ friendship

BY

Dorien Grey

DORIEN GREY

ZUMAYA BOUNDLESS   AUSTIN TX

2007

THE DREAM ENDER
© 2007 by Dorien Grey

ISBN 13: 978-1-934135-62-4
ISBN 10: 1-934135-62-3

Cover art and design by Martine Jardin

Library of Congress Cataloging-in-Publication Data

Grey, Dorien.
  The dream ender : a Dick Hardesty mystery / by Dorien Grey.
     p. cm.
  ISBN-13: 978-1-934135-62-4 (alk. paper)
  ISBN-10: 1-934135-62-3 (alk. paper)
  1. Hardesty, Dick (Fictitious character)--Fiction. 2. Private investigators--Fiction. 3. Construction workers--Crimes against--Fiction. 4. Motorcyclists--Fiction. 5. Gay men--Fiction. I. Title.
  PS3557.R48165D74 2007
  813'.54--dc22
                    2007020103

To those who were lost, and those who fought to save them.

Dreams define humanity. They give us hope and point us to the future. They are our birthright, and they affect not only us but those we love and who love us.

Some dreams are universal and live on from generation to generation, but an individual's dreams most often die with the dreamer. Death and the end of dreams is the price we must eventually pay for the gift of life.

Because of our need to understand that which cannot be understood, we often refer to death in human terms by capitalizing the word and giving him a number of appellations—primarily, The Grim Reaper, which creates a vivid image of both Death and his purpose. The Reaper has a variety of scythes at his disposal for ending dreams, and illness has always been one of the sharpest and most dreaded. And when AIDS appeared in the mid-1970s, the Reaper strode through the gay community, ending the lives and dreams of tens of thousands of gay men and sending waves of helplessness and fear through us all.

Because we could not depend on our government to protect us, we tried to protect ourselves by establishing an unwritten code of ethics to which we were honorbound to adhere. Those who were aware they had contracted the disease were obligated by our common humanity to inform prospective partners of the risk. Most did, but incredibly, a few who knew they were sick chose to ignore the code and wittingly infect others. By so doing, they incomprehensibly and unforgivably forfeited their humanity and usurped the Reaper's dominion as the Dream Ender.

Dick Hardesty

I

"How's he doing?" I asked as Jonathan returned to bed.

"He'll live," he said, pulling the sheet up to his chin. "It's all your fault, you know."

"My fault?" I asked. "And exactly how did you reach that conclusion?"

"That kid can con you out of anything and he plays you like a fiddle. You had to let him have another piece of birthday cake!"

"Well," I said in my own defense, "it was only a very small piece and it *was* his birthday, after all. He doesn't turn five every day." It was a weak excuse and we both knew it. "He told me you said it was okay," I added lamely.

Jonathan spun onto his stomach and plumped his pillow a little more vigorously than was probably necessary.

"The defense rests," he said.

It was hard to believe Joshua had been with us for nearly a year. While I was truly amazed at how well he had outwardly adjusted to his parents' death, there was ample if subtle evidence of how deeply it had affected him. One obvious manifestation of this was his being an absolute sponge for affection and reassurance. While both came naturally to Jonathan and me, he was not above occasionally provoking us or pitting us against each other, as if testing to see if we really did love him anywhere near as much as his parents had.

His fifth birthday had been, therefore, a cause for special celebration. The Bronson sisters, who ran the daycare center Joshua attended, had a party for him with milk and cake and games. Then, because it was a Friday, our little clique of Phil, Tim, Mario, Bob, Jake and Jared stopped by after dinner for another small party with another birthday cake. Joshua was his usual subdued self, bouncing off the walls, running from present to present, generally

1

hamming it up and finding time somehow to convince everyone that of all the people in the room, the one he was conning at the moment was his very favorite. So, I guess I really should have known better when, as I was in the kitchen rinsing off the dishes and putting them in the washer, he came in and asked for another piece of cake.

"I don't think that's a very good idea, do you?" I said, glancing through the door at Jonathan, who was engaged in conversation with the guys.

"It's my birthday," he answered plaintively, in case I may have forgotten. "Uncle Jonathan said it was okay," he added, climbing up onto his chair at the kitchen table.

Hey, would a five-year old kid lie?

So, rather than interrupt Jonathan for verification, I cut him a small piece and gave him a juice-glass of milk to wash it down. He finished it in under a minute and hopped down from the chair to run back into the living room for more attention.

Bob and Mario left early, since they both had to work at their respective bars. At about eight-thirty, it being my turn to get Joshua ready for bed, I excused myself and went into his room for his pajamas then led him, under protest, into the bathroom for the evening undress-bath-pajamas-toothbrush ritual.

When we emerged, the others were getting ready to leave—it was a Friday night, after all, and they had places to go. I reflected yet again on the time before Joshua entered our lives, when Friday night was more than just another evening at home, and had just a twinge of nostalgia for the "good old days."

Both Jared and Jake had been uncharacteristically quiet during the evening, and I'd wondered if anything might be wrong. They'd been gone no longer than a minute when Joshua came running over.

"Look what I found!" he said, holding up a wallet.

"Where did you get that?" Jonathan asked.

"Over there," he said, pointing to where Jared had been sitting.

"Thank you, Joshua." Jonathan took the wallet from him then turned to me. "Maybe I can catch him," he said and hurried from the apartment.

I took Joshua into his bedroom, listened while he said his prayers and tucked him into bed with Bunny, his favorite stuffed animal. He'd already picked out a book for Story Time—another evening ritual—and I'd just sat down on the bed and picked up the book when Jonathan returned.

"Catch him?" I asked, and he nodded. "Everything okay?"

"Tell you later," he said.

About halfway through Story Time, Joshua announced he wasn't feeling very well, which he shortly thereafter demonstrated by vomiting what appeared to be half a birthday cake.

To the bathroom, bed sheets changed, re-pajamaed and returned to bed, Joshua insisted that one of us stay with him for comfort and moral support, and Jonathan volunteered, joining me when Joshua finally fell asleep.

"So, did Jake and Jared say anything about why they were so quiet tonight?" I asked.

He sighed. "One of their friends died this afternoon. He was thirty-one. He'd only been sick for two months."

I didn't have to ask the cause of death. By that point, with friends and acquaintances dropping like flies, no gay man had to ask the cause of the sudden death of another.

"Jeez, I'm sorry!" I said, and meant it. "It's getting really scary out there."

Jonathan moved closer to me and put his arm across my chest.

"That's one more reason I'm so glad I have you," he said. "Even if you do let Joshua get away with murder."

AS I'VE OFTEN SAID, HAVING A KID AIN'T LIKE HAVING A PUPPY, AND THERE'S ONE HELL OF A lot more involved in the way of responsibilities than many—probably most— gay men would want to deal with.

It was a pretty busy time at work, and I was concentrating on squirreling away cash—kids are also expensive—against the next dry spell, which this business has taught me was always just around the corner. Jonathan, too, was putting in quite a bit of overtime, which meant a lot of juggling of schedules and logistics to pick Joshua up each day from daycare.

But we managed, though it didn't leave nearly as much time as we'd have liked for going out or getting together with our friends. And weekends were devoted to those things we didn't have time for during the week: laundry, grocery shopping, housecleaning, etc.

Since living in an apartment is pretty limiting for a small boy, we made an effort to set aside at least one weekend afternoon to do outdoor things with Joshua—the zoo, street fairs, picnics, hikes, swimming and the like. Then, before we knew it, it would be Monday again, and we'd start the whole process over.

About once a month we were able, with effort, to squeeze in a just-the-two-of-us night out for dinner or a movie, thanks to seventeen-year-old Craig Richman, son of a senior officer with the city police. Craig was at the very top of Joshua's list of favorite people—an admittedly long list—whose services as a babysitter were indispensable.

We did get to see Phil and Tim a couple of times, either having them over for dinner or going to their place, and we talked to Bob and/or Mario, who worked nights, on the phone, but when I suddenly realized that nearly a month had gone by without any word from Jake or Jared, I began to get concerned.

So, after dinner Tuesday night, while Joshua and Jonathan were feeding the goldfish and watering the plants, I gave Jake a call. He wasn't home, so I left a message on his machine then decided it was worth a long-distance call to Jared in Carrington, where he taught Russian literature at Mountjoy College.

He answered after the third ring. "Hello?"

"Hi, Jared," I said, "it's Dick. Haven't heard from you in a while so thought I'd give you a call."

"I've been meaning to call you, too," he said, "but I've been really busy getting ready for the next term."

"I understand. We really should have called sooner. How's Jake?"

There was a slight pause, then: "He's fine. He was up last weekend. He's got a couple of new construction projects going on, and he's been working his tail off, so…"

I detected something in his voice, though I couldn't put my finger on it.

"I didn't have a chance to tell you I was sorry to hear about your friend. Jonathan told me."

Another pause. "Ah…yeah, thanks. Mike was a great guy. Always on the go, always making plans to climb some mountain or other. It was all so damned sudden. One minute he's here, the next minute he…isn't. We saw him just before he…found out…and two months later he's dead."

Hesitation is not characteristic of Jared's speech. And I suddenly realized what I'd heard in his voice—fear. *Jared* and *fear* were two words I would never put together on my own.

"Life really sucks sometimes," I said. "But you're okay?"

"What do you mean, am I okay?" he asked, a little sharply, and I realized how he had misinterpreted my question.

"I mean, you're handling his death okay?"

"Ah. Yeah. Sorry. I misunderstood." He sighed. "Yeah, I'm fine. It's just that dying at thirty-one…and he's not the only one."

I quickly changed the subject, thanking him for the kid's tool set he and Jake had given Joshua for his birthday.

"He loves it," I said. "Now if we can just keep him from trying to saw the legs off the chairs, we'll be okay."

We both laughed, and the tension seemed to ease.

After another few minutes of general chitchat, I turned the phone over to Joshua for a quick personal thank-you and then to Jonathan. The conversation ended with promises to get together soon.

Though I didn't say anything to Jonathan, the conversation had bothered me. I knew that while Jared and Jake were devoted to one another they had a totally open relationship and often engaged in three-ways and group sex. From the tone of Jared's voice, I got the distinct impression they may have known Mike more ways than one, in which case Jared's comment they had seen him shortly before he found out he was infected was truly chilling. I hoped I was just reading my own paranoia into all this, but I couldn't escape the fact that Jared was obviously worried.

When Jake returned my call the next night, he was his usual upbeat self and gave no indication of sharing Jared's unspoken concern, which made me feel a little better. Then, once again, daily existence moved in like a snowstorm, effectively covering over any crevices of worry.

Most of my recent jobs had been of the legwork variety. I had a number of lawyer clients, including the city's top gay lawyer, Glen O'Banyon, who would have me run around verifying alibis, checking facts or tracking down information or witnesses on pending cases. Hardly the stuff of mystery novels, but the money was just as green.

The Wednesday following Jake's call, I went directly from home to the Hall of Records for some research for one of my clients. I got to the office at around ten-thirty and had just opened the door when the phone rang. I hurried across the room to answer it.

"Hardesty Investigations."

"Hi, Dick, it's Jared."

Jared? What's Jared doing calling me on a Wednesday morning at work? I had no idea why he was calling, but I instinctively knew it couldn't be good.

"Hi, Jared! This is a surprise. Aren't you teaching today?"

"No, I don't have any Wednesday classes. I thought I'd come into town and maybe have lunch with you, if you're available."

Actually, there were several things I had scheduled for the day, but they could wait.

"Sure," I said. "When and where?"

"How about the Carnival around noon? I've got a couple errands to run first."

"Noon it is," I said. "See you there."

I hung up and stood by my desk, looking out the window. I couldn't remember the last time Jared had called me at work. And what would bring him down from Carrington during the week? It was only an hour's drive, true, but...

And if he was coming down, wouldn't he have tried to have lunch with Jake? He'd said Jake was busy with a couple construction projects, so maybe he couldn't make it. But then, why...?

I stopped myself right there. No point running off on tangents. I'd find out at lunch. But I didn't like it.

THE CARNIVAL ALWAYS DID A GOOD LUNCH BUSINESS. IT WAS A LITTLE OFF THE BEATEN path, but not that far off, and it had a parking lot. I got there about quarter-till and there was already a fairly good crowd. I asked the waiter to save us a table on the patio and went to the bar to order a Bloody Mary. I don't usually drink during a workday, but something told me I might need it.

What in the hell are you getting so worked up over? a mind-voice—the one in charge of logic—demanded. *A friend called you for lunch. Period. No big deal.*

The bartender brought my drink, and I fished a bill out of my wallet to pay for it. I glanced at my watch and saw it was still only eight minutes until noon, assuming Jared would be on time, which he usually was. I sat there idly pushing an ice cube around the inner edge of the glass with the celery stalk, occasionally removing the stalk to tap the liquid off and take a large crunch out of it. I became so absorbed in pushing the shrinking ice cube around that the hand on my shoulder made me jump.

"Easy, boy, easy!" Jared said with a smile, which I returned. I set my drink aside to get up and exchange a hug. At over six feet and with the build of a linebacker, he was as spectacular as the first day I'd met him, when he was delivering beer to Bob's bar—a long story I won't go into at the moment.

The waiter came over to ask if we were ready for our table. Jared gave his drink order to the bartender and asked to have it brought to the table, and I picked up my drink as we followed the waiter out into the patio.

"Well," I said when we were seated, "this was a pleasant surprise. We just don't see enough of one another."

He grinned. "Well, we might if you hadn't gone monogamous on me." Then his grin faded, and he added, "Which may not have been such a bad idea."

Before I met Jonathan, Jared and I had gotten together regularly for a little no-holds-barred horizontal recreation, which was made all the more enjoyable by the fact neither of us had any romantic designs on the other. I'd had the same type of relationship with both Tim and Phil, as well. Though I'd never mentioned it to Jonathan, I know he knew; and bless him, he never let on, or let it cloud his own friendship with them.

Jeezus, you were a slut! one of my mind voices said.

Luckily, a couple others came to my defense. *Bullshit! You were just a healthy, red-blooded American boy. Sex was fun. It still is. You've just limited the number of players.*

The waiter brought Jared's drink and asked if we'd like some more time to look at the menu. We said yes, and he left.

We sat in silence for a moment. I knew Jared wanted to say something and decided I'd give him time to do it.

"I'm worried," he said finally, not looking directly at me.

"I know," I said. "Mike."

He nodded. "Mike. And he's the third one I know of to die from the Male Call crowd in the last four months. A couple others have just dropped out of sight, and I've heard of a couple others who are sick."

The Male Call was the city's most popular leather bar, and one of Jared and Jake's hangouts whenever what Jared called their "leather mood" struck them.

"They closed the back room," he said, referring to a poorly lit walled-off rear section of the bar where anything and everything could and did go on. "Sort of like locking the barn door after the horses got out. Business has really dropped off. Guys are scared. I'm scared."

"Did you have sex with Mike?" I asked, though I really didn't have to.

He nodded again. "Just before he found out," he said.

I couldn't help myself; I had a sick feeling in the pit of my stomach.

"Isn't there some sort of test you can take? Do you know anything about it?" I asked.

He sighed. "There isn't any test. Jake's brother Stan is an immunologist at Mercy Memorial, and he just returned from a year with the CDC, so he's right there on the edge of things. He mentioned they're working on a way to test for it, but…Mercy's treating more AIDS patients than most people know. They've set aside a special floor for them. Some nurses refuse to work on it. Some doctors, too, if you can believe it. The hospital keeps it all real quiet."

He said nothing for another moment then continued, "But even if there was a test, Jake says he wouldn't take it. 'If I don't have it, there isn't any reason to,' he says. 'And if I did have it, it'd be too late to do anything about it.' I have to admit he has a point."

The waiter came to take our order, though I was not the least bit hungry. I waited until he left before I said, "Neither one of you has had any…physical problems…have you?"

He shook his head. "No. We're both healthy as a horse. It's just the idea of the thing. You don't know how lucky you are that you and Jonathan have the arrangement you have."

I knew.

"Well," I said, "I'm sure you don't have anything to worry about as long as you're careful."

"We are," he said. "Now. We even use a rubber with each other. But that's just been since Mike. Again, horses and the barn door."

"Jake's right in that there really isn't any point to worrying about it. You can't go back and change the past. All you can do is be careful from here on out."

"Believe me, we will be," he said. He looked me directly in the eye and held it. "Thanks, Dick," he said.

"For what?" I asked.

"For being here for me. I'm not the kind of guy to go around crying on other people's shoulders, but I had to talk about it and I knew I could talk to you."

"I appreciate that, Jared," I said. "And you know I'm here any time you need me."

He nodded again as the waiter brought our food.

II

I REALLY DON'T LIKE TO KEEP THINGS FROM JONATHAN AND FELT GUILTY FOR NOT mentioning my having had lunch with Jared when he called to say he would be about an hour late getting home. I rationalized that it was more a way of respecting Jared's confidence than in keeping something from Jonathan.

I'd picked up Joshua after daycare, which he insisted on calling "school." We had talked about putting him in a public school kindergarten when the new school year started in September but decided his current daycare offered a learning experience equivalent to what he would get in a public school. Plus, taking him out of daycare would create even more logistical problems considering our work schedules. We knew we'd have to face those problems when time for first grade arrived, but until then...

Okay, I know I'm telling you more about raising a kid than you probably need or care to know, but it just underscores how much of my life was now involved in things I never would have dreamed of even two years earlier.

Since Jonathan was going to be late, I decided I'd fix dinner, so Joshua and I stopped at the store on the way home. I made the mistake of asking him what he'd like, as if I didn't already know, and on cue he replied "Macaroni and hot dogs!" Maybe I'd asked him because I *knew* what he'd say, and macaroni and hot dogs don't exactly require a degree in gourmet cooking.

There was a message on our machine from Phil and Tim; and figuring that, since I'd pretty much mastered the art of boiling water, I could put off starting dinner until just before Jonathan was due home, I gave them a call right away.

Phil answered.

"Hi, handsome," I said. "Is your lover home?"

"No. Why don't you come on over? I'm horny as all hell, and I don't get

9

nearly enough attention lately. I'd been hoping you'd call and I'm dying to see you…Who is this, by the way?"

We both laughed.

"I see you've been taking prick-teasing lessons from Tim again," I said.

"Never know when they might come in handy," he replied, followed by a sharp "Ouch! It's Dick, okay?"

I heard Tim in the background saying, "I knew that. You just deserve a good punch every now and then on general principles."

"Boys! Boys!" I said. "Play nice!"

"I am playing nice!" Joshua said, looking up from his coloring book.

"I know you are, Joshua," I said. "I was talking to Uncle Phil and Uncle Tim." I paused to shake my head before returning to the phone. "Well, now that everyone is thoroughly confused," I said, "I was just returning your call."

"Yeah, we were wondering if you guys might want to come over for dinner tomorrow night. Tim's got an urge to make lasagna and you know he always makes enough to feed the Bulgarian army."

"Does Bulgaria have an army?" I asked.

"Not since his last lasagna," Phil replied, followed by another loud "Ouch! Quit beating on me, you little twerp, or I'll whip your ass!"

I heard Tim's voice again: "Promises, promises!"

I laughed. "I'll have to check with Jonathan—he should be home shortly—but let's count on it, and if he's got something else planned for us, I'll call you back. Otherwise, what time?"

There was another muffled exchange between Tim and Phil, then: "Seven? That be too late for Joshua?"

"Seven's fine," I said. "He's used to going to sleep at your place anyway, and once he's out, he's out, though he's getting pretty heavy to throw over my shoulder. But we'll manage."

"Great. We'll see you then."

We hung up, and I went to the kitchen to fill two pans with water and turn on the stove.

"Come on, Joshua, let's set the table," I called.

We'd been using a set of Melmac dishes so, if they were dropped, they wouldn't break. But Joshua was getting pretty adept at holding on to things and seemed to actually enjoy helping us around the house.

Have I mentioned he's a pretty good kid?

WE ARRIVED AT TIM AND PHIL'S RIGHT ON TIME, AND JOSHUA IMMEDIATELY RAN TO THEIR large aquarium to watch the fish while Phil fixed us drinks: a Manhattan for me, a Coke for Jonathan, bourbon-sevens for himself and Tim and a small glass of Coke with a maraschino cherry for Joshua.

"You got a new fish!" Joshua declared, pointing to a small, bright pink fish about three inches long. How he was able to spot one new fish in a tank with dozens I didn't know.

"Yeah," Tim said. "He's a pink veil-tail oscar. We just got him."

"His name is Oscar?" Joshua asked, obviously enthralled.

Phil, Jonathan and I sat around the kitchen table talking while Tim puttered getting everything ready, then moved into the dining area for dinner. Tim had made two huge pans of lasagna, which was served with a large salad and garlic bread and wine (another Coke for Jonathan and milk for Joshua). Needless to say, it was all wonderful, and I remarked yet again that if Tim ever decided to leave his job as an assistant medical examiner with the coroner's office, he should open a restaurant.

After dinner we sat around the living room talking, while Joshua alternately ran to the fish tank and sat on the floor with a box of crayons and the coloring book we'd brought along. Around eight-twenty, he crawled up on the couch between Jonathan and me and, after a valiant effort to keep awake, began a slow but increasing list to port until his head was in Jonathan's lap and he was asleep, Jonathan's arm over his shoulder.

"Have you talked to Jared and Jake?" Tim asked.

"Yeah, we called both of them a couple days ago," Jonathan said, sparing me having to find a way to avoid saying I'd had lunch with Jared the day before. "Did they tell you about their friend?"

Phil sighed. "Yeah. As we were going down to the cars after we left your place, I asked why they'd been so quiet all night and they told us. We met him once, I think, when we went out bar-hopping with them. I think it was at the Male Call."

Again I resisted the temptation to say anything.

"Oh, yeah," Tim said. "I remember him now. A real hunk!" He paused and shook his head. "What a damned shame!"

"Neither Jake nor Jared said anything, but I think it really rattled them, especially considering how active they are."

"It's like Russian roulette," Tim added. "The more times you pull the trigger, the greater the risk you're taking. I'm not trying to sound holier than thou here, but the worse this thing gets, the more glad I am I'm not out there on the streets anymore."

"Amen to that," said Phil, who, like Jonathan, had been a hustler when I first met him.

WE LEFT AROUND NINE-THIRTY, ME CARRYING A STILL-SOUND-ASLEEP JOSHUA LIKE A SACK OF potatoes and Jonathan a large aluminum-foil-covered tray of lasagna.

As we'd done before on similar occasions, rather than trying to put Joshua in his pajamas and get him cleaned up, we postponed the ritual until morning and put him to bed in his underwear, making sure Bunny was at his side.

When we went to bed ourselves, Jonathan snuggled up close, putting his arm around me to draw me even closer.

"Can we have sex?" he asked

"Since when do you have to ask?" I said, somewhat taken aback by the question but sensing something behind it.

He sighed, the flat of his hand moving slowly back and forth across my chest.

"I'm scared," he said, "and I don't want to have to be afraid of sex. I guess I just need a little reassurance."

I pulled his head to me and kissed him on the forehead.

"You've got it," I said and then we didn't talk anymore.

THE DAYS CLICKED BY. WE'D HEARD NOTHING FURTHER FROM JAKE OR JARED, BUT THAT wasn't all that unusual. Bob called on a Thursday to ask if we'd like to join him and Mario for an after-church brunch at Napoleon, our favorite gay restaurant, on Sunday and we accepted, conditional on our being able to get Craig Richman to come watch Joshua for a couple of hours.

Every Sunday, Jonathan took Joshua to services at the local gay Metropolitan Community Church. As a confirmed agnostic, I did not feel comfortable with any organized religious service so I never went, but since Joshua's parents had taken him to church regularly before they were killed, Jonathan thought it was important to keep up the tradition. On those occasions when Craig, who was openly gay, babysat for us on a Saturday night, he often, with his parents' full approval, stayed overnight and would then accompany the two J's to church. He usually attended services with his family at a non-gay church, so he always welcomed the chance to go to the M.C.C. whenever he could.

When we called to ask if he was available, Jonathan made arrangements to meet him at the church and bring him home for babysitting after.

Just after we'd put Joshua to bed and were sitting in the living room watching TV, the phone rang. Since I was closest, I picked it up.

"Hello?"

I almost didn't recognize the voice. "Dick, it's Jared. Are you busy?"

I instinctively felt as though I'd suddenly jumped feet first into freezing water. "No, we're just watching some TV. What's up?"

"I...uh..." That damned hesitation again! "I had to come in to see Jake."

The chill had reached my bones. "See Jake?" I repeated inanely.

"Yeah. He's...in the hospital. He's got pneumonia."

Oh, Jeezus!

III

"W HERE ARE YOU?" I ASKED, TRYING TO SOUND CASUAL, BUT WHEN I SAW THE LOOK ON Jonathan's face I could tell he knew something was wrong. He got up and came over to stand beside me.

"I just left the hospital," Jared said. "I'm going to go spend the night at his place, but I thought maybe you could meet me for a beer somewhere?"

"Which hospital?" I asked.

"Mercy Memorial, where Jake's brother Stan works."

"That's not far from here," I said. "Why don't you come over here?"

"I don't want to upset Jonathan. I know what a softie he is," he said, and I could tell he meant it as a joke. It didn't work.

"It's no bother at all," I said. "And he'd feel bad if you didn't."

There was a long pause, then a sigh. "Yeah, but it's a work night for him and…"

"Don't worry about that," I said. "Just come over."

He paused only a moment before saying, "Okay. I'll be there in about twenty minutes."

"I'll keep the beer cold," I said.

Jonathan said, "What's wrong?" before I'd even put the receiver down.

"Jake's in the hospital. He's got pneumonia. It's probably nothing," I lied, noting the look of shock on his face..

"Bullshit!" he snapped. "Damn it, Dick, I wish you wouldn't always try to protect me! I'm not made of glass!"

The sharpness of his tone, and the fact that he almost never swore, not only pulled me back to reality but made me realize he was right—I was trying to protect him. I was always trying to protect him and Joshua. That's what I was there for.

Oh, come on, Tarzan, several of my mind voices said in unison, *Jonathan's your partner, not your kid.*

I reached out and pulled him toward me, wrapping my arms around him.

"I'm sorry, babe," I said. "It's just that I'd do anything to keep you from being unhappy. You know that."

He raised his head off my shoulder and looked into my eyes. "I know that and I appreciate it...I do. But we've got Joshua, and one kid in the family is enough." He kissed me on the tip of my nose and broke our hug. "Come on," he said, indicating the scattered books and newspapers around the room. "Let's pick up some of this mess before Jared gets here."

"SO WHAT HAPPENED?" I ASKED AS I HANDED JARED HIS BEER AND SAT DOWN.

He leaned back in his chair and shook his head. "He's been trying to juggle two big jobs at the same time, and he just bit off more than he could chew. He was working sixteen hours a day and weekends, and about two weeks ago, after all that rain you had down here, he caught a really bad cold. But he wouldn't let it slow him down, and then one of his foremen up and quit, so Jake had to work even harder to fill in for him. I kept telling him to talk to Stan, and when he did, Stan put him right in the hospital."

"So it's just regular pneumonia?" Jonathan asked. "Not...that other kind?"

"Pneumocystis?" Jared said, then shrugged. "Yeah, I'm afraid it is."

"But that doesn't mean...?" Jonathan began, but couldn't bring himself to say the word.

Jared shook his head. "We don't know. It might just be the overwork that's affected his immune system. Stan says he's going to try to get that test they're working on for him as soon as it's available, but he doesn't know when that might be." His voice was calm, but the strain was clearly evident.

"How long will he be in the hospital?" I asked.

"It depends on how he responds to the treatment. Probably a couple of days. He just needs to rest up."

"We'll go see him tomorrow, if that's okay," I said.

"I'd rather you didn't. He doesn't want anyone to know he's in the hospital or make a big deal out of it. When he gets a little better..."

"Of course," I said. "Just let us know, though. We do want to see him as soon as he's up to it. I assume you haven't told the rest of the gang?"

"No, there's no point in worrying them. Everybody is so skittish about this...this whole business, they assume the worst when someone sneezes. So, please don't say anything."

"We won't," Jonathan and I said in unison.

"I'm taking some time off from work," Jared continued, "just to make sure that Jake takes it easy when he gets out. I know damned well he's going to want to go directly from the hospital to work, and I'm going to make sure that doesn't happen."

"Maybe you can take him home and tie him down," Jonathan suggested with mock seriousness.

Jared grinned. "Been there. Done that. Often," he said. "But don't think for one minute I won't if that's what it takes."

Jonathan's comment had eased the general tension, and by unspoken mutual agreement, we switched the conversation to other topics.

Jared left around eleven-thirty to head over to Jake's for the night. Normally, I would have invited him to stay with us, but now that Joshua had taken up residence in the guestroom, sleeping on the couch would have been a little impractical for someone Jared's size. And I sensed that he would feel more comfortable at Jake's.

When he left, we merely exchanged hugs—I didn't say anything about calling if there something he or Jake needed or that we could possibly do to help. I'd already said that when we had lunch and there was no point in belaboring the obvious.

We went to bed shortly after Jared left and neither of us said much. There really wasn't anything either of us could think of to say. But as soon as we got into bed, Jonathan turned on his side facing away from me and reached behind him to take my hand and pull me into our favorite "spoon" position, my right arm around his chest and our clasped hands between his cheek and the pillow.

And so we slept.

I REALLY DO TRY NOT TO WORRY ABOUT THINGS UNTIL I'M SURE THERE IS, INDEED, something to worry about, but I couldn't get Jake and Jared out of my mind. AIDS, as it was now being called, was like a gigantic stormcloud hovering over all our lives, with ominous flashes of lightning advancing over the horizon. But the prospect that it might strike someone close to me had been incomprehensible. I continued to tell myself that just because Jake had pneumonia didn't automatically mean he had AIDS; I was probably worrying for nothing. But that didn't keep me from worrying.

Right after dinner on Friday we called Jake's apartment and left a "just checking in" message. We figured Jared would be at the hospital until they kicked him out and that he'd get the message when he got back.

"We've got to get tested," Jonathan said after we'd returned to the living room from putting Joshua to bed.

"You heard Jared. There isn't one yet," I said.

"Why the hell isn't there?" he demanded, and again the fact that he almost never swore showed the intensity of his feelings. "People are dying, and they can't even test to see if they have it or not?"

"They will," I said.

"Sure they will. You know as well as I do that the government doesn't give a damn about a bunch of faggots dying. Good riddance! And I read that not everybody who has it gets sick right away, and they carry it around with them for who knows how long."

His bitterness was shared by much of the gay community. I knew that we'd both been pretty—well, *promiscuous* is kind of a prissy word, but it's fairly accurate—before we met and that could potentially be a problem. Even though we'd been monogamous since we first got together, I, too, had heard rumors that in some cases there was apparently a long incubation period.

It was quite possible the disease—and we all thought of it as a disease now rather than a series of unrelated illnesses taking advantage of a weakened immune system—had been like a seed just waiting to germinate. Like just about everything else relating to that disease, no one knew how long the seeds had been waiting to germinate. But once they did, the Reaper was not far behind.

I knew what was behind Jonathan's concern, and he finally expressed it.

"We've got Joshua to think about," he said. "We've got to be sure we'll be here for him until he grows up."

I reached out and took his hand. "We will be," I said. "Trust me."

JUST BEFORE WE WENT TO BED, JARED CALLED. JAKE HAD RESPONDED WELL TO conventional treatment, and his brother was hopeful that if he continued to improve, he could be released Monday. We asked if he was up to receiving visitors and, on being told yes, said we'd be over Saturday morning.

Because children were not allowed on patient floors, we brought along enough things to hopefully keep Joshua occupied while we took turns going up to see Jake. I sent Jonathan up first while Joshua and I sat in the main floor waiting room.

"I'm hungry," Joshua announced after noticing the waiting room led to the hospital's cafeteria.

"We had breakfast just before we left the apartment," I said.

"Well, I'm hungry anyway," he said. "I'm a growing boy. Uncle Jonathan said so."

"Well, when Uncle Jonathan comes back maybe you and he can go in and get something to keep you alive until lunch."

"When's he coming back? I'm hungry now!"

"Be brave," I said and, recognizing a losing battle when he saw one, he reluctantly returned to his coloring book.

Jonathan returned about ten minutes later.

"How is he?" I asked, although I'd be seeing for myself in a minute or two.

"He looks a little tired, but otherwise he looks the same as always."

"Jared there?" I asked in a classic example of a dumb question.

He nodded as Joshua hopped down off his chair and tugged on his shirt.

"I'm hungry," he said. "Uncle Dick promised you'd take me to get something to eat as soon as you got back."

Jonathan shot me a look, and I merely rolled my eyes toward the ceiling.

"You two work it out," I said. "I'll meet you here..." I paused and nodded toward the cafeteria. "...or there in a few minutes."

JAKE WAS IN A PRIVATE ROOM ON THE TENTH FLOOR. JARED SAT ON THE EDGE OF ONE SIDE OF the bed, and on the other side stood a spectacularly handsome specimen of manhood in a white doctor's lab coat. I didn't have to ask who it might be—the resemblance to Jake was clear.

Jake grinned, and Jared stood up when I came in.

"Dick!" he said. "Good to see you."

I hurried over to shake hands with him, then with Jake, who still was hooked to an IV.

"Dick, this is my brother Stan. He just stopped in to pester me about going hunting this fall."

We reached across the bed to shake hands, and I was a little ashamed of myself for a quick rush of erotic fantasies.

Jeez, Hardesty, this is a hospital, fer chrissakes! one of my mind voices scolded.

Hey, hot is hot! another responded.

I noticed that Stan wore a large silver wedding ring. Oh, well, so much for that.

"Hunting?" I asked.

"Yeah," Jake said. "We go deer hunting every fall. We've been trying to talk Jared into coming along this year. Especially since he has a cabin close to where we normally go."

Jared grinned and shook his head. "Not fair to the deer," he said, looking mildly uncomfortable.

"He was a sniper in Special Forces in the Army," Jake explained.

I didn't even know Jared had been in the service.

"Yeah, well, that's a part of my life I'd just as soon forget," he said.

I decided it was time to change the subject and turned back to Jake.

"You look great," I said.

"Thanks to my big brother here," he said.

We talked in generalities for a few minutes until Stan excused himself.

"I wish you were the only patient in the hospital," he said to Jake, "The nurses tell me you've been acting like it. But since you're not, I've got a few other people to look in on." He offered me his hand again and said, "Nice to have met you, Dick. Jared, you keep Jake in line, hear?"

When he'd gone we picked up our conversation in mid-generality. Not a word was said that might even imply the potential seriousness of Jake's situation, and after a few more minutes, a good-looking male nurse came in to give him some medicine. Jake, Jared and I exchanged glances and knowing smiles, which were not lost on the nurse.

As the nurse was leaving but was still within earshot, Jared grinned at me and said, "Damn! And I forgot the condoms!"

The nurse paused at the door and turned around with a grin.

"Maybe next time," he said and left.

One thing you've gotta say for gay men—you can knock us down, but you can never count us out.

IV

I WAS SURPRISED WHEN, JUST BEFORE NOON ON SUNDAY, WHILE I WAS READING THE paper and Jonathan and Joshua were at church, I answered the phone to hear Jonathan's voice.

"What's up?" I asked.

"I wanted to get your okay on something."

He had me. "Okay...like what?"

"Well, Craig's here with his friend Bill—we met him once at the Cove when we were having breakfast with Craig after church."

"Yeah, I remember."

Bill had been with a bunch of gay teens around Craig's age, and the two of them had spent the entire time we were there cruising each other. When Bill and his group finally got up to leave, Jonathan told Craig to catch him before he left and get his phone number. Apparently, it had worked out.

"And?"

"And Craig wants to know if Bill can come over while he watches Joshua. They want to go to a movie after. It's okay with me, but I didn't want to say yes until I'd talked to you."

Well, now, that was something of a dilemma. Craig was a great kid and I trusted him completely with Joshua, but I also remember when I was seventeen and had the chance to be alone with somebody I was hot for. Raging hormones tend to be stronger than common sense. Yet if I said no, Craig would understandably think we didn't trust him, and that's the last thing I wanted.

It wasn't easy being a horny gay teenage boy living at home—the options for spending some private time with someone were limited. But by the same token, his parents trusted me not to put him in a position where he might do something they would object to.

Do you trust him or don't you?

"Okay," I said.

BRUNCH WITH BOB AND MARIO WAS GREAT, AS ALWAYS. AS A BAR OWNER AND BAR manager, respectively, they always have an endless string of stories and we all laughed a lot—something I, for one, definitely needed.

But eventually, as all conversations at the time tended to do, talk turned to AIDS and the countless rumors and speculations circulating through the bars.

"There's a new one going around that's really unbelievable," Mario said. "I don't know if Bob's heard it, but I'd guess so."

"What's that?" I asked.

"That someone is going around deliberately spreading AIDS."

Bob nodded.

"Yeah, I've heard it, too."

I shook my head. "How can people believe that shit?"

Mario looked at me. "I thought that, too, until I was talking with one of my regulars who had just lost his best friend. The friend told him he got it from a really butch guy who refused to use a condom, and after they'd finished and the guy was leaving, he stopped at the door and casually said, 'Oh, and I've got gay cancer. Welcome to the club.' And he left. The friend thought it was just a really cruel joke, but then he got sick."

"Who could do something like that?" Jonathan asked, incredulous. "It's bad enough that other people want to see us dead, but our own people? I can't believe it!"

Bob shrugged and sighed. "I'm afraid it might be. I've heard similar stories," he said, "and sad as it is, I wouldn't be surprised if some of them were true. I guess some guys just want to lash out at everyone else when they know they're going to die. They figure somebody gave it to them and they're getting even, somehow." He was quiet a moment then added, "But the interesting—and disturbing—thing is, now that I think of it, several of the rumors involve the Male Call. A lot of their regulars have been getting sick, I hear."

Jonathan just shook his head, and I hastily changed the subject.

WE MADE A QUICK STOP AT THE HOSPITAL ON THE WAY HOME. JAKE WAS CHOMPING AT THE bit to be released, but Stan had insisted he stay until Monday.

All seemed to be well at home. Craig and Bill were in the living room on the couch watching TV with Joshua wedged between them. Typical. I suspected he was probably a little jealous of Bill for diverting Craig's attention.

"So, you guys are going to the movies?" I asked and instantly wished I hadn't, since Joshua immediately wanted to go, too.

Bill gave Craig a meaningful glance that said *I hope not!*

"Yeah," Craig said, apparently oblivious to Bill's glance. "We're going to catch an early show of *Ghostbusters.* I hear it's great."

"I like ghosts," Joshua volunteered eagerly.

"I thought you wanted to see *The Muppet Movie?*" I said, trying to head him off at the pass. "Kermit? Miss Piggy? Remember, we said we'd go tomorrow night right after supper?"

We hadn't, but I was desperate. Jonathan looked at me but said nothing.

I gave Craig a little extra so they could get a pizza after the movie, and they went on their way.

TIME PASSED. ODD THING ABOUT TIME—EVERY SINGLE DAY SEEMS CHOCK-FULL AS WE'RE going through it, yet looking back it's often hard to tell one from the other. But there is definitely something to be said for a comfortable routine.

Jake went back to work and Jared went back to Carrington, and after the jolt of the initial scare, all seemed to have settled down. The gang kept in touch, mostly by phone, with an occasional brunch or dinner. Jared and Jake became much more cautious—for them. They cut back on their group sex encounters, and they wouldn't have anything to do with anyone who wouldn't use a condom. Still not a total guarantee of safety, of course, but a solid start.

Then, one Sunday morning while Jonathan and Joshua were at church, Jared called from Jake's, where he'd been spending the weekend. A couple of minutes into our conversation, he said, "Oh, and I wanted to give you a heads-up. You might be getting a call from Carl Brewer."

"Carl Brewer? The owner of the Male Call?" I'd been there a couple of times in my single days—usually with Jared, since I was never much into the leather scene—so I knew who Brewer was but had never officially met him.

"We stopped in there last night for a drink and were talking with him," Jared explained. "It's obvious he's got some serious problems. You know the Male Call—it's usually packed on a Saturday, but the place was practically empty. There's a rumor going around that somebody there is deliberately spreading AIDS, and it's scaring everyone away.

"To be honest, we'd been staying away ourselves and only went in last night because we felt guilty. Carl's one of the good guys and has always been a straight shooter with us and we wanted to show him a little support. He doesn't deserve to lose his bar because of rumors. He told us he's sure somebody's deliberately out to drive him out of business, and we mentioned your name. So you might be getting a call from him."

"Thanks, Jared," I said. "I appreciate it. I'll let you know if he calls."

We talked for a few more minutes until he announced that Jake was out of the shower and dressed and waiting for him to going out to breakfast. We signed off with mutual promises to talk again soon.

Carl Brewer, eh? Well, trying to figure out if someone might, indeed, be out to shut a business down through rumor would be a real challenge. More of a challenge would be what to do if the rumors proved to be true. In either case, I wasn't sure what Brewer might be able to do with the information.

Working for Brewer and tracking down the source of the rumors would put me closer to two areas in which I was woefully lacking practical experience—the leather scene and AIDS. The leather scene didn't bother me. AIDS did.

Don't get me wrong about the AIDS thing. Life wasn't one big sturm-und-drang Wagnerian opera, totally revolving around it. While it was an ominous cloud on everyone's horizon, it was largely separate from our daily lives so long as it kept its distance and did not affect us directly. It did, however, become something of a ritual in the community to scan the obituaries for familiar names among the ever-longer columns reporting the deaths of single men, most of whom were between 20 and 35. The cause of death was never mentioned. It didn't have to be. The fear had not subsided; it merely became one more fact of life for gay men.

Realistically, though, I didn't expect Brewer to follow up on Jared's and Jake's suggestion—far more advice is offered than taken. So I was rather surprised, when I arrived at the office on Monday morning to find a message waiting for me...from Carl Brewer.

I checked the phone book to see if the number he left was the Male Call. It wasn't, which meant, one, that it must be his home and, two, if it was, he would probably be there at this time of the day. There was also the three that if he worked until the bar closed at two a.m. he may well be asleep and not welcome being awakened by a phone call at 8:35. But what the hell, he'd called me and asked me to call him, so I did; he hadn't specified a time.

The phone rang three times before I heard the receiver being picked up, followed by "Brewer."

"Mr. Brewer. This is Dick Hardesty of Hardesty Investigations returning your call."

"Ah. Yeah. Glad you called. I was talking to Jake Jacobson and Jared Martinson about you. They think you might be able to help me out with a problem."

"I'll be glad to help if I can," I said. "Would you like to get together and discuss it?"

"Yeah, the sooner the better," he said. "What's your schedule?"

"I've got something on for this morning," I said, remembering some papers I had to run by Glen O'Banyon's office. "But I should be free from noon on."

"Good. Why don't you come by here, say, one-thirty?" He gave me his address, and I assured him I'd be there.

With his being the only message on the machine, I settled into my morning routine—fixing a pot of coffee and sitting at my desk to read the paper. I took my time doing the crossword puzzle—in pen, a small concession I make to vanity even though I occasionally have to scratch out one letter or word to squeeze in another—and spent an hour or so doing miscellaneous paperwork.

Around half-past ten I headed to Glen O'Banyon's office with the material I'd gathered for him for one of his cases. He was, not surprisingly, in court, so I left the packet with the office receptionist with the request she give it to his secretary, Donna.

Since I still had quite a bit of time to kill before going to Brewer's, I called Evergreen, the nursery where Jonathan worked, to see if he might be available for lunch. Often, he'd be out on some landscaping project, but occasionally he would be working in the nursery yard. I try not to disturb him at work as a rule, but there were exceptions; and his boss didn't seem to mind as long as he didn't abuse the privilege.

Luckily, it was a yard day for him, so I arranged to pick him up at eleven-thirty.

We'd been together now for—What? Three years?—and especially now, with Joshua, the chance to steal a little private time with him still gave me that hard-to-describe rush you get when you've just started dating someone special. Okay, so I'm a marshmallow. Sue me.

V

I'D THOUGHT THE ADDRESS BREWER GAVE ME SOUNDED FAMILIAR AND IT WAS—2720 Foster was two blocks south of Arnwood, where many of the city's gay bars, including the Male Call, were located. The Male Call itself was in the 2700 block of Arnwood. I wish I lived that close to my work.

Though Arnwood was heavily commercial and not by any stretch of the imagination fashionable, Foster was a typical residential street of mostly older single-family homes. Unlike its neighbors, 2720 was surrounded by a thick but neatly trimmed hedge, broken only by a wood-gated front entrance and hedge-lined driveway leading to a single-car garage at the rear of the house.

The front gate was not locked and I saw no sign of a bell, so I just walked through and up to the porch of the story-and-a-half house. The front door was open behind the screen door, and I could hear music coming from somewhere inside. I was looking directly through the living room into a hallway and what I assumed to be the kitchen at the back of the house. I knocked, and a moment later a large backlit form appeared in the hall and moved toward me. As it got closer, I recognized Carl Brewer from the bar.

Tall, shaved-head bald with two large, heavy-looking silver hoop earrings—he was probably in his late 50s or early 60s, and some of the mass of his torso had moved south, but he wore tight faded jeans and a black leather vest with no shirt to display his tattooed shoulders.

Opening the screen with his left hand, he extended his right as I entered.

"Thanks for coming," he said as we shook. "Come on back to the kitchen."

I followed him through the house, noting that it was a lot neater than our place and obviously masculine without being overpoweringly butch. The kitchen table, I saw as we entered, was covered with newspapers on which some sort of engine was being eviscerated, with a confusing number of screws, bolts and mysterious assortment of unrecognizable parts scattered around.

"Fixing one of my bikes," Brewer explained, indicating the table. "Like a beer?" he asked. "Or coffee?"

I noticed a partially filled cup of coffee on one side of the table and a half-full carafe in the coffeemaker on the counter. A small radio beside it was tuned to the Big Bands station, playing Glenn Miller's "String of Pearls."

"Coffee'd be good," I said. "Black."

He gave me a slightly raised eyebrow of what I took as approval then moved to the cupboard above the coffeemaker for another cup.

"Have a seat," he said, indicating one of the large round-topped wooden spindle chairs on my side of the table. I pulled one out and sat down as he filled my cup and refilled his own, returning the carafe and taking his own seat, leaning forward to set my cup in front of me.

Resting both forearms on the table, he said, "So, I've got a problem."

"So I heard," I said. "It's getting rough out there."

He shrugged and took a swallow of his coffee. "No shit."

I didn't say anything, waiting for him to get to it at his own pace. Finally, he looked up from his coffee and directly at me.

"Look," he said, "I'm not stupid. I know this AIDS thing is spread through sex and I know that a lot of my customers don't come to the Male Call just for the beer. I shut down the back room to cut back on sex in the bar itself and I lost some business because of it, but I can only do so much. I'm not these guys' mother. If they want to stick a loaded gun in their mouth or up their ass and pull the trigger, I can't stop them. They're gonna do what they're gonna do, and the only thing I can do about it is try to see they don't do it in my bar."

He paused. "Jeezus!" he said. "This whole thing is a fuckin' disaster! I've had the Male Call for twenty years and there's never been a problem. Guys come in, they meet friends, they drink, they shoot the shit, they use the back room if they want to get their rocks off and then they go home. But now..." He shook his head slowly. "Now these guys are dying! Guys I've known for years! That's not bad enough without me hearing shit about somebody from my bar deliberately spreading AIDS? I can't believe it!"

We each took another swallow of our coffee before he continued, again prefacing his remarks with a deep sigh.

"Like I said, I'm not stupid. I know that some of my customers must have it without knowing it and that they're probably passing it on to their tricks. That's one of the reasons I shut down the back room. I wish to hell there were something more I could do to prevent it, but there isn't.

"But having AIDS and spreading it accidentally is one thing. Deliberately…" He shook his head disbelievingly. "If I can't prove who's behind these rumors and do something about it," he said after a minute, "I won't have any customers left. But I'm not about to lose my bar because of gossip that someone from the Male Call is deliberately killing people."

I took a swallow of coffee. "Which brings me to the question of exactly how you intend to stop the rumors? Spreading rumors isn't a crime."

"No, but slander is, and I've got the best lawyer in the city, who I'll bet can find a whole shitload of other grounds to sue the ass off whoever's responsible."

Being able to pin a rumor to just one source struck me as a classic case of the needle in the haystack. I was pretty sure the lawyer he was talking about was Glen O'Banyon but didn't say anything.

"I gather you have an idea of who might be responsible?"

He nodded. "Pete Reardon. No question. But unless I get some proof…"

Reardon and Brewer, I knew, had been bitter business rivals for years. Reardon had spent two years in prison following the firebombing of his bar, the Dog Collar—the deadliest fire in the city's history—which killed twenty-nine gay men, including a friend of mine. He'd been convicted of criminal negligence for violation of safety codes that contributed to the high death toll.

Though the bomber, whose identity was common knowledge in the community, had never gone to trial for reasons too complicated to go into here, Reardon refused to accept that he had acted alone, and always believed Brewer had a hand in it. When he got out of jail, he opened a new leather bar, the Spike, to try to pick up the competition with the Male Call where it had left off.

But the Spike never remotely achieved the popularity of the Dog Collar, probably because Reardon was too closely associated with the disaster. He refused to accept that and blamed Carl Brewer for the bar's lack of success. So, I had to admit, he would probably be at the top of any list of suspects.

But I also fully knew, as I'm sure did Brewer, that there could be any number of other people who had a real or imagined grudge against the Male Call and/or its owner. The Male Call wasn't a bar for sissies, and a lot of ultra-butch types tended to bear ultra-butch grudges.

I wasn't quite sure how to bring up my next point, but as usual when I don't know how to do something, I just went ahead and jumped in.

"What if it's true?" I asked. "What if someone from the Male Call is deliberately spreading AIDS?"

"No," Brewer said emphatically. "I can't accept that. I won't. The idea that somebody's out to ruin me's one thing. But that anybody from the Male Call could be sick enough—and I don't mean physically—to deliberately spread AIDS…no, I won't buy it."

I could appreciate his position, but I learned long ago not to rule anything or anyone out.

We sat in relative silence, finishing our coffee, until Brewer said, "Well, you think you can help me?"

I drained my cup and pushed it far enough onto the table it couldn't easily be knocked off.

"I'll do my best," I said.

"That's all I can expect," he said. "And if there's anything you need from me, just let me know."

"As a matter of fact, there is," I said. "You and your crew can start making a list. Every time you hear anyone mention the rumor, try to pin down exactly where and from whom they got it. I'll do the same and check with my connections at some of the other bars. I know they've all heard the same story and will be glad to help. We can work backwards from there. It's a really long shot, but it's worth taking."

I thought a minute before adding, "And you might also make me a list of anyone other than Pete Reardon you think might have a grudge against either you or the Male Call. Have you fired anyone lately? Any trouble in the bar?"

"Well," he said, "the Male Call ain't exactly nursery school, but it's not one continual brawl, either. Every now and then a couple of the guys will square off, but it's usually more show than substance. And I've had to fire a couple of bartenders over time, sure. That's the nature of the bar business. But I can't think of anybody other than Pete, or any incident that might have given anyone reason to start this kind of shit."

"Well, if you could get me a list of the guys you've fired and anyone you've eighty-sixed over the past three or four months before these rumors started, I'd appreciate it. And I'd also like a list of the Male Call's customers who've become sick or died."

Brewer nodded with each point I made, and I hoped he would remember them all. He'd better—his business future depended on it, not to mention the lives of his customers.

"So," he said, "we need a contract or something?"

"I'll write one up and bring it in to the bar tonight around ten, if you'll be there," I said.

He nodded. "I'm there every night."

"Okay," I said as we stood. "I'll see you later, then."

"And I'll start making up those lists," he said as we headed for the front door.

"I'LL WAIT UP FOR YOU," JONATHAN SAID AS I PICKED UP THE ENVELOPE CONTAINING Brewer's contract and got ready to leave. Joshua was already asleep. "You won't be gone long, will you?"

"I certainly don't expect to be." I'd told him about my meeting with Brewer and everything we'd covered. "But you go on to bed. How long I'll be depends on whether he wants to go over anything else. And, of course, on whether a couple of those leather guys decide to tie me up and do all sorts of unspeakable things to me."

"Hey!" He scowled in mock seriousness. "I'm the only one allowed to do unspeakable things to you! Remember that!"

I gave him a big hug and a kiss. "How could I forget?" I said. "But don't wait up—you've got work in the morning."

He sighed. "Okay. But you be careful."

I didn't ask what he thought I should be careful of, but I appreciated his concern and merely smiled. "I promise," I said and left.

GRANTED, MONDAY NIGHT ISN'T TYPICALLY A BUSY NIGHT FOR ANY BAR, BUT I WAS STILL surprised when I walked into the Male Call at exactly ten and found no more than ten guys in the place, including the bartender. Normally, there'd have been at least twice that many.

Carl Brewer sat at the far end of the bar talking with a guy in full motorcycle drag—I'd noticed a bike parked by the door. Since there were two or three other customers in regular street clothes, I didn't feel too out of place as I went to the bar to order a beer. I'd just paid the bartender, a shirtless hunk whose thick forest of chest hair couldn't hide a magnificent set of pecs, and taken a swig when Brewer looked up and saw me. Saying something to the guy he was talking with, he swung around on his stool and got up to come over to me.

"Punctual, I see," he said as we shook hands.

"I try to be."

He gave a nod to indicate the envelope I'd laid on the bar in front of my stool. "Why don't you bring that into the office. I've got a couple of things for you, too."

I picked up the envelope and, carrying my beer, followed him around the end of the bar and down a long and typically dimly lit hall with a pay phone, a cigarette machine, two side-by-side doors, each marked RESTROOM—gender specification unnecessary. A pair of closed double doors with a hand-lettered cardboard sign saying CLOSED I knew from having visited the bathroom when I was last there with Jared led to the famous (or infamous, depending on where you stood on the prude scale) back room.

And at the very end of the hall was a door marked PRIVATE.

Brewer unhooked a set of keys from his belt and did an expert rosary through them as we approached, finding the right one and inserting it into the lock in one seamless motion. He opened the door and reached in with one hand to turn on the lights. I noticed it was pretty much a carbon copy of just about every bar office I'd ever been in—small, cluttered, one entire wall lined with stacked cases of booze and beer. The obligatory desk, chair and locked file cabinet. Beside the file cabinet, three cases of vodka sat atop a black cast-iron safe, and crammed into the narrow space between it and the crate-lined wall were two collapsed folding chairs.

Brewer pulled one out and set it up for me beside his desk then took his own seat. I handed him the envelope with the contract, and he in turn gave me a manila folder from one corner of his desk.

We each studied our materials independently. The manila folder contained three sheets of yellow lined notebook paper. The first listed the names of five bartenders fired in the past four months—a pretty hefty turnover rate, I thought, but then realized that on busy weekends there were sometimes as many as three bartenders on duty at the same time. I also knew bartending tended to be a high-turnover occupation.

One of the five was canned for either coming in late or not showing up for work at all, two had been tapping the till, one was caught several times shortchanging customers—especially the drunk ones—and one had gotten in an argument with Brewer and threatened to punch him—not the wisest of career moves. He thoughtfully supplied addresses and phone numbers for all five men.

The second sheet was labeled 86'D, beneath which were four more names together with the dates or approximate dates they were kicked out and the reason. Only two had first and last names, the others just a first name. No addresses or phone numbers given. The reasons ranged from a history of being drunk and belligerent to stealing a billfold one of the patrons had left on the bar to pissing in the hallway when there was a line for the bathrooms.

But it was the third sheet which got to me. There were fifteen names on it—fifteen!—divided into two categories: "Dead"—nine names—and "Sick"—six names. And those were just the ones he knew about. Jeezus!

I became aware Brewer was watching me.

"That's not for publication," he said, indicating the sheet I was looking at.

"I understand." I was sure every bar owner in the city had lost customers to AIDS, but fifteen? Even for a bar as busy as the Male Call was—or used to be—fifteen was a sobering number. There were phone numbers for fewer than a third of them.

I put the sheets back in the folder. Brewer signed and handed me the contract, and I co-signed both copies, returning one to him.

"I haven't had a chance to start the list on where the rumors are coming from," he said, "but I clued Andy, who's behind the bar tonight, to start paying attention and asking questions and will tell the other bartenders when I see them."

"I appreciate it," I said, putting the signed contract in with the notebook sheets, then got up from my chair. "I'll get started on this tomorrow" I extended my hand.

He got up, too, shook my hand and reached over to open the door.

"If you have any questions, give me a call," he said.

I picked up my beer and edged past him. "Likewise," I said and he nodded.

I went down the hall to the main room, drained my beer, set the bottle on the bar and left.

VI

FIRST THING TUESDAY MORNING, AFTER MY COFFEE-NEWSPAPER-CROSSWORD PUZZLE ritual, I checked the phone book for the names on Brewer's list of the Male Call's dead and ailing customers. While I really hated to bother anyone so deeply effected by the situation, I thought they or, if the phones of the dead were still in service, any lovers or roommates might be able to give me some information. I was able to find numbers for a little more than half of them and wrote them down beside the names.

Waiting until about ten-thirty, I called Brewer to see if he had any idea where his fired bartenders might be working currently. I had their phone numbers, but thought it might be a good idea to try to drop in on them where they worked now.

"Val works days at the Spike—I'm sure a lot of the rumors come from there and from him. The guy's an asshole, and I'm not surprised Pete Reardon would have hired him. Ted Murray's at the Tool Shed. Scotty was at Daddy-O's last I heard, but that was his second job since he left the Male Call; no idea if he's still there. Ray's at Venture. I haven't heard anything at all about Clayton—I think he may have left town. God knows he ripped me off for enough to afford to go first class."

I took notes on everything he said, finding it interesting that one of the fired bartenders was now working at Venture, which was managed by our friend Mario, Bob Allen's partner. I had been planning to call Bob and Mario later anyway.

"Did you know any of the guys on the...the other list...well enough to know anything about them? Lovers? Friends? Where, other than the Male Call, they hung out?"

There was a slight pause. "I probably knew most of them, or at least knew who they were. But there were only a couple I knew really well. Stu Elliot had been a friend for years. His best buddy, Mark, still comes in frequently. I can put you in touch with him if you'd like. John Ellysse was one of the roughest, toughest studs I ever knew. Nobody messed with John. I don't think he went anywhere else. He didn't have time. What hardly anybody but me knew was that he lived with and took care of his sister, who has Down syndrome. She was his life." He paused again, longer this time, then said, "Christ! What a fucking waste!"

I could clearly hear the bitterness and anger in his voice.

"I'll tell you one thing," he continued. "If I ever found out that somebody was actually going around deliberately giving AIDS to other guys, I swear to God I'd kill him myself!"

I WAITED UNTIL I WAS SURE MARIO AND BOB WOULD BE UP THEN CALLED. BOB ANSWERED, and from the faint sound of a lawnmower in the background I assumed he was at the kitchen phone by an open window.

"Got the farmhands out on the south forty, I hear," I said.

"Hey," Bob replied, "he's younger than I am. Besides, he needs the exercise. I get all I need doing dishes. To what do we owe the honor of a midweek daytime call?"

"Two things," I said. "I've been hired to look into the source of these rumors about somebody deliberately spreading AIDS, and I need your and Mario's help."

"Sure!" He didn't ask who had hired me, but I hadn't expected him to. Bob never pushed. "These rumors are everywhere," he continued, "and they're making everyone even more skittish than they already were. It's hurt all our businesses, but I understand it's been really hard on the Male Call. What do you need?"

"I need to know everything I can about who's spreading the rumor and where they heard it. I'm going to try to track it backwards to see if it points to anyone in particular. Could you and Jimmy..." Bob's fulltime bartender at Ramon's. "...make some sort of list for me? I know it's a lot to ask, but there's a lot on the line here. If it's just a rumor, I want to know who started it, and if it's not a rumor somebody's got to find and stop this guy."

"Of course, we'll help," Bob said, "but if there is somebody deliberately spreading AIDS, there really isn't very much anybody can do about it. It isn't a crime—that I know of."

He was right. Deliberately kill someone with a gun and there's no question you'll face a murder charge. Deliberately kill someone by giving them AIDS and…Gee, fella, that wasn't a nice thing to do. Possibly some civil suit or other could be filed, but I wasn't sure what the basis would be, or who would file it—the victim often didn't live long enough to go through the suing process.

"I'm not sure what can be done about it," I admitted. "But people have to know the truth. There's very little of it around these days, and these rumors are hurting everybody."

Bob sighed. "I agree. It was bad enough when we had to live in fear of the police. Now we have to be afraid of one another."

I no longer heard the sound of the lawnmower in the background, and a moment later there was the creak of a spring as, I assumed, the screen door to the kitchen opened.

"Is Mario handy?" I asked. "I've got a question for him."

"Sure," Bob said. "He just walked in. Here he is." I heard a lowered-voiced "Dick wants to talk to you" followed by Mario's, "Hi, Dick. What's up?"

"Bob can fill you in on most of it, but I wanted to ask you something about one of your bartenders—guy named Ray."

"Ray Croft? What do you want to know?"

"Do you know where he worked before he came to Venture?"

"He last worked at the Male Call," he said. "Why?"

I really didn't like the idea of maybe getting someone into trouble, but I was curious as to what reason Ray may have given for leaving the Male Call.

"Did he say why he left?" I asked.

"Yeah, he told me he'd threatened to punch out the owner and got canned. Brewer's got a reputation for being really tough on his employees, so while I can't approve of what Ray did, I can understand it. But I'd been in there a couple of times while he was on duty and he's a damned good bartender, so when he came to Venture, I hired him. We get along fine."

"Have you heard Ray badmouthing either Brewer or the Male Call—or linking the rumors of someone spreading AIDS to the Male Call?"

"Not that I've heard. I always tell our bartenders they're there to listen not to talk. But now that I think of it, what Bob said at brunch is true—a lot of the rumors do seem to involve the Male Call. Care to tell me what's going on?"

"I explained it to Bob, but I've been hired to track down the source of these rumors and find out if there's any truth behind them. He can fill you in on what I need."

Like Bob, Mario didn't ask who hired me, but I don't think he had to.

"I'll be glad to do whatever I can," he said.

We talked for a few more minutes then said our goodbyes and hung up.

I made a list of other bar owners, managers and bartenders I knew well enough to ask for help and decided to devote a night to making the rounds to talk to them. I figured maybe Jonathan and I could make a night of it and also made a note to call Craig Richmond to see if he might be available to watch Joshua either Friday or Saturday night.

And so the day passed in lists and notes and planning just how best to go about my investigation.

MY LIST OF BARS, OF COURSE, INCLUDED HUGHIE'S, A HUSTLER BAR CLOSE TO MY OFFICE and for a while a regular afterwork hangout, not because of the hustlers but for the fact they serve dark beer on tap—and in frosted mugs, no less. It was at Hughie's I had met Jonathan.

I seldom went to Hughie's anymore, now that I had a reason to go right home from work, plus I knew Jonathan didn't want to be reminded, even by proxy, of his brief hustler days.

While Hughie's and the Male Call didn't have much of a crossover clientele, I that there wasn't much in this town going on that Bud, Hughie's perennial bartender, didn't know about. So, I left the office an hour early and walked the two blocks to the bar.

I hadn't been there in a couple of months, and while the interior had not changed by so much as a replaced burned-out lightbulb, I sensed…something different…and for some reason, that felt very, very strange. Hughie's never changed. Never. I always thought of it as a time warp. Hughie's today was Hughie's five years ago and Hughie's five years from now. *Different* and *Hughie's* didn't belong in the same sentence.

One of the things I noticed as I walked to the bar—Bud had, as usual, seen me enter and reached into the cooler for a frosted mug—was that it was a little after four yet there was practically no one in the place. Usually, the hustlers started drifting in between three and four o'clock, anticipating the arrival of johns as soon as the offices started closing. Now, there were only two guys I could have spotted as hustlers from a block away and two or three regulars—the same guys who had been there the last time I was, sitting on the same stools.

Bud had my beer waiting when I reached the bar, and I dug a bill out of my pocket to hand him.

"How's it goin', Bud?" I asked, as I did every single time I came into the place.

"Pretty good, Dick. You?"

"Pretty good. Really busy, but otherwise pretty good." I looked around the bar. "Where is everybody?"

He shrugged. "Business is off lately," he said, and he didn't have to explain why.

"I wanted to ask you about that," I said. "You got a minute to talk?"

He slowly looked up and down the bar. "What do you think?"

I grinned.

"So, what do you want to know?" he asked, putting both hands on the bar.

"What do you know about these rumors of somebody deliberately infecting other guys?"

"I've heard stories," he said noncommittally.

"Any specifics? People? Places?"

He lowered his head, thought a minute, then looked back up at me.

"You know how rumors are," he said. "They're all over hell, and they can be damned bad for business. The hustlers don't talk about it—at least when the johns can hear. It's bad for business. A lot of the johns who come in here, they're straight, but even they're becoming aware of AIDS and they're getting skittish. And the minute they hear one story about somebody handing out AIDS like breath mints, they're gone.

"You never hear definite names, though, which is typical with rumors. There's hints that it's this one or it's that one."

I nodded. "Well, could you do me a real favor and try to remember any specific names you might hear? I'm trying to track down the source of these rumors and to find out if there's any truth to them."

"Sure," he said. "It does seem that I hear the Male Call come up more often than any other bar, though. Rumor has it a lot of guys from there have it."

"Has Hughie's lost any yet?" I asked.

He shrugged. "Only one that I know of. But it's hard to tell. This place is pretty much a revolving door. Hustling's a high-turnover and competitive business. Most of these guys are loners...I don't know where they came from before they got here or where they go after they leave. It's none of my business. I just serve beer."

A thirty-something guy in a business suit walked in, and Bud left to take his order as one of the hustlers picked up his own beer and sidled over toward the newcomer.

Let the games begin!

I finished my beer, put another bill on the bar for Bud and left.

THAT EVENING, HAVING TALKED WITH JONATHAN AND CALLED CRAIG TO VERIFY THAT HE'D BE available Friday night—he and Bill were going to a dance for gay and lesbian teens at the MCC's Haven House on Saturday—I called Jared in Carrington. Luckily, he was home.

We talked for a minute or two before I got to the main reason for my call.

"Carl Brewer's hired me to check into all these rumors about someone from the Male Call spreading AIDS." I'm not normally that open about discussing my business, not even with Jonathan, but I knew I could talk to Jared, especially about something which by extension involved both him and Jake. "He wants to find out if there's any validity to them," I continued, "and if there is, who might be responsible."

"I sure as hell hope it's only rumor," Jared said. "I can't comprehend anyone spreading this thing knowingly!"

"Well, one thing I'm going to try to do is track your friend Mike's sexual partners."

"Good luck on that one!" Jared said.

"I know," I agreed, "but I'm going to do the best I can. Do you know of any of the guys Mike had sex with before he got sick?"

There was a pause. "Other than me and Jake, you mean?"

"Yeah. Did he ever mention any names to you?"

Another pause. "Not that I can think of," he said. "But…I do remember him bragging at a party that he'd finally landed Cal Hysong. That was maybe six weeks before he…found out."

"Who's Cal Hysong?" I asked.

"Well, Cal's sort of the alpha butch at the Male Call. As you know, a lot of the guys who go there do it for the fantasy. They put on being butch like they put on their leather. But not Cal. He's the real article, and to land Cal is like landing a Great White. I've seen him just snap his fingers and have guys drop down and lick his boots."

Actually, I'd bet there were a lot of guys who'd be more than willing to lick Jared's boots if he wanted them to but set my fantasies aside to let him continue.

"He doesn't like to take no for an answer, and I've had a couple of run-ins with him in the past. Remember when you had to bail me out of jail after that row at the Male Call a while back?"

"Yeah?"

"Well, it was Cal I got into it with. He's a first-class prick. We nearly got into it again last time we were in there."

"What happened this time?"

"Pretty much a carbon copy of the first time. Cal was hitting on some guy who was way out of his league playing butch. Cal wanted to take him into the back room and the guy didn't want to go. I finally stepped in and told Cal that if he didn't back off, I'd kick the shit out of him...again. We would have gotten into it right then if the owner hadn't stepped in."

"I'm sure I've seen him, but I can't picture him off-hand."

"Well, you don't go to the Male Call that often. Like most predators he has his own territory, and the Male Call's it for him. Every now and then he'll go out to the 'faggot bars' and 'troll for fucks,' as he puts it. That fishing analogy's his, by the way. He doesn't have any friends that I know of. He's a biker, but while he'll go on a run with some other guys every now and then he still stays aloof. But I guess the king doesn't need friends as long as he's got people intimidated."

"I gather he's not your type,?" I said. "Not that it's any of my business."

"Nope," Jared said. "He's just a little too serious about it all for my taste. Sex should be fun and I don't think *fun* is a word I'd associate with Cal. Jake's always thought he was hot, though."

Knowing that Jake and Jared had a very open relationship and that they sometimes didn't see each other for a week or so, I wondered if Jake had ever had the chance to act on his attraction. But that was far more my erotic fantasy than it was my business, so of course, I didn't ask.

"Who was at the party where Mike said he'd been with Hysong? Can you remember? Did Mike have sex that night with anyone there?"

"Well, okay, so it was more of an orgy than a regular party. I think just about everybody was with just about everybody else at some point in the evening. I saw Mike with Jim Prescott and Ted Wills and Monty..." He paused to think "...Sherman. Oh, yeah and Brad Scott. And Jake and me."

"Sounds like some party," I said.

"Oh, yeah." He was quiet for a long minute before he said, "When I think that Mike might have had it even then, and that he might have passed it on to some of the guys there that night...Jesus, that's scary!"

"Do you know if any of the guys you mentioned have...had any problems?"

"Not that I know of. We've seen most of them—I can't remember which ones, exactly—at the Male Call at one time or another since then, and they all seemed to be fine."

I'd reached for a pencil and written down the names Jared had mentioned. I'd try to check on them. "You got phone numbers on any of these guys?"

"Some of them," he said. "I'll check my book and get them to you. And maybe Jake's got some I don't have."

We made plans for brunch on Sunday—Jared was coming in to spend the weekend with Jake.

"He's working his ass off again," he said, exasperation clear in his voice. "I should stay up here this weekend to get some things done, but I know he'd be working Saturday if I didn't come down there and keep him from it. These bullheaded Norwegians never learn."

VII

WEDNESDAY MORNING WAS SPENT ROUGHLY PLOTTING OUT FRIDAY NIGHT'S BAR TOUR and who I hoped to talk to at each stop. There were a couple of places I did not want to take Jonathan—the Male Call and the Spike among them. Okay, I know we just went through that "I'm over-protective" thing, but, damn it, I don't want to expose him to any situation that could lead to problems.

Actually, I realized, a lot of it had to do with the fact that I didn't trust myself not to slip into my possessive "Me Tarzan. Him Boy. Boy mine!" Scorpio mode if some pseudo-butch number made a pass at him. I'm not particularly proud of it, but it's there and I have to live with it.

We couldn't really hit very many bars in one night, anyway. Most started filling up around ten, so I figured we could make it more of an "us two" night out by going to dinner first, which would still let us get to at least one or two of the bars before the bartenders and/or owners got too busy. We'd hit Daddy-O's, a nice little neighborhood bar where Brewer said DeVose, one of his fired bartenders, worked, then go to Venture—I made a note to call Mario to be sure Ray Croft would be on duty—and move on to Bob Allen's bar, Ramon's, to talk to Jimmy, Bob's primary bartender. Jimmy could be waiting on a customer at one end of the bar and not miss a word of a conversation going on at the other end. Then we'd wrap up the evening at Griff's, which I saved for last because it was our favorite piano bar.

After I got back from lunch—I just ran downstairs to the diner in the lobby for a grilled ham and cheese, fries and coffee—I pulled out the list I'd made of the Male Call dead and ill. There are times in this job that I wished to hell I didn't have to do something, and this was right up there at the top of them.

Luckily, I'd separated the two groups, and while it was the ill who were most likely to give me the information I needed, I hated the idea of having to pry into how they got the disease they knew would undoubtedly kill them and probably soon.

So, I decided to start with those already dead to see if their friends or partners could give me any information at all on how they might have contracted it.

I'll spare you the details of each and every call. As a matter of fact, I ws only able to make three before I had to give up simply because I couldn't deal with having my guts ripped out by the grief of those the dead left behind. But as for useful information, there were some interesting comments.

Though I knew they were all patrons of the Male Call, I asked if they were regulars at any other bars, or if they had any indication where and how they had contracted it. Three were directly traceable to the Male Call's back room and, most telling of all, two mentioned the name of the bar's "alpha butch," as Jared had called him—Cal Hysong. Each of the two had considered being screwed by Hysong something of a feather in their cap. Actually, it might have been a nail in their coffin.

But even though Hysong might, indeed, be infected and while it might indicate that the rumors about someone spreading AIDS from the Male Call could have some validity, there was no proof it was being done deliberately. A very fine and weak line in the end result, but a major one in the difference between the unwitting and the morally criminal. Even so, I made a note to call Brewer and alert him of the possibility in case he wanted to have a talk with the man or take some sort of action.

Talking to the friends of the dead was draining, and a thought occurred to me as I sat staring at my notes. Mario had said something about one of his regulars at Venture telling him about a best friend who claimed he'd gotten it from a "really butch" guy who told him "I've got gay cancer—welcome to the club."

Jeezus! Why hadn't I picked up on that sooner? I cursed myself for being so dense. I'm supposed to be a detective, fer chrissakes, and I let the possibility it might very well have been Cal Hysong go right over my head. Outside chance, but still, I should have followed up on it.

I wondered where all this had taken place. The description of the setting all but ruled out the Male Call's back room. Maybe the baths? If it was Hysong, it could well have been during one of his "trolling for faggots" outings.

I immediately dialed Mario and Bob's number. After four rings, I got their machine and left a message asking Mario to give me a call as soon as he could.

Of course, it was way too early to start zeroing in on Hysong, and I had to be careful not to let myself try to put a square peg in a round hole. Everything I knew at that point did indicate Hysong, but I actually knew very little right then. If it did turn out to be Hysong, the tie-in to the Male Call would be established.

I was still mulling all this over when the phone rang.

"Hardesty Investigations."

"Dick. Mario. Sorry to have missed your call—we're out working on the coach house. I just came in to get some ice tea. What's up?"

I asked him if he remembered anything else about the "gay cancer" story he'd reported at brunch.

"I'm afraid not. To be honest with you, I didn't give it much credit at the time—the rumors were just starting at that point. But I can probably put you in touch with the guy I heard it from."

"That'd be great," I said.

"His name's Allen, and he comes in for Happy Hour several times a week and usually on the weekend. I don't remember his last name, but the minute I see him I'll try to get his number and give it to you, or give him yours and ask him to call you."

"Either way's fine," I said. "I'd really appreciate it."

"No problem. Oh, and on the rumors. No specific names or details, just the typical grapevine stuff—'the friend of a friend' or 'these guys were talking and….' You know the kind. But I'm keeping my ears open."

"I owe you," I said. "But now I'd better let you get to your ice tea."

"Thanks," he said. "I've got to go in tonight around five to break in a new bartender."

I had one more thought. "Oh, before you go. Jonathan and I are planning to stop at Venture Friday night. Will Ray be working? I'd really like to talk to him for a minute."

"Yep, he's on. Nice that you two are actually getting out for a change."

I felt a slight pang of guilt to realize how right he was.

We exchanged goodbyes and the usual "give my best tos" and hung up.

I know I should have started calling those on the Male Call's "ill" list next, but I just couldn't bring myself to do it, to rub their noses in something of which they were excruciatingly aware every single moment—that someone had given them a fatal disease. I wasn't infected—please, God!—but the very thought of what that knowledge could do to those who were was almost more than I could bear. So, while it may have violated every rule in the Good Detective's Handbook and possibly delay my getting to the bottom of the

42

matter, I determined that I'd call the ill only as a last resort.

I remembered Brewer had told me that one of his fired bartenders—Val, I think his name was, I'd check my notes—now worked days at the Spike. I'd only been there once, with Jared. It was a watered-down version of the Male Call, spartanly butch. Its focal point was a raised, cordoned-off platform against the wall at one end of the bar on which, perched under a spotlight, was a gleaming classic blue 1956 Harley-Davidson double-glide Panhead, the pride and joy of the bar's owner, Pete Reardon. He drove it in every Gay Pride parade, at the head of a pack of gay bikers. The wall behind it was covered with photos of bikers on their bikes, individually and in groups.

I definitely wanted to talk with Reardon, but I preferred to see what other people had to say first. I looked at my watch and decided I had time before the end of the day to run over to the Spike. I mainly wanted to talk to Val right now. If Reardon happened to be there, too, I'd play it by ear.

Like the Male Call, the Spike was on Arnwood, though at the opposite end of the strip of gay bars. I left the office around three and headed over. I was counting on the fact there wouldn't be much of a crowd at that time of day, and I was right. There were maybe four guys in the place, including the bartender, who if I had seen him on the street I would have easily pegged as a bartender in a leather bar—black skin-tight T-shirt over a solid body, a rugged, heavily pockmarked face, close-cropped black hair, overtly butch. In this town's leather bars, image may not be everything, but it beats whatever comes in second by a mile.

He looked up from putting a case of beer in the cooler under the bar as I approached.

"What'll it be?" he asked, eschewing such fruity preambles as "Hi."

"A Bud," I said, and he nodded, reaching back into the cooler.

I handed him a bill and my card, which he glanced at only cursorily.

"You're Val, right?" I asked.

He nodded.

"You got a minute to talk?" I asked.

He looked at me suspiciously. "About what?"

"I'm a private investigator," I said, indicating my card with a nod of my head, "and I'm looking into the rumors about someone deliberately spreading AIDS."

"I don't repeat rumors," he said.

"I wasn't saying you did," I replied. "But you hear them, and I'd like to know if you've heard any specific names mentioned, either people or places. I know you're sharp enough to be able to tell which stories have some truth in them and which are just made up."

"Why did you come to me?" he asked, suspicious.

I didn't want him to make any connection between me and Brewer.

"Because I understand you worked at the Male Call and you probably have a better idea than most guys of what was going on over there."

He seemed to relax a bit. "Yeah," he said finally, "Maybe I did. And they're a lot more than just rumors."

"How do you know?"

He glanced up and down the bar to see if anyone needed attention, and seeing they didn't, he leaned forward, putting both forearms on the bar. I automatically moved forward on my stool.

"Too many guys from the Male Call getting sick. That's why I left."

Actually, I knew he left because Brewer fired him for tapping the till.

"Yeah, well, a lot of guys are getting sick," I said. "I'll wager every bar in town's been affected by it."

He nodded. "Sure. There's been a couple I know of from here—but they all used to go to the Male Call, too, and I'll be willing to bet that's where they got it."

"I'm afraid I don't follow," I said. "Do you have any proof?"

"Well, I got a buddy came to visit me from San Francisco four months or so ago. I was workin' the Male Call, and he came down while I was on duty. The rumors were already starting, so I warned him against goin' into the back room. One night he decided to go to the baths and said he'd made it with a guy he recognized from the Male Call, although the guy didn't recognize him.

"Anyway, Bart said the guy was really hot but a little weird. For one thing, he wouldn't wear a condom, and for another, as soon as they got in the room and before the guy took his towel off, he unscrewed the light bulb so the room was totally dark. Bart thought it was pretty strange that a guy that butch wouldn't want to be seen totally naked.

"Anyway, he told me that when they were through and he was leavin' the room, the guy puts his towel back on and says to him, 'I gave you a little somethin' to remember me by.' Bart thought the guy was just referring to the screwing. He didn't think much of it until last week, when he called to tell me he's got it. He said he realized the minute he found out that's what the guy in the bath meant."

It occurred to me that if his friend lived in San Francisco, it was just as likely, if not more so, that he contracted it there. But I decided just to hear Val out.

"I don't suppose he got the guy's name," I said. "The one from the bath?"

He looked at me as though I were not quite bright, and he was right—baths are not a place for exchanging names.

"He didn't have to. When he described him and said the guy wouldn't use a rubber, I knew who it was."

"So, who was it?" I asked, though I was pretty sure I knew.

"Cal Hysong. You know him?"

"I know of him," I said. "Did you say anything to Carl Brewer? He might want to know."

He shook his head. "I don't owe him shit."

I shrugged. "No, you don't. But if it *is* Cal, what about all the guys he might be passing it on to?"

"That's not my problem. If they're dumb enough to have sex with somebody who won't use a rubber, they've only got themselves to blame. Even Bart. Problem is, Cal's so fucking butch most guys'd throw safety out the window to get him into bed. Cal's the boss—he says, you do, and you don't argue or he'll drop you like a hot rock and get the next guy in line."

"But in order for someone to pass it on, they have to have it themselves," I said. "You think Cal's got it, then?"

He paused, his forehead wrinkled in thought. "Well, he looks okay," he admitted. "But what about that—what was her name? Typhoid Mary? She didn't look sick, but she killed a lot of people."

He had a point.

"And you haven't spoken to Cal about it personally, I assume?" I asked.

He looked at me and shook his head slowly. "Are you fucking crazy? You say somethin' he doesn't want to hear, he'll kick your ass from here to next Tuesday without blinking!"

"But you're sure it's him?"

"All I'm saying is he'd better watch his ass. Anybody who brags about handing out AIDS won't have to worry about dyin' of it—somebody's gonna see to it he never lives that long."

A guy at the far end of the bar signaled for a drink, and Val pushed away from the bar and moved off toward the waiting customer.

SINCE JONATHAN WANTED TO STOP ON HIS WAY HOME FROM WORK TO REGISTER FOR HIS final semester at Grant Tech, I'd volunteered to pick Joshua up from daycare; I made it just in time. Several of the parents were arriving as I did, and we exchanged smiles and hellos as we walked up onto the porch to begin collecting our various kids, who ranged in age from two to five years.

I thought again of just how lucky we were to have found the place. The Bronson sisters, Bonnie and Estelle, who owned and operated Happy Day Daycare, were former schoolteachers who, being lesbians themselves, wanted to start a daycare specifically for the children of gay and lesbian parents.

Since Happy Day was right on Jonathan's way home from work, he normally picked Joshua up. Whenever I did the honors Joshua and I engaged in a little ritual involving my giving him a piggyback ride to the car.

"I'm tall," he proclaimed from his lofty perch on my back.

"Yeah, and you're getting heavy, too," I said. "How about next time you carry me?"

"Sure!" he said, undaunted.

JUST BEFORE DINNER, MARIO CALLED TO SAY THE GUY HE'D MENTIONED TO ME—ALLEN somebody—had been in for Happy Hour, and Mario had given him my work number. The guy had said he'd call.

Not having heard anything from him by half-past ten Thursday morning, I took out the list of the Male Call's fired bartenders. I dialed the number Brewer had given me for first name on the list, Ted Murray. No answer and no machine. I figured if he was working at another bar, he might still be sleeping, so I made a note to call later.

Even though I'd put Daddy-O's on our Friday bar tour, I decided that as long as I was on the phone, I'd try to give Scotty DeVose a call and maybe be able to substitute another bar on Friday. However, I got a "the number you have reached is no longer in service" message, and information had no new number for him. I knew Daddy-O's didn't open until around four, so made a note to call there when I got home to see if Scotty was still around.

I'd already talked to Val and planned to talk to Ray Croft during our bar rounds on Friday. The last name on the list was Clayton Poole, the one Brewer thought might have left town. His number, too, was disconnected, and again, information didn't have a new number for him.

I took an early lunch then tried Ted Murray's number again. I was in luck.

"Yeah?" a voice said after the third ring.

"Ted Murray?" I asked.

"Yeah? Who's this?"

"My name's Dick Hardesty," I said, "and I'm a private investigator. I understand you worked at the Male Call."

"Yeah? So?"

"So, I'm checking with everyone I can locate from the Male Call about these rumors of someone from there deliberately spreading AIDS. Bartenders hear everything, and I wondered what you might have heard."

"Hell, you know rumors. I normally just ignore 'em, but this one's coming out of the woodwork. I'm at the Tool Shed now, and I'm still hearing 'em."

"Any specifics?"

"Like I said, you know rumors—they're pretty short on specifics. But they all involve the Male Call."

"Any idea why?"

"You've been there, right?"

"Yeah."

"Well, then, you know it's almost a glorified bath house for all the sex that went on there before they closed the back room. You remember how dark that back room was? Two lousy little twenty-five-watt light bulbs, plus any light that might come in when the doors opened."

I didn't tell him I'd never actually been in the back room, but I did remember the dark hallway and thought that even opening the door all the way wouldn't have let in much additional light.

"Well, somebody was always unscrewing the two bulbs so the room would be pitch black—everything's done by feel, if you know what I mean. There might be ten, fifteen guys in there at any one time. Not knowing who you're with adds to the mystery, I guess. Carl always threw a shit fit when that happened—fire laws say every room has to have some sort of illumination.

"Anyway, I started hearing stories from guys who'd been in the back room when all the lights were out saying that someone was going around screwing guys in the pitch dark, then whispering "And now you're dead" after he'd finished."

"And nobody wondered what he meant by that?" I asked.

"Who knows why anybody says anything?"

"Any idea who it was?"

"Hard to tell in the dark, other than that the guy was really big. The Male Call's got a lot of really big guys as regulars, and a lot of them were in and out of the room. But I'll bet you anything it was Cal Hysong."

I was beginning to suspect that might be a fairly safe bet. But whether it was Hysong or not, if what Murray said was true it would clinch both the rumors of someone deliberately spreading AIDS and the tie-in to the Male Call. I couldn't be sure Val wasn't just saying it to get back at Brewer for firing him, but it could be a significant piece of the puzzle and I wasn't about to let go of it.

We talked for another minute or two, then I thanked him for his help and we hung up.

A few minutes later, the phone rang.

"Hardesty Investgations," I said after the third ring.

"Yes. This is Allen Gilford calling. The manager at Venture gave me your number and asked me to call. I understand you have some questions about my friend Jesse's death."

"That I do," I said, "and I really appreciate your calling. I understand your friend…Jesse…told you he thought someone had deliberately given him AIDS?"

There was a pause, followed by a sigh. "Yes." Another pause. "I couldn't believe it. I still can't. How could anyone do something like that? But Jesse said it was true, and he's dead and…"

"I'm very sorry for your loss," I said, and I truly was. "But can you tell me everything you remember about what he said? Did he get the guy's name? A description? Where did they meet? Anything at all you can tell me will help."

"Jesse and I had been friends since high school," he began, "and he was always fascinated by butch men—leather men, in particular. But though he wasn't at all feminine, he never went to leather bars because he thought he wouldn't fit in. One night he went to the Tool Shed—it's as close to being a leather bar as he felt comfortable going to—and met this guy. Jesse said he couldn't believe his luck. He said the guy was the butchest guy he'd ever seen."

Another pause and sigh, then: "Jesse wasn't stupid. He was always very careful. Ever since AIDS came along, he always insisted his partners use protection. But when they got to Jesse's place, this guy insisted Jesse turn all the lights out before they got undressed—and then he refused to wear a condom. 'You want to get fucked with plastic, go get yourself a dildo,' he said.

"Jesse knew better! He did! But here's this guy who represented every sexual fantasy he'd ever had and…well, he let him. And then—" He stopped talking, and I gave him time to recover himself. "And then as the guy was leaving he stopped at the door and turned around and said 'How does it feel to be a dead man?' And then he left, and Jesse didn't have any idea what he was talking about, but it scared the shit out of him."

There was another long silence before he continued. "He called me immediately, and I did my best to reassure him the guy it probably didn't mean anything, but two months later, Jesse developed Karposi's sarcoma, and then he got pneumonia and he was dead within six weeks. Six weeks! That guy knew he had AIDS and that he'd given it to Jesse! How could anybody do that to another human being? I just pray that guy is dead now, too and burning in hell!"

I really didn't know what to say, so I just restated my condolences, thanked him for his time and hung up, feeling like I had a bowling ball where my heart should be.

VIII

C AL HYSONG. IT ALL CAME BACK TO CAL HYSONG.
 And who else could it come back to? my mind voice in charge of logic asked…logically. *Who else have you even considered?*

It had a point, of course. Cal Hysong was hardly the only ultra-butch guy out there. And not all of them were gay. What about some straight guy who somehow got infected—they were beginning to say it could be spread through blood transfusions, and some hospitals were refusing to allow gays to give blood. So, maybe it's some straight guy out to get revenge on gays.

All evidence to the contrary, part of me simply could not accept the thought that one of our own people could do this.

Okay, so for whatever reason, Hysong was the only name I had. I promised myself I'd stay as objective as I possibly could and not close the door on any other possibilities. I'd continue to go with it until another came up.

From what I could tell, whoever it was never came right out and said he was giving his partner AIDS. Still, it didn't take much of a stretch to realize what he meant by "a gift" or "leaving" them something. And all the incidents I'd heard of had happened at least a couple of months ago. AIDS was killing guys within a matter of weeks in some cases. Whoever said it could well be dead himself by now. Cal Hysong, was from all reports, as healthy as they come.

Val had mentioned Typhoid Mary. Maybe it was possible for someone to carry AIDS around with them and give it to others without being sick themselves. But then how would they know they had it if they weren't sick? There was no test yet. Maybe it just progressed slower in some people than in others. Who knew?

Which was exactly one of the major problems. If anybody did know, they weren't telling the rest of us.

One very interesting thing I remembered about both stories was that the guy insisted all the lights be turned off before having sex. Was that just one of his hangups, or might it have another meaning? And was there some tie-in to the turning off of the lights in the Male Call's back room?

Cal Hysong yes or Cal Hysong no, I decided to check to see what Brewer knew about him.

"BREWER," THE VOICE ON THE OTHER END OF THE LINE ANNOUNCED.

"Mr. Brewer," I began—I always address a client formally unless and until asked to do otherwise, and Brewer thus far hadn't—"it's Dick Hardesty. I've got a couple of questions for you."

"Shoot."

"I've heard several references to a guy whose description I understand fits one of your regulars—Cal Hysong—and his name's come up a couple of times. What can you tell me about him?"

"Cal? He's why leather bars were invented. He's one mean, tough sonofabitch and nobody messes with him, but he's never been a real problem." He paused. "You're not saying Cal's behind these rumors?"

"No…at least, not directly. I assume he used the back room while it was open?"

"Who didn't?" Brewer answered.

"And I understand you had some problem with guys unscrewing the lights in there."

"Yeah, and that really pissed me off. If the fire inspectors came in and caught that, they could have my license!"

"Did you ever hear any stories about what happened back there when the lights were out?"

"What do you mean? Same thing went on when the lights were out as when they were on, only maybe with a little more intensity, if that's possible."

"Nobody reported some guy screwing them and then telling them they were dead men?"

There was a long pause before a very unconvincing: "No."

"Look, if I'm going to help you get to the bottom of this thing, you're going to have to be honest with me."

"Well, okay, yeah, one or two of the guys mentioned they'd heard something like that, but I didn't believe it. Some of these guys have a strange sense of humor, and I figured it was probably just some bastard joking around. A lot of these guys like to play the intimidation game."

"That's a pretty sick joke," I said.

"Yeah, I'll admit telling somebody you've just fucked that he's a dead man is pretty sick, but I can't imagine anyone seriously meaning it—or anyone taking them seriously, for that matter. And if you're thinking it might be Cal, all you have to do is take a look at him. Six-four, two-forty if he's a pound, not an ounce of fat on him—solid muscle. He's a steelworker on the Century Tower project, swinging I-beams into place all day. He's as healthy as a horse."

"You don't have to look sick to be sick," I pointed out.

"No, but..." A long pause, then: "No. Not possible. I can ask him what he's heard about all this, but I don't know what good it might do."

"Well, I'd be curious as to his reaction to the question," I said. "What else can you tell me about him?"

"He's an arrogant son of a bitch. I can't remember him ever saying anything positive about anything."

"How about his friends?" I asked, though I remembered Jared telling me Cal didn't have any.

"He's got a little circle of guys he tolerates or rides with, but he doesn't let anybody get too close. For the most part, he could be straight. He's got nothing but contempt for 'faggots.'"

"Is he into S and M?" I asked.

Brewer shrugged. "You sure might think so to look at him and listen to him talk, but his contempt extends to anybody putting labels on him."

"So, what does he do in bed?" I wondered.

"Any damned thing he wants to."

EVERY NOW AND THEN I DO SOMETHING TOTALLY OUT OF LEFT FIELD, AND WHEN I HUNG UP from talking with Brewer I found myself doing it again.

I checked in the phone book for a listing for a Dr. Stan(ley?) Jacobson. There was none. Well, Jake had said his brother just got back into town after a year at the CDC, so I looked up the number of Mercy Memorial and called, asking to be transferred to Dr. Jacobson's nurse.

"Dr. Jacobson's office," a pleasant female voice said.

I knew I didn't stand the chance of a snowball in hell of actually talking to him right then, so I said, "Could I leave a message for Dr. Jacobson, please?"

"Of course."

"Would you ask him if he could please call Dick Hardesty when he has a moment? I met him the other day while his brother was a patient."

"Do you need to make an appointment?" she asked.

"No," I said. "But it is rather important, and I would very much like to talk with him if I could. By phone would be fine."

I gave her both my office and home numbers. I felt a little guilty about bothering him, considering how busy he had to be dealing with an increasing number of AIDS patients, and didn't hold much realistic hope he'd call, but I had a couple of questions about AIDS he would be uniquely qualified to answer—if there were any answers. To date, answers to questions about the disease were in agonizingly short supply. But, I rationalized, he might be able to help me do at least a little something to stem the tide.

After hanging up, I agonized again about calling the numbers on my "ill" list. What in the hell could I possibly say to them? "Hey, I was wondering if you might know who killed you?" These poor guys had enough to worry about: I couldn't see adding to their anguish. I knew I probably would have to do it eventually. Just not now.

I did pull out the list of the nine—nine!—Male Call patrons who'd already died. I'd already talked to friends/roommates/lovers of three of them, and tried to look up the phone numbers of the other six. I found five. The first two I called were disconnected—including Mike Brisco, Jared and Jake's friend. On two others I got answering machines, but at least that meant someone would get my message and, I hoped, reply. I left both my work and home numbers.

I was able to only actually talk with one roommate of the dead, who had not been a roommate long and who had little of significance to report, other than to verify that the man had, indeed, been a Male Call regular, which I already knew. One did say, however, that his roommate seldom went to any other bar.

JOSHUA HAD JUST FINISHED SAYING HIS PRAYERS AND HUGGED HIS PARENTS' FRAMED photograph and climbed into bed for Story Time when the phone rang. I told Jonathan to start without me and hurried into the living room to answer it.

"Dick? This is Stan Jacobson. I got your message. What can I do for you?"

"I really appreciate your calling, Doctor—"

"Stan," he corrected.

"Stan. I'll get right to the point. There are rumors going around the gay community of someone deliberately spreading AIDS, and I've been hired to track them down to see if there's any validity to them."

"Unfortunately, I wouldn't be surprised," he said.

"From what I've heard and those cases I know of, the time between becoming aware of being infected and death is pretty short. But I know of someone who might have been deliberately spreading it for several months and is still alive and apparently healthy."

He sighed. "Yes, that's possible. There's so much we don't know yet, and until we can test for it reliably—and we're very close now—we can't really be sure of anything. As you said, the time between infection and death can be a matter of months, if that. But apparently some people are carriers without knowing it or becoming ill, or somehow manage to hold the symptoms at bay. I have a patient right now who has had Karposi's sarcoma for at least four months without its spreading, or without falling prey to the other opportunistic diseases so common in AIDS patients.

"You have no idea how frustrating this is for everyone in the medical establishment. The only thing we're certain of is that we can't be certain of anything. We're learning, but about all we can do is work as hard as we can to deal with each opportunistic disease as it arises then wait for the next one to show up and deal with that one."

I wanted to ask him about Jake but couldn't bring myself to do it. Maybe if we just ignored it, it would go away.

Suddenly, I found myself thinking of a link between the stories the now-dead Bart and Jesse had told—the guy's insistence on the lights being out before they had sex. And the lights being turned out at the Male Call. Of course!

"Stan, I know you can't give out any information on your patients, but I have one question I hope to God you can answer for me. The guy with Karposi's—can I ask what part of his body is involved?"

There was a long pause. "That's an odd question. Why would you ask it?"

"Because the guy I was telling you about won't let his partners see him without a towel around his waist and always insists on having the lights out during sex. If you don't want to be specific, could you at least tell me if I'd be right in guessing that it's somewhere on his lower torso or upper legs?"

"I don't know, Dick. I . . ."

"Look, Stan, I understand your situation. I do. But if I'm right, maybe we can find a way to keep him from giving AIDS to anybody else. It would sure as hell make your job easier."

He sighed again. "Well, I'm afraid getting one carrier off the streets is like trying to lower a lake by taking out a cup of water. But the answer to your question is yes."

"Thank you!" I said, and I'd never meant anything more sincerely.

"You're welcome," he said. "I wish you luck. Oh, and I'd just as soon you didn't mention this call to Jake."

"Of course," I replied, though the fact he had said it sent a chill up my spine.

IX

I WOKE UP FRIDAY MORNING THINKING. I HATE THAT, ESPECIALLY WHEN I HADN'T SLEPT all that well, probably because I'd been trying to sleep and think at the same time. Not easy.

I was still thinking as I waited for Jonathan to get out of the shower. Okay. Dilemma time. I was now as certain as I could be without pulling his pants down for a visual check that Cal Hysong had Karposi's. Maybe I could sneak up behind him...

Jeezus, Hardesty! a mind-voice snapped. *How can you joke about something like that? Hysong may be a total asshole, but he's still a human being!*

It was right, of course. But I'd just gotten out of bed and somehow found it difficult to feel charitable toward someone who was deliberately trying to kill guys.

Anyway, back to the dilemma. Since Carl Brewer had paid me to find out if there was any truth to the rumors, I was obliged to tell him what I had discovered. It wasn't a comfortable position to be in. And there was still the outside chance it wasn't Hysong. I've fallen flat on my face more than once jumping to conclusions. I didn't want to do it again, especially when the stakes were so high.

I decided I'd just lay it all out for Brewer and leave it to him. I remember his saying that if he ever found out someone from the Male Call was deliberately infecting others, he'd kill the guy himself. I'm sure it was just a heat-of-the-moment comment, but it still gave me pause.

I decided I'd put off talking with him until Monday, which would give me a few more days to see if anything else might come up to make me consider someone other than Hysong.

CRAIG'S DAD DROVE HIM OVER AROUND SIX-THIRTY FRIDAY EVENING. WE'D ALREADY FED Joshua—chicken potpie, a close runner-up to hot dogs and macaroni-and-cheese on his list of gourmet foods—and I was just putting him into his pajamas when Craig arrived. We'd told Joshua that if he promised not to give Craig an argument when it came time to go to bed he could help Craig make popcorn later. Of course, Joshua considered Craig his best buddy and was almost always on his best behavior around him.

We had made reservations at Napoleon, our favorite restaurant and were just heading for the door when the phone rang. I had to head Joshua off at the pass to beat him to it.

"Hello?" I said, displaying my keen sense of originality.

"Dick Hardesty?"

"Yes?"

"This is Mel Franklin, Tom Kester's roommate. Sorry I didn't get back to you sooner; I was out of town. What did you want to know?"

"I appreciate your calling, Mr. Franklin..."

"Mel," he corrected.

"Mel," I said. "While it's really none of my business, could I ask about your relationship? Roommates? Friends? Partners?"

"We were best friends since high school," he replied, "which always amazed both of us, considering how very different we were."

"In what way?" I asked.

"Tom was the classic extrovert, never afraid of anything. He was up for any adventure and liked living on the edge."

"I understand he was a regular at the Male Call," I said.

Franklin laughed. "Oh, yeah. He loved his leather. He loved the fantasy of it."

"And you?" I asked.

"Not me. I always found the leather scene kind of silly. Tom would drag me along with him to the Male Call every now and then, but...I was afraid that exactly what happened would happen."

"So, you think he contracted AIDS from the Male Call?"

"I'd bet every penny I have, and I'll bet you I know exactly how he got it and who gave it to him."

That got my adrenalin pumping! "Who do you think it was? And how do you know?" I asked as calmly as I could.

"Like I said, I always thought the leather scene was just one big fantasy trip for most guys," Franklin said. "That butch thing is a real turn-on for a lot of guys, and there's one guy there who takes it well past the limit. His name, I think, is Cal…"

He paused a second, during which my adrenalin level kicked up a notch.

"And?" I prompted, though I knew he'd continue when he was ready.

"And like just about every other guy in the place, Tom wanted him. Bad. And one night he got him. Tom was walking on air, and he described it all to me in glowing detail. They did it in the back room of the bar, which wasn't exactly what Tom had hoped for, and he said the guy had refused to wear a condom. Tom never went anywhere without a condom, and he always insisted the guys he went with wear them. But he was so hot for this Cal character that he went along with him."

He paused again. "That was it. I know it was. Tom knew it, too, the minute he found what he thought was a bruise on his forearm, about a month later. He died the third of July. He was thirty-four years old."

"Do you know if the guy said anything to Tom after they'd had sex?"

"Not that I know of. Tom didn't say anything. Why?"

"No reason," I lied. "Oh, and did he say anything about the lights being on?"

"Yes, he did say that when they went into the room there was only one small light on, and that the guy went over and unscrewed it before they had sex. There were a lot of guys in the room, but no one said anything."

They wouldn't have dared, I thought. Cal Hysong did what he wanted.

"That took a little of the excitement out of it for Tom," Franklin continued. "He liked to watch the person he was having sex with."

THE PHONE CALL WITH MEL FRANKLIN HAD, ON THE ONE HAND, CONFIRMED MY EARLIER belief it was Cal Hysong who was deliberately spreading AIDS. Stan Jacobson had said Hysong had had evidence of Karposi's for at least four months. There's no way he could not have known he had AIDS, yet he kept on insisting on having unprotected sex. He had to have known he was spreading it. At best, he just didn't care. At worst, he was doing it deliberately, and I was willing to bet it was the latter from what he'd been telling guys he'd have sex with.

I tried my best to push the conversation aside long enough to enjoy our dinner, which was made a little easier by the fact Jonathan had gotten a haircut on his lunch hour and was wearing a new shirt. He looked so spectacular that as we were looking at our menus I blurted out, "Jeezus, I love you!"

He looked up from his menu, gave me a small smile, said "I'm rather fond of you, too," and went back to the menu—but I felt his foot rubbing up against my leg.

It was eight-thirty when we left Napoleon and drove to Daddy-O's. I'd called Thursday when I got home to verify that Scotty DeVose, one of Brewer's fired bartenders, was still employed there. I was determined that despite my conversation with Mel Franklin I would try to cling to my objectivity.

Daddy-O's was a pleasant little neighborhood bar not too far from The Central, the city's main predominantly gay district. I'd not been to Daddy-O's in years, but like most neighborhood bars, it hadn't changed much. It was early, so there were probably eight guys sitting at the bar. A lesbian couple was playing darts, and another was deeply engaged in conversation in one of the booths.

We took seats at one end of the bar as the bartender came over to take our order. His long hair was pulled tightly back into a rubber-banded ponytail, and he had a short chin-strap beard.

"What can I get you gentlemen?" he asked.

"A draft for me and…" I turned to look at Jonathan.

"Tonic-and-lime," he supplied.

"A man after my own heart," the bartender said with a smile. "Comin' right up."

As he moved off for our drinks, I took a bill and a business card out of my billfold and laid them on the bar.

"Do you have a minute?" I asked when he returned. I pushed the card toward him, and he picked it up.

"A PI, huh?" he said. "We don't get many of those in here. What do you need?"

"I'm looking into these rumors about someone deliberately spreading AIDS. Do you know anything about them?"

He put the card back on the bar. "I've heard them, of course," he said. "But I can't believe anybody would do something like that."

"Have you heard any names mentioned?"

He shook his head. "Just some names of guys who claim to know someone who knows someone—you know how rumors are. I can't remember anything specific about any of them. The Male Call is mentioned a lot, though, now that I think of it. I used to work there, it's a pretty rough place, so I'm not surprised."

"Do you have any reason to think, having worked there, there's anything to the rumors?"

"I couldn't say. I was drinking too much back then and a lot of it's sort of a blur. It took my getting canned to pull my act together." He indicated Jonathan's tonic-and-lime with a nod of his head. "That's as strong as I go now.

"But as for the Male Call, like I say, it's a pretty rough place, and a hell of a lot goes on there that wouldn't be tolerated in other bars. So, it's not surprising the place would be a rumor mill."

"So, nothing specific about anybody specifically getting AIDS from someone there?"

He glanced up and down the bar to see if anyone needed another drink then said, "Look, guys who go to leather bars either are tough or want everybody to think they are. Intimidation and control are all part of the game. You have to take it all with a pound and a half of salt."

He picked up the bill I'd set out and headed for the cash register.

"Keep the change," I told him.

"Thanks," he said over his shoulder.

WE MADE QUICK STOPS AT TWO OTHER BARS BETWEEN DADDY-O'S AND VENTURE, NEITHER of which produced any useful new information, and arrived at Venture shortly after ten. The place was just beginning to fill up, and I knew that by eleven it would be jammed.

We looked around for Mario but didn't see him. The smaller bar by the dance floor wasn't open yet, but there were three bartenders at the main bar. I had no idea which one might be Ray, but we walked over to the nearest and ordered. After three beers, I'd switched to a weak bourbon-seven, and I was sure with all the quinine Jonathan was consuming in his tonic-with-limes he'd never have to worry about malaria.

Just as we were picking up our drinks, Mario appeared and, spotting us, came over.

"Let's move over here," he said, leading us to the far end of the bar. He indicated the bartender closest to us, one my crotch had pointed out to me when we entered—blond crew-cut, obviously tailored short sleeve white shirt that molded his impressive biceps, probably older than he looked. "That's Ray," he said. "I'll get him for you in a minute."

Though Mario was as relaxed as if we were sitting in his living room, we knew he was working, and that riding herd on a busy gay bar wasn't the easiest of jobs. Sure enough, less than two minutes into our conversation one of the other bartenders flagged him down, telephone in hand, and Mario excused himself. On the way down the bar, he stopped to say something to Ray, who looked in our direction and nodded then went back to fixing a drink.

A few minutes later, he came over.

"I'm Ray," he said, extending his hand to first Jonathan then me. "Mario says you have some questions for me?"

"Yeah," I said, noticing his eyes kept moving back to the customers near his station. "We won't keep you long. I'm trying to track down the source of these rumors about somebody deliberately spreading AIDS."

"Yeah, Mario told us all to start paying attention to them. Lots of talk, little substance."

"I understand you worked at the Male Call," I said.

"That's right. And if you know that you know I got canned for threatening to deck the boss. Is that what you wanted to talk to me about?"

"No," I said. "I'm only interested in getting to the base of the rumors. A lot of them seem to wind their way back to the Male Call."

"Well, I don't know who's spreading them, but I know it isn't me." he said. "Carl Brewer's a prick, and I wouldn't piss on the Male Call if it was on fire, but saying someone from there was deliberately spreading AIDS—no way, unless I knew for a fact it was true. And I don't."

"Well, I've heard a couple names mentioned from the Male Call."

He nodded. "Cal Hysong, I'll bet."

I hoped my surprise didn't show. "What makes you say that?"

"Well, for one thing, compared to Cal, every other guy in the bar is a drag queen, and if you doubt it just ask him. I don't know what there is about that guy everybody finds so fucking hot, but they sure as hell do. And the guy's an arrogant asshole. He treats everybody like shit, and they'd still fall on their backs and throw their legs up in the air anytime he snapped his fingers."

"Well," I said, "he's not the only ultra-butch guy at the Male Call."

"No, but he's the only one I know of who didn't start wearing condoms as soon as they figured out how it's spread. Man, that's asking for trouble these days. And anybody who would let him get away with it is asking for it, too. I'd really hate to think that anybody would knowingly infect somebody else, but if anybody would, my bet's on Cal Hysong."

Increasingly, so was mine.

EVEN THOUGH THE EVENING WAS FAIRLY FRUSTRATING FROM THE STANDPOINT OF FINDING out anything I hadn't either already known or suspected—and that in itself bothered me because I couldn't be sure exactly how objective I was really being, or whether I was just accepting things because they fit in with what I already thought—the time with Jonathan was very pleasant. Talking with Jimmy and Bob at Ramon's was nice, though not even Jimmy, who attracted rumors like a magnet attracts metal shavings, could supply any new additional information, and spending time at Griff's listening to Guy Prentiss sing old show tunes was, as always, a great pleasure.

We got home around one to find Craig curled up asleep on the couch in front of the TV. I wasn't sure if we should wake him or just let him sleep, but he woke up when Jonathan turned the set off.

"Hi," he said sleepily. "How was your evening."

"Great," Jonathan said with a smile. "Joshua behave himself?"

"No problem. I read him a story before bedtime and he 'read' me one. He's got 'em all memorized."

Jonathan got the couch ready while Craig excused himself and went into the bathroom. He came padding out a minute later in his shorts, his clothes over one arm; he laid those carefully out on a chair.

I must say, Craig was definitely crossing the threshold between being a kid and a young man. Jonathan saw me looking at him and gave me a small grin then mouthed the words *Don't drool,* which fortunately Craig didn't catch. We said our goodnights and went to bed.

"Was I ever that young?" I asked as we got under the covers.

"Oh, come on, Gramps, it's not that bad," Jonathan said, moving closer. "Besides, Craig and I aren't all that far apart in age."

"Rub it in," I said and turned off the light.

X

W E'D ARRANGED WITH CRAIG TO COME OVER SUNDAY AFTER CHURCH AND STAY WITH Joshua while we met Jake and Jared for brunch at Rasputin's, one of the places we used to go fairly regularly BJ—before Joshua. They were there, sitting at the bar, when we arrived and got up for an exchange of hugs.

"Hey, Jonathan," Jake said, taking him by the shoulders and stepping back to arm's length. "You been working out? You're lookin' good!" Then he turned his head to look at me. "You...eh!"

Jonathan blushed furiously as he did every time Jake flattered him.

"No, just working," he said. "And I think Dick looks great."

Jake grinned at me. "He'll do."

While I had a lot of questions I wanted to ask about what they might know about the Male Call and its clientele, I determined I wouldn't say anything if neither of them brought it up, and they didn't. We talked about everything *except* the Male Call and the rumors and the shadow I could sense even now had fallen over our two friends.

But when Jake excused himself to go to the bathroom while we were finishing our coffee, Jared reached into his shirt pocket and brought out a piece of paper.

"The phone numbers you asked for," he said.

I took it without a word and put it into my own pocket.

I'M PAID TO GET INFORMATION. I HAVE NO CONTROL OVER WHAT THAT INFORMATION MIGHT be or what the person hiring me might do with it once I give it to him. Contrary to what Brewer had suspected, I hadn't found any indication of a direct tie-in to Pete Reardon or anyone from the Spike as being instrumental in spreading the rumors. But every bit of information I had gathered thus far on who might be deliberately spreading AIDS pointed directly at Cal Hysong.

I was more than a little conflicted. I felt Brewer had a right to know what I'd found out so far, but I still had some other leads I wanted to follow—specifically, talking to the guys on the list Jared had given me at brunch. But, I reasoned, at least I could give Brewer a heads-up.

I waited, again, until ten-thirty Monday morning before dialing his number.

"Brewer."

"Mr. Brewer, Dick Hardesty. I'll be writing up a full report later but wanted to give you a quick rundown on what's going on."

"Yeah, I've been wondering."

"Would you like to get together for a few minutes today?" I could as easily do it over the phone, though I really always prefer to talk to clients face to face.

"I've got a busy day today. Can we just do it over the phone?"

"Sure."

"So, what have you got?"

"I've still got several leads to follow," I said, "but there's one constant in everything I've found out so far, which is why I'm mentioning it now."

I then laid out for him what I'd been doing, to whom I'd talked, what they'd told me and what I'd deduced from it. I pointed out again that there were still paths to follow, but that I could find no evidence Reardon or anyone from the Spike was engaged in a concerted effort to put the Male Call out of business. More important, I told him, at this point, everything centered on the strong probability that Cal Hysong had AIDS and was knowingly giving it to the men with whom he had sex.

I did not tell him about my conversation with Stan Jacobson, but I did mention the fact of Hysong's insistence on sex in the dark and on wearing at least a towel in the baths.

When I finished, there was a long pause—to the point where I was beginning to wonder if he was still on the line. Then, just before I spoke, Brewer said, "Okay. I'll take it from here. You can send me your bill."

Send him my bill? Whoa, there, cowboy!

"Uh," I said. (I hate saying "uh," it makes me look like I've been caught by surprise. Well, I had been.) "We still don't know without question that it's Hysong. It's your decision, of course, and I'm certainly not out to pad my bill, but…"

"No," Brewer said, "You only confirmed what I suspected."

"Can I ask what you plan to do?" I said, wishing to hell I hadn't even called him until I'd at least checked with the guys on Jared's list.

"I'm not sure. But the first thing I'm going to do is to permanently eighty-six Hysong and tell him that if I ever catch him within two hundred feet of the Male Call, I'll blow his fucking head off."

His voice was calm, but I could sense the anger under the calm. I hoped to God he wasn't planning on doing something stupid. And if he was serious about my sending him my bill, that meant I'd just managed to talk myself out of a client.

I'd give it a couple of days to see if he might call. In the meantime, though, I wouldn't pass up any other offers.

WHEN BREWER HADN'T CALLED BACK BY THURSDAY, I FINISHED WRITING UP MY REPORT TO him—most of which I'd told him on the phone already—and prepared my bill. I still felt a little—what? Guilty? No, more ill at ease—over the idea that I hadn't taken the case as far as it could possibly have gone if Brewer hadn't chopped it off. I really hadn't expected him to do that, but I should have learned by now that people don't always do what I expect them to do.

Friday night, just as we were finishing dinner Bob called to invite us—Joshua included—to a barbecue at their place on Sunday, and we accepted with thanks.

"Oh," he said after we'd gotten the what-time-and-what-can-we-bring (I volunteered potato salad) details out of the way, "have you heard the latest rumor going around?"

"Great," I said. "That's all we need, another rumor going around. What's this one about?"

"About a guy named Cal Hysong. He got eighty-sixed from the Male Call for spreading AIDS."

Well, Brewer certainly hadn't wasted any time. I hadn't a doubt in the world about the source of this tidbit. I wouldn't be surprised if he'd been handing out fliers.

"No, I hadn't," I said. "But guilty or not, I wouldn't want to be in Hysong's shoes. People will be avoiding him like the plague—no pun intended—and he probably won't be able to walk into any bar in town."

"Yeah, but if he is guilty, at least when he shows up anywhere, people will know the fox is in the henhouse."

"So much for innocent until proven guilty," I said.

"You think he's innocent?" Bob asked, sounding incredulous.

"Frankly, no, I don't. But I'd just like to be absolutely sure before we start forming a lynch mob."

"Agreed, but under the circumstances, better safe now than maybe sorry later."

"Yeah, but that's the tragic part—no one's safe."

SATURDAY AFTERNOON WE MADE A FAMILY PROJECT OF MAKING POTATO SALAD TO TAKE TO Bob and Mario's barbecue. While I've never been on Julia Childs's Christmas card list, I do make a mean potato salad—a throwback to my single days when I'd make a huge batch and eat it all week long, and I learned that the flavor is always better if you make it the day before you start eating it. We let Joshua "help" by mixing the chopped onions, celery and olives with a long wooden spoon in a deep pot to keep spillage to a minimum. Then, when we had it in the bowl and sprinkled with paprika, we let him arrange egg slices and whole olives on top.

We got to Bob and Mario's at around two, to find Jake and Jared already there. Tim and Phil pulled into the drive right behind us. Joshua insisted on carrying in the potato salad. Mario held the screen door open for the five of us as we entered the kitchen.

"Look what I made!" Joshua announced to the others sitting around the kitchen table, then marched it over to Bob, who stood at the kitchen counter making hamburger patties.

Bob wiped his hands on a towel and took the bowl. "This looks great, Joshua," he said. "And you made it yourself?"

Joshua nodded. "Yep," he said then, looking quickly at Jonathan and me, added, "Almost."

At that point, one of their two cats—I couldn't tell if it was Butch or Pancake (long story)—made the mistake of walking into the room, and Joshua was off like a shot.

"Joshua!" Jonathan cautioned, "Take it easy!"

"That's okay," Mario said with a grin. "They can take care of themselves." He put the potato salad into the fridge and took out beers for Tim, Phil and me and a Coke for Jonathan. "I've got lemonade when Joshua's ready."

When Bob had finished making the hamburgers, we all moved out into the fenced-in backyard. I noticed the grill and the picnic table were already set up. Joshua had been reluctant to leave the cats, who were not allowed outside, but he soon became engaged in looking for the box tortoise that Mario assured him was somewhere in the yard.

AS ALWAYS, A GREAT AFTERNOON. A LOT OF CATCHING UP AND LAUGHING AND STORIES AND good food. Tim had made one of his Bavarian tortes that, as usual, disappeared in a matter of minutes. Everyone was in good spirits, and I noticed again with some relief that Jake appeared totally recovered from his bout with pneumonia.

While we'd been visiting him in the hospital, he had mentioned that he and his brother Stan were setting up a hunting trip. Jared, it seemed, had reluctantly agreed to go along, so they could all stay at his cabin.

"Why don't we make it a group outing?" Jake suggested. "Any of the rest of you hunt?"

"I used to," Bob said, "but I haven't in years. I don't even have a rifle anymore."

"That's okay," Jake said. "Stan and I just bought two new Winchester 94s, so we've still got the old ones any of you would be welcome to use."

"Well, thanks, but I don't know..." Bob said.

"Hey, you wouldn't even have to hunt. It would just be great for all of us to get out of the city for a weekend. Think about it."

"It sounds like fun," Jonathan agreed, "but I'd feel funny about leaving Joshua with someone for a whole weekend."

"Ah, the joys of parenthood," Jake teased, then said, "You can bring him along. It would do him good to get out into nature for a couple days."

I didn't know if he had any real idea of what he was suggesting. The guys were all used to being around Joshua for relatively short periods of time, but for an entire weekend? And the prospect of eight guys being cooped up with a hell-on-wheels five-year-old...

"We'll think about it," I said.

The conversation segued into Mario and Bob telling bar stories, and Mario—I'm sure without thinking—brought up the subject of the rumors.

"What do you think of the latest about the Male Call?" he asked.

"What's that?" Jared asked. "We haven't been out in a while, both of us have been so damned busy."

"About Cal Hysong getting eighty-sixed."

I was glad he caught himself before adding "for spreading AIDS."

I shot a quick glance at Jake and saw just the flicker of something I definitely did not like.

I decided I'd better jump in before we started down the slippery slope.

"I suspect this particular rumor is Carl Brewer's attempt at damage control. Rumors have been killing him and to eighty-six someone for being behind them, whether it's true or not, is a good way of saying 'Okay, guys, you can all come back now. The bogeyman's gone away.'"

"But why Hysong?" Phil asked.

Having set off on a little journey of evasions and half-truths, I thought I'd better just keep on going.

"Probably because the guy is an arrogant prick and has always been something of a recruiting poster for the Male Call. I'd imagine he's probably the first person anyone thinks of when they think of the place."

"What's an 'arrogant prick?'" Joshua, who I hadn't seen come up behind me for a refill of lemonade, asked.

"That's a not-nice man," Jonathan said as he shot me a dirty look. "And you should never call anyone that, okay?"

"Uncle Dick did," Joshua pointed out logically.

"Well," Jonathan said, reaching for the pitcher of lemonade, "grown-ups sometimes say things they shouldn't."

"Okay." Joshua held out his glass.

To counterbalance the great weather of the weekend, we had three solid days of unrelenting drizzle with a downright chill wind. Wednesday night, just as we were getting ready for bed, the phone rang. I do not like telephone calls at that hour of the night. Nine times out of ten, they portend bad news.

The minute I heard Jared's voice, my heart sank.

"Jake's in the hospital again," he said. "And if Stan hadn't called me, I never would have known. I'm so fucking mad at Jake I could kill him! He never fucking learns! He went to work every single day this week, in all this rain. He knew damned well what was going to happen and then acts surprised that it did."

"Jeez, Jared, I'm sorry," I said. "I can understand your being worried, but…"

Jonathan had come over to stand beside me, and I tipped the phone so we could both hear what was being said.

"That's not the worst part," Jared said.

"What do you mean?"

There was a very long, almost palpable pause.

"He had sex with Cal Hysong."

XI

J EEZUS!
  "When?"

"A couple of months ago. You know our arrangement—we can screw around with anyone we want to and I knew he was hot for Cal, so I probably shouldn't have been surprised."

"How do you know for sure?" I asked.

"He told me. After Bob and Mario's barbecue. He hadn't heard about Cal being eighty-sixed, and he swore he had no idea Cal was a carrier."

"And Cal didn't use a condom."

"No. The good thing—if it's possible for there to be a 'good thing' in all this—is that Jake wouldn't let Cal screw him without one. But he blew him."

I was mildly ill. Not by picturing what went on—jeez, no gay man would find that the least bit strange. On the contrary, it would be a turn-on for most.

What disturbed me was knowing what Cal might have passed on to Jake in the course of it. Nobody knew for sure the exact details of transmission, but there was a lot of talk about what they euphemistically referred to as "exchanging bodily fluids." Well, oral sex certainly exchanged bodily fluids.

"I told Stan," Jared continued. "He's been doing his best to have Mercy Memorial be one of the hospitals on the viral test trials list and he thinks he can do it—he's expecting to hear from the CDC any day now. Jesus, Dick! If he does have it, I…What the hell are we going to do?"

"Look, Jared," I said, as calmly as I could, "I know you've got every right to be upset, but we both also know jumping to conclusions is the quickest way to drive yourself crazy. It won't do anybody any good. Nobody knows for sure if Cal even has it or not—it's all just rumors at this point. And even if he does, that doesn't automatically mean he gave it to Jake. Jake'll be fine. I'm sure of it. Just take it easy."

"But what if he does have it?" Jared asked.

A detached corner of my mind found it interesting, even in the middle of such a surreal conversation, to realize that the fear of AIDS was so great in the community that the name itself was almost never used. AIDS was simply "it," and everyone knew what "it" was.

"Then you'll...we'll all...just have to find a way to deal with it. But please, please, try not to let worrying about it get the best of you right now. Okay?"

Another long pause, then: "Okay."

"Can we go see him?" I asked.

"No, not just yet. And please don't say a word to the guys. I'm doing enough worrying for all of us."

"Well, promise you'll keep us posted. And if there's anything at all..."

"I know," he said. "And I appreciate it. I'll call you as soon as I find out anything."

I hung up the phone feeling oddly calm. Of course, Jake didn't have AIDS. Jared was just overreacting. Understandably so, but overreacting nonetheless. Anybody could come down with pneumonia working in a cold rain for three days, especially if he'd just gotten over a bout a short time before. Even if it was pneumocystis again, that didn't mean it was AIDS. Jake was an idiot to press his luck, but he'd be fine.

He couldn't *not* be fine.

"He's got it," Jonathan said, his voice flat, his face expressionless. "And if Jake's got it, Jared's got it."

I took him by the shoulders and turned him to face me. "We don't know that," I said, looking him firmly in the eye, "and until and unless we do know..."

He sighed and turned his head away. I felt him relax just a bit, and I released his shoulders. "You're right, of course," he said. "But..."

"No buts," I said. "We don't go running off in all directions until and unless we know. Okay?"

He nodded.

I'M AFRAID THAT, LIKE MOST PEOPLE, I'M MUCH BETTER AT GIVING ADVICE THAN TAKING IT. I couldn't stop thinking—and worrying—about Jake even as I went through the rituals of a series of phone calls and yet another trip to the Hall of Records to gather information for a lawyer client. I found I was reluctant to leave the office in case I might miss a call from Jared, but when I did get back there was no message from him. I assumed he had taken more time off from work and was here in the city with Jake, but he hadn't specifically said so when we'd talked.

The afternoon was marked by a phone call from Estelle Bronson at Happy Day, reporting that Joshua had gotten into an altercation with another boy and called him an "arrogant prick," which meant we'd have to have a little family meeting that night. I told Estelle I was sorry and said we'd see to it that Joshua issued a formal apology to the boy the next day.

Though I was mildly angry at Joshua for his behavior and more so at myself for having used the term in his hearing, it was, in fact, a welcome distraction.

I'll spare you the drama of our talk with Joshua that evening before dinner. Suffice it to say it involved a relatively low level of histrionics, not a few tears, a little well-taken recrimination ("Uncle Dick said it first!") and some major sulking. The punishment was banishment to his room from right after dinner until bedtime and his promise of a sincere apology to the other boy in front of Estelle Bronson. As a bargaining chip, we agreed that if he withstood his exile nobly we would not deprive him of Story Time.

We'd just returned to the living room after Joshua's reluctant surrender to sleep when Jared called.

"Jake's doing better," he said, "and Stan got word today that the CDC has approved Mercy Medical for inclusion in the testing program. Stan says it isn't foolproof yet, but it's a step in the right direction. We should know about Jake before he leaves the hospital."

"Well, you know we've got our fingers crossed. How much longer do you think they'll be keeping him?"

"Probably another couple of days."

"Be sure to let us know as soon as we can see him," I said. "How are you going to handle your teaching? I'd imagine they'll only let you have so much time off, now that school has started."

"I'll manage. And when Jake comes home, I'll just commute for awhile until I can trust him not to be such an idiot. I hope he's learned his lesson on this one."

An hour each way between here and Carrington was quite a commute, but I knew a lot of people in the bigger cities did it as a matter of course. Still…

"I've been hearing from several of the guys we know from the Male Call," Jared continued. "They don't know about Jake's being in the hospital, but they're all up in arms over this rumor about Cal. One of 'em suggested we all get together to talk about it and about what we can do."

I sighed. "Well, I don't know if there is much anyone can do."

"We could kill him," he said with a casualness I found chilling. "If he gave it to Jake, I'll kill him myself."

I felt a shock not unlike sticking my finger into an electric outlet. I knew he was just letting his emotions run away with him, but...

"Jared! Come on, get serious! Don't even think about anything so stupid! We still don't know for sure that Jake has it, and if he does, we can't prove Hysong did it."

He sighed. "True. But if it looks like a duck and quacks like a duck...That's why a meeting might not be a bad idea. If we all got together and pooled everybody's information maybe we could make a list of everybody we know who's had sex with Cal—I know at least two of the guys I talked to have. Maybe we could convince Stan to test them. Or at very least, we can warn anybody else we know and it might keep other guys from having sex with him. It's just a thought, but..."

Actually, it wasn't a bad thought at all, especially now that Stan had access to the test. It took what I'd been trying to do ever since Brewer hired me a step further. If I were still on the case, which, I had to remind myself, I wasn't...

After we'd hung up and I'd filled Jonathan in on our conversation, the air slowly went out of the enthusiasm the news Stan had access to the test had pumped into me. All a test could do was show whether Jake had AIDS or not. If he did...

Well, I couldn't let myself think about that.

SEX SHOULD NEVER BE CLINICAL, BUT AS JONATHAN AND I FOUND OUT SHORTLY AFTER Joshua entered our lives—and as most straight couples realize after their first trip to the delivery room—the opportunity for spontaneous sex more or less goes out the window. So, for someone as testosterone-driven as me, I frequently, in moments of circumstance-based frustration, found myself contemplating the different primary elements of sex (lust, fun, need—and if you're lucky, love) and how their mix and proportions vary with each encounter.

All this is to preface the fact that, after my talk with Jared, I became aware of another element—reassurance. We sometimes look to sex for comfort and the assurance that we are not alone. Usually, it was Jonathan who required it from time to time—just to hold and be comforted by and feel physically a part of another human being. So, while I initiated it as soon as we closed the bedroom door behind us, it was obviously a mutual need, and it was really very special.

And if talking about sex as being "special" isn't being clinical, I don't know what is.

He said only two words: "He's positive."

"Positive?" I asked, not sure how to react. "That's good or bad?" I honestly, at that point, didn't know.

"He's positive for the virus. They're pretty sure he has it." His voice was frighteningly calm.

"Pretty sure? What does that mean?"

"Well, the test they gave him is called ELISA. Stan said what that stood for, but I can't remember. It has a pretty high rate of error. So, then they did something called a Western Blot which is supposed to tell if the results were accurate. According to that one, they were. But there's just so damned much they don't know!"

I didn't know what to say, or how to say it. I can't even describe what I felt, if I felt anything other than numb.

"So what...what now? What did Stan say?"

There was a slight pause and then, still calmly: "Well, Stan says all it means is that he has the virus in his body. From what they can figure out at the CDC, the virus itself isn't what kills you. It just lowers your immune system and opens the door to allow anything that comes down the pike to take a foothold in your body and wreak hell. We're lucky that Stan is an immunologist—he can keep minute-by-minute tabs on Jake and says there are all sorts of things Jake can do to protect himself. Diet, exercise, preventive medications, immune boosters—he says it won't be easy, but he's pretty sure it's doable. He's putting the best possible face on it, I know, but we'll take it. I thank God he's there for Jake."

It was probably my state of something akin to shock that made the whole thing surreal and therefore enabled me to be almost as objectively calm as Jared was.

"And what about you? Is Stan going to test you, too?"

"He did. Today. We'll see by Monday."

There was a long pause while I tried to come up with something to say. But before I did, Jared spoke first.

"Oh, and guess who I saw coming out of the hospital just as I was going in?"

"Who?"

"Cal Hysong," he said casually—and it was the casualness that had the effect of a bucket of ice water poured on my head. Surreal was gone. Real was back.

"And?" I finally managed to say.

"And nothing. I just thought it was interesting."

Interesting? You've just found out your partner has AIDS—okay, has the virus—and you run into the guy you think gave it to him and you find that interesting?

"Jared! Come on! This is me you're talking to! I know you. You didn't just find it 'interesting.' What did you do?"

"I didn't do anything. He didn't see me, and we didn't speak. I just walked right by him. Stan won't—or can't—tell me, but I think Cal's one of his patients."

I remembered my conversation with Stan in which he'd practically confirmed my suspicions about Hysong's having Karposi's sarcoma.

"So, what are you *thinking* about doing?" I asked.

"Nothing," he said. "I just think we should have that meeting I told you some of the guys from the Male Call wanted. You know, keep it small—just the guys who lost friends from there."

"Jared," I said as calmly as I possibly could, "I don't think that's a good idea right now."

"Yeah? When do you think it might be?"

"Look, I…At least, if you do decide to have it, let me come."

A long pause before: "Well, I haven't decided yet, for sure, but if I do…"

"Let me come."

"I appreciate your interest, but you aren't a Male Call regular."

"No, but I have a friend who has…the virus."

"True," he said. "Well, we'll see if I even decide to have it first."

"Okay, but let me know."

"I will. Look, I'm calling from the phone in the lobby. Jake asked me to pick him up some magazines, so I'd better be getting back."

"Okay. Any idea when he might feel up to visitors?"

"Maybe Sunday. I'll ask and let you know."

"Thanks. Give him our best. And you take care of yourself, too."

"I will. Thanks. See ya." And he hung up.

TO TELL OR NOT TO TELL—THAT WAS THE QUESTION I PONDERED ON THE WAY HOME. I really didn't want to tell Jonathan; I knew he'd be devastated. But not telling him would only put off the inevitable. He'd have to find out sooner or later, and he'd be rightly upset with me for keeping it from him.

I told him while we were watching the news before dinner. Joshua was playing with the tool set Jake and Jared had given him for his birthday, trying to "fix" a small broken orange crate he'd found behind our building while coming home from school. Maybe it was just a tad unfair of me to do it then, but I knew Jonathan would not allow himself to show his emotions while Joshua was around—it was one of the things I have always admired about him.

I emphasized that Stan's being an immunologist certainly gave Jake an edge and that having the virus was not the same as having AIDS. It may have been a fine line, but if it could give people something to hang on to, it was well worth it. I know I had a tight grip on it and wasn't about to let go.

I did not mention Jared's having seen Cal Hysong, or of the talked-about meeting of Male Call regulars who had lost friends possibly because of Hysong. Just the thought of the potential ramifications of such a meeting made me shudder. But I hoped that if there was one, I would be able to be there. I realized the chance of that was remote in the extreme—Jared was right, I wasn't a Male Call regular. I probably wouldn't know anyone there besides him and, assuming he was out of the hospital, Jake.

Jared was one of the most level-headed guys I knew. He certainly was not given to letting his emotions run away with him. But this situation went far beyond everyday emotions. It's human nature to want to lash out at those who hurt us or those we love. There was no vengeance grieving friends could exact upon the Grim Reaper—he was an abstraction. But Cal Hysong was all too mortal, and while the Lord may have said vengeance was His, I was sure there were more than a few men from the Male Call who would be eager to take over the job.

XII

JARED CALLED SATURDAY TO SAY JAKE WOULD BE GOING HOME MONDAY AND SUGGESTED we might get together at Jake's for a drink Monday night. I said we'd be delighted to, if we could find someone to look after Joshua.

"You're welcome to bring him along," Jared said. "I know Jake would like to see him." Then he paused. "Unless you'd rather not."

Sometimes what isn't said conveys a lot more than what is. I knew what the "unless you'd rather not" meant, and I made a giant leap of faith in assuming Jonathan would agree when I replied, "Sure, if you think Jake's up to dealing with a five-year-old."

"He'll manage," he said. "About seven-thirty, then?"

"Sounds good," I said. "Give our best to Jake."

When we'd exchanged our goodbyes and hung up, I relayed our conversation to Jonathan, and I could see concern on his face. I knew he wanted to say something but was hesitant to do so.

"What?" I asked

He sighed and shook his head. "I'm really ashamed of myself for even saying this, but I wish we had had a chance to talk about it before you said we'd bring Joshua. I mean, I understand why you said it, but...do you really think we should take him? There's so much nobody knows about AIDS yet, and Joshua is only five years old, and we've got to protect him and..." His expression changed from concern to anguish as he tried to deal with his feelings.

I moved over to him and hugged him.

"I know you're concerned, babe—so am I. It's totally natural. But we're entering into a whole new world now, and we can't shut ourselves or Joshua off from it, much as we might like to. If I thought there was any real danger—

hell, if Jared thought there was any danger, he never would have asked. Jake's life has just changed forever, and he'll need his friends now more than ever. The very least we can do is not treat him any differently than we always have."

Jonathan clasped his hands behind the small of my back and pulled me closer.

"You're right, of course," he said, then sighed. "It's just…"

"I know," I said, and kissed him on the bridge of his nose.

At that point, Joshua, who had been busy with one of his toys, came running over.

"Hey, where's my hug?" he demanded.

We showed him.

MONDAY EVENING, WE DECIDED TO SAVE A LITTLE TIME BY GOING OUT TO ONE OF THE 397 or so local Cap'n Rooney's Fish Shack franchises—each one of them a personal favorite of Joshua's because of the large fish tank they all had in the center of the dining area. We arrived at Jake's right on time, having explained to Joshua that Uncle Jake was kind of tired from working hard so he— Joshua—should refrain from instigating their usual roughhousing and using Jake as his personal Mt. Everest.

Jonathan's comment on the way over that we'd never been to Jake's apartment caught me rather by surprise when I realized he was right. Not that it mattered, of course; it had just worked out that way.

Jake lived in a very nice neighborhood, and his apartment was on the ground floor of a newer four-story building. He met us at the door looking tired but otherwise pretty much usual Jake. Our cautions to Joshua went right out the window when Jake scooped him up and tossed him in the air, to Joshua's delight; but I noted that rather than tossing him several times as he normally did, he set him down after the first one.

"You're getting to be too big a boy to throw around, Joshua," he said with a smile.

"No, I'm not," Joshua objected.

Jake tousled his head. "Well, that's one of the prices you have to pay for growing up," he said.

Turning to Jonathan and me, he gave us both a hug. "Jared's on coffee duty in the kitchen," he said. "I've sort of given up on the booze for a while. But I can make you a Manhattan if you want, Dick, or get you a beer."

I shook my head as we moved into the living room. "Coffee'll be fine," I said.

The apartment was small but very comfortable, and I was mildly surprised but pleased to see that Jake had several framed photos of himself and Jared, including one of the five of us we'd taken at a picnic right after Joshua had come to us. At one end of the room I noticed a large lighted display cabinet with bevel-glassed doors, behind which were mounted five or six what I assumed to be hunting rifles, though they looked a little strange. Jake had said he collected them.

Joshua, of course, was immediately drawn to it and stood staring up at the highly-polished stocks and gleaming barrels.

"Are you a cowboy, Uncle Jake?" he asked eagerly, obviously associating the guns with his favorite Westerns on TV. "Where's your horse?"

Jared entered the room at that point and grinned at Joshua, who ran over for a hug.

"That'd be me," Jared said.

"You're not a horse!" Joshua declared. "You're silly!"

"Well, Uncle Jake works me like one," Jared replied.

"Uh-huh," Jake said.

"Interesting collection," I said, knowing next to nothing about rifles. "Which one's your new one?"

Jake laughed. "Those are all antiques," he said. "I keep the two newer ones locked away in the bedroom."

We all sat down, and I was feeling mildly uncomfortable, wondering how we were going to dance around the 900-pound gorilla in the room. Luckily, that issue was resolved when Jake said, "So, Jared told you?"

Neither Jonathan nor I said anything, just nodded.

"It's going to be quite an adjustment," Jake said matter-of-factly. "Thank God for Stan—he's going to walk me through it. Not very many people are lucky enough to have one of the top immunologists in the country as a brother. Jared and I were just going over some of the new rules before you got here. No more fifteen-hour workdays, a lot more delegation of the work itself. Stan's working out a diet for me, which I'm sure I'll probably hate, figuring out which vitamins and supplements I should start on to help boost my immune system—that sort of thing."

Jonathan was staring at him. "You're incredible!" he said. "I could never take all this so calmly."

Jake shrugged. "I don't have much of an alternative, really. I've always liked challenges, and this is just another one. A big one, I'll admit, but…

"What I'm not going to do is let it take over my life. And the fact that you guys are here—and that you weren't afraid to bring Joshua…" He paused a second and gave a small smile. "…or that you brought him anyway, means a hell of a lot and will make it a little easier. I'll have to tell the rest of the gang, and I hope they'll take it as well as you have."

"You know they will," I said.

The tension eased, and the conversation moved on to other things.

When Joshua began to get fidgety, Jared got up and said, "Come on, Joshua. We'll go get the coffee, and I see somebody left us a cherry pie. You can help me cut it—but I don't suppose you're hungry after dinner, are you?"

Joshua immediately hopped off the sofa and headed for the kitchen. "Yes, I am!"

WEDNESDAY'S WORK MAIL BROUGHT A CHECK FROM CARL BREWER—NO NOTE, JUST THE check with "Thanks" written on the memo line in the lower left-hand corner.

I'd really made a concerted effort, after our Monday visit with Jake and Jared, to put this AIDS thing out of my mind as much as I could. But every morning, while driving to work, I had to pass the construction site of the new Century Tower office complex and, inevitably, was reminded Cal Hysong worked there. I'd just as soon forget about Cal Hysong.

That, of course, would remind me of Jared's proposed meeting of Male Call regulars with every right to have a grudge against Hysong. Jared hadn't said any more about it, and if he'd discarded the idea, as I hoped he had, I didn't want to replant it by asking him about it.

Thursday evening we got calls from both Phil and Tim and Bob and Mario. Jake had called them to give them the news about Jake's status. They'd all done their best to hide their shock and concern and to go along completely with Jake's expressed confidence in Stan's ability to protect him.

Whether Jake believed it himself was another matter. The little dances that humans go through in trying to protect and support their friends is one of our stranger and more admirable qualities.

Because we owed Tim and Phil a dinner, we invited them over Friday night and they readily accepted. It was rather like Joshua's seeking reassurance from Jonathan and me the way our friends sought reassurance from one another. Reassurance of exactly what we probably could not say.

SO, ALL WENT RELATIVELY WELL UNTIL I SAT DOWN AT THE OFFICE THE FOLLOWING TUESDAY morning to read the paper and my eye went directly to an article on the bottom half of page one.

WORKER DIES IN FALL

The fall was from the under-construction Century Tower, and the worker, it turned out, was one Cal Hysong.

I wasn't quite sure what my reaction was—the fleeting shadow of sorrow that accompanies the news of any death; relief that Jared would not need to have that meeting he talked about, which could not have led to anything positive; a certain sense of vindication in knowing that if it had been Cal Hysong deliberately spreading AIDS to others he had gotten his comeuppance and would not be the ender of anyone else's dreams.

The article went on to say he had been working on a beam on the Twelfth floor of the tower, had not been wearing his safety harness and had somehow fallen. My quick thought that it might have been suicide was only mildly comforting.

But none of it mattered. He was dead, and the world would move on without him.

I was tempted to call Jake but thought better of it. What would be the point? He'd probably see it on the evening news.

Tim called that evening right after dinner, while Jonathan and Joshua were busy feeding the fish.

"You saw the news on Cal Hysong?" he asked.

We had discussed Hysong at length on Friday.

"Yeah," I replied. "I hate to see anyone die, but in his case, I'm almost willing to make an exception. Did you work on him?"

"That's one of the perks in having achieved my exalted station at the coroner's office," he said. "I can occasionally ask to work on a case that interests me."

"And Hysong interested you?"

"In a way, yes. And I thought I'd let you know, just between us, that you were right—he had Karposi's sarcoma, and apparently for some time, though it's hard to tell. But that's not the interesting part."

"Oh? What is?"

"That the fall killed him, but he had help."

He had me.

"Help? Somebody pushed him?"

"Indirectly. He was shot."

XIII

H E WAS SHOT? OFF AN I-BEAM TWELVE STORIES OFF THE GROUND?"
"Yep. We almost missed it—we were looking for evidence of a stroke
or embolism as cause of death and found the bullet in his chest. Came as
quite a surprise."

"I can imagine," I said. "So, I don't suppose there's much chance of its
being an accident."

"I suppose it could have been a freak accident involving someone's just
firing a gun into the air. The bullet was a .38 calibre, and they're doing a
match to see exactly what kind of gun was used, but from what I've heard
about Cal Hysong, I'd say its a little unlikely it was an accident. But that's not
our job to say. We just report what we find. What happens then is out of our
hands."

"Well," I said, "at least a lot of guys can sleep easier knowing there's one
less going around spreading AIDS."

Tim sighed. "I just wish I could be more confident he wasn't the only one
spreading it deliberately."

"Jeez, Tim! That's a terrible thing to think."

"I know, but my job always reminds me what one human being is willing
to do to another. I wish it weren't so, but that damned reality always gets in the
way of what we'd like to believe."

I knew he was right, of course, and not for the first time, I did not envy him
his job.

I WAITED UNTIL AFTER STORY TIME AND JOSHUA WAS ASLEEP TO TELL JONATHAN WHAT TIM
had said, though when he said "Well, at least it's over," I left out the part about
Hysong's probably not being the first or the last to deliberately spread the

81

disease.

"Are you going to call Jared and Jake?" he asked.

"Not tonight," I said. "It's getting late. It can wait until tomorrow."

It was not until the words came out of my mouth that I realized I had a reason other than the hour.

Hysong had been killed, obviously, as a result of Brewer's leaking Cal's name to the rumor mills. And the killer was undoubtedly someone Hysong had infected, or someone seeking revenge on behalf of a victim. And I could not avoid the likelihood that Hysong had infected Jake and that both he and Jared had to be included in the list of those potentially out to seek revenge.

I was both shocked and disgusted with myself that I could even think either Jared or Jake could have been involved, but as Tim so rightly put it, "that damned reality always gets in the way of what we'd like to believe."

I also couldn't help wondering if Jared had called that meeting of Male Call regulars he'd talked about and not invited me. He certainly wasn't under any obligation to do so, but I was curious and thought I just might ask.

I glanced at the clock beside the bed to see it was 12:43. I assumed Jonathan had been asleep a long time before, so I was startled when I felt his hand slide over my chest, and to hear him say, "Don't worry. They didn't do it."

I turned to face him. "What are you doing still awake?"

"I was waiting for you to fall asleep first," he replied. "I know you're worried."

I didn't even try to deny it. "I can't help it," I said. "I know they couldn't have been involved, but I know damned well if there is much of an investigation into this, they'll be on the list. And they don't need to be hassled any more than they've already been. Especially Jake!"

"Well, there's nothing you can do about it tonight. Try to get some sleep."

"I've been trying. But I'm wound up tighter than a watchspring."

"Maybe I can help there," he said, and his hand slid down my stomach.

"Babe," I said, "I appreciate the thought but..."

"Shhhhh!"

Did I had mention in my listing the different benefits of sex the one that had always been a strong one for me—relaxing tension?

When Jonathan came back up next to me I started to move to reciprocate, but he pushed me back onto the pillow.

"I'm fine. Sleep now," he said.

I did.

WHILE HYSONG'S DEATH HAD WARRANTED ONLY THE BRIEFEST OF MENTIONS WHEN IT WAS assumed he had fallen, the discovery he had been shot made the morning news on every TV and radio station in town—and every one of them included a sound bite from our new district attorney, Victor St. John, who, having risen to the post only after the forced resignation of his predecessor, had his eye on the upcoming elections. He was already notorious as a headline grabber, his aspirations to higher office well known.

When my office phone rang at nine-thirty that morning, I was not at all surprised to recognize the voice—Detective Marty Gresham of the city police.

"Marty!" I said. "To what do I owe the honor?"

"I've got a case that might interest you."

I wasn't about to let on that I knew it was Cal Hysong, since I wasn't supposed to know he'd been shot.

"Oh?" I said non-committally.

"Yeah, a guy named Cal Hysong. You know him?"

"The guy who fell off the Century Tower?" I didn't like playing games with Marty, but I didn't want to risk getting Tim in any trouble.

"Yeah, but he didn't just fall, he was shot first. Didn't you watch the news?"

"Yeah, I did. But what does that have to do with me?"

"Lieutenant Richman wants to know if you can come by headquarters this morning. He'd like to talk to you."

"Sure," I said. "But can you tell me what it's about?"

"Dick, it's me, Marty. Neither one of us just fell off the turnip truck. You can figure it out."

"Yeah, I guess I can." Obviously, they knew I knew something about Hysong, but I had no idea what or how they'd found out. "What time?" I asked.

"Ten-thirty? I've got a couple things to check out first."

"So, you'll be there, too?"

"Hey, we haven't seen each other in ages. How could I pass it up?"

"Ah, Marty, you finally got your BA in bullshit, I see."

He laughed. "I'm going for my masters," he said. "So, see you in an hour?"

"Right." And we hung up.

Lt. Richman was Mark Richman, Craig's dad. I'd known and worked with him since the early beginnings of the detente between the police department and the gay community following years of police harassment, mutual tension and distrust. Though, now the tension levels had nearly dropped off the scale, the police were able to work more easily in and with the community, I still served as a very informal liaison between the two when the police needed more access or information than they felt they could get on their own.

I'd known Marty Gresham since he was a rookie, and for some reason he'd always credited me with helping to fast-track him to his current status as a detective.

Rather than take my car and, as I normally did, park it in the lot beneath Warman Park then walk the two blocks to the City Annex, which housed the police department, I decided to take the bus. It dropped me off in front of the City Annex at 9:50 and after being okayed by the security desk, I took the elevator to the fifteenth floor and Mark Richman's office.

On the way up, I reflected briefly on the little protocol games we humans seem to enjoy so much. On those rare occasions when we met outside of police headquarters, and if he was not in uniform, I called Lt. Richman "Mark" and was comfortable doing so. But I would never dream of doing it when he was acting in his formal capacity. Marty, on the other hand, was always "Marty," unless, again, it was in a direct-police-related situation where others were present.

As Joshua was recently fond of saying, "That's silly," but that's also people.

KNOCKING ON LT. RICHMAN'S DOOR, I ENTERED ON HIS "COME" TO FIND HIM WITH MARTY Gresham and Marty's partner, Dan Carpenter. I shook hands all around and was gestured to a seat. Marty and Dan took chairs on either side of me and Lt. Richman sat behind his desk.

"Detectives Carpenter and Gresham are working on an interesting homicide," he began then paused, looking at me.

"Cal Hysong," I supplied.

"You knew him?"

I couldn't help but smile. "Do you have any idea how many gay men there are in this city?" I asked. "I know a lot of them, but not all."

"So, you didn't know him?"

"Not personally," I said. "I knew of him."

"And what did you know?"

Well, we could keep playing Twenty Questions all day, but I figured we might as well cut to the chase.

"I knew he was suspected of deliberately spreading AIDS."

Marty and Detective Carpenter exchanged quick glances, but the lieutenant didn't bat an eye. Whether they had known about the AIDS thing before I mentioned it I couldn't tell.

"A fairly good motive for murder, I'd say," Richman observed.

"So would I," I agreed.

"So, here's our problem," Marty said. "None of his coworkers knew much about him—or, apparently, even that he was gay. They described him as a tough-guy loner who nobody dared to mess with. Basically the same story from his neighbors, though a couple said they knew he was gay. We started checking the bars. Apparently, those rumors of someone spreading AIDS have been going around for a couple months, but in the last week or so, they started to zero in on Hysong. We learned he mainly hung out at the Male Call, but the owner denied knowing anything except that he'd eighty-sixed Hysong because of the rumors."

He paused, apparently waiting for me to say something, but I still wasn't sure where this was going and remained silent.

Finally, Carpenter picked up where Marty had left off. "The autopsy on Hysong showed he had AIDS himself, and if he was deliberately infecting others we're looking at a pretty big suspect pool here. We can use your help in narrowing it down. The most logical place to start is the Male Call, since we heard that was Hysong's main stomping ground. What do you know about it and, specifically, about any of its clientele?"

Okay, kids, it's tightrope-walking time, I thought. I was positive Brewer would never have mentioned hiring me, but I didn't want to risk Marty or Richman finding out later and think I was hiding something from them.

"The Male Call's normally a little out of my league," I said. "But Carl Brewer, the owner, hired me to try to find out who was behind the rumors that someone from the Male Call was responsible, since the rumors were destroying his business. Everything I found out pointed to Cal Hysong, and I probably made a mistake when I told Brewer before I had really exhausted all possible leads. Brewer said he didn't need me to look further, and I suspect it was him who started pointing the finger directly at Hysong and led, I have no doubt, to Hysong's murder."

"Well, Brewer's got an alibi for the time of the murder—he was taking inventory at the bar with one of his bartenders until about three."

"So, do you know any of the Male Call's regulars?" Marty asked. "It might be a good idea for us to start asking around, and if we had some specific names to start with it would help."

Shit! How the hell was I supposed to get around that one? The only ones I really knew were Jared and Jake, and if the police found out Jake had sex with Hysong and was now positive for the virus, I might just as well paint a bullseye on their backs.

"I know several guys who go in there from time to time, but I wouldn't call them regulars. Brewer'd be the one to ask about that."

Please, please don't push it! my mind pleaded.

"Yeah," Marty said, "we asked him for a customer list, and he said he'd make up one for us."

Great, I thought. Jared and Jake will undoubtedly be on it...but I'd worry about that later.

"We just thought you might have some other ideas as to where we should be looking," Marty continued. "We hoped maybe you might have known Hysong personally. And you don't know of anyone who might have a grudge against him?"

Time for a major sidestep. "For deliberately infecting other guys with AIDS?" I asked. "Like I said, there are tens of thousands of gay men in this city. Take your pick."

I really hated being so damned evasive, but I just didn't see how else I could avoid not only dragging Jake and Jared into a murder investigation but having them be high on the suspect list. I did give the detectives the names of the guys I'd talked to in the course of my truncated investigation and what little I'd learned from them—most of it implicating Hysong.

I also did not mention Brewer had said that if he found out Cal was spreading AIDS he'd kill him himself. I didn't think it a wise career move for a private investigator to go around siccing the police on former employers without a lot better reason than something said in the heat of the moment. If I'd seriously thought he meant it it would be different, but for now I'd let the police do their job.

Lt. Richman, who hadn't said anything but had, I noted, been watching me carefully, said, "Look, Dick. I understand your position here. But a guy getting shot off a downtown construction site is the kind of high-profile case the DA loves. He's jumped on this thing, and he wants a conviction. If this Hysong did what you and the rest of the gay community seem to think he did, he deserved to be punished. But you know as well as I do that nobody deserves to be murdered."

Unless it's the criminal justice system doing it, my mind added. Of course, he was right, but I'd rather he think I was protecting the entire gay community rather than knowing I was trying to protect my friends.

"All I can tell you, Lieutenant, is that from what I was able to find out, Hysong infected at least fifteen men from the Male Call; and I know of a couple others away from it. How many more there are, I don't know or want to think about. But every single one of these men has friends and partners who are totally justified in wishing Hysong dead, and any one of them is as likely a suspect as any other. I really wish I could narrow down the potential suspects, but I can't. I can promise you I'll let you know anything I hear that might be helpful."

And I knew full well even as I said it that no matter what I did, Jake and Jared were bound to be caught up in the investigation. Damn!

Nobody said anything for a moment, and I felt it about time to make my exit. But before I got up to leave, I couldn't resist asking, "Have you found the murder weapon, by any chance?"

Richman shook his head. "No. All we know is that it was most likely a hunting rifle—a Winchester, probably a Model 94."

I was glad I wasn't standing when I asked the question—the answer might have made my knees buckle.

ASSUMING THAT JARED WAS COMMUTING BETWEEN JAKE'S AND CARRINGTON AND PROBABLY wouldn't get back into town until dinner time, I held off calling Jake's place. I'd rather talk to both of them at once. They may well have heard of Hysong's death but probably didn't know it was murder, or that a murder investigation was now underway and that there was no way they could avoid getting caught up in it. I knew stress was the last thing either of them needed, but since there was no way to avoid it, I could at least give them a heads-up.

I called at around seven. Jonathan was at his first night of class, and Joshua and I had just finished the dishes. Jake answered and when he verified Jared was there, I asked him to put Jared on the bedroom phone so I could talk to them both at once.

There was a pause, then Jared's voice: "Hi, Dick. What's up?"

I told them. They had heard of Cal's death, and neither seemed particularly surprised to learn he'd been murdered.

"It was only a matter of time," Jared said.

"I've got to ask you something," I said. "Did you ever have that meeting with the guys from the Male Call?"

There was a pause, then: "Well, yeah. Not a meeting, really. A couple of the guys came over last Thursday, and we just talked about it. I know you wanted to be there, but…"

"No, that's not what I'm concerned about. What does bother me is that if the police find out about it, they might jump on it with both feet."

"All we did was talk," Jake said. "Nobody said anything about killing him…well, not seriously, anyway."

"What did you talk about, if I can ask? And believe me, if I'm curious about it, you can be damned sure the police will be, too."

"It was just general bitching, mostly," Jared said. "We talked about going around to every bar and bath owner in town to tell them what was going on and to ask them to eighty-six him if he showed up. We also talked about maybe forming teams of two to follow him around everywhere he went. If he went into a bar, we'd go in, too. If he hit on anyone, we'd warn the guy what they were in for. We just wanted to make life as miserable for him as we could."

"And no one mentioned killing him?"

"Not seriously, no."

"But you did talk about it?"

"Well, yeah, but that's hardly surprising given what that bastard was doing."

"So, no specifics as to how it might be done?"

"No."

I sighed. "Look, guys, I'm not trying to drag out the rubber hose here, but I know damned well I'm not asking anything the cops won't ask. I'm between a rock and a hard place here. They called me in to ask if I had any thoughts about who might have done it. I've developed a good relationship with the police over the years, and I don't want to jeopardize it. They wanted specific names of guys who might have had a grudge against Hysong, and the only actual names I could think of other than Carl Brewer were yours—and I wasn't about to tell them that."

"Well, thanks for that," Jared said, "And we appreciate your telling us all this. But you don't have to protect us. We've got an alibi if we need one. We went up to my cabin over the weekend and didn't get back until late Monday."

"Well, I sure hope it doesn't reach the point where you'd need an alibi," I said. I didn't want to muddy the waters by asking how they had both gotten off work on Monday. Sometimes, being a PI sucks.

"Oh, one last thing," I said. "Hysong was killed with what they think was a hunting rifle like yours."

"What do you mean, like mine?" Jake asked.

"They think it was a Winchester Model 94."

"Well, it sure wasn't mine."

"Of course not," I said. "But the thing is, the police will quite probably be checking to see if anyone from the Male Call has one, so be prepared."

XIV

THURSDAY PASSED WITHOUT INCIDENT. I WAS, OF COURSE, CURIOUS ABOUT HOW THE police investigation was going, but while under other circumstances I may have been tempted to call Marty Gresham to ask him, I didn't want to even consider it now. The further I kept away from things, the better.

I was just getting ready to walk out the door for work on Friday when the phone rang.

"Hello?"

"Dick, it's Jake. We've got a really big problem."

Shit!

"What's wrong?" Stupid question.

"The police just left. They showed up with a search warrant for my gun."

I was a little surprised but tried to offer some reassurance. "I told you they might ask you if you had a hunting rifle. But that they'd have a search warrant is a little extreme, I'd think."

"That's not the problem! When I went to get it for them, it was gone!"

"Gone?" I echoed, immediately feeling stupid for doing so. "When's the last time you saw it?" I also immediately thought of the meeting they'd had with the other guys from the Male Call.

"The last time I saw it was when I put it under the bed right after I bought it. I didn't have any need to take it out until hunting season." He paused, then: "I should have looked for it when you told me about it on the phone. I at least could have reported it stolen before the police showed up looking for it.

"And what's worse, if that's possible, is that the warrant wasn't just for a Winchester hunting rifle. It was specifically for a Model 94 Chief Crazy Horse Commemorative. They're a limited issue."

"Chief Crazy Horse?" I asked. "Why in the world would you want a Chief

Crazy Horse Commemorative rifle?"

"Winchester does commemoratives all the time," he explained. "When Stan and I were kids, we always played cowboys and Indians, and Stan always insisted on being Chief Crazy Horse and me being General Custer. I know they didn't have anything to do with each other in fact, but you know how kids' minds work.

"We had been talking about buying new rifles this year anyway, and when Stan heard about this particular commemorative, he insisted we get it. How could the police have known I even had one?"

Good question. Obviously the police had been doing their job.

"I'd imagine they tested the bullet taken from Hysong's body and that it came from a Winchester 94," I said. "You said it was a pretty new model—apparently, they were able to pin the spent bullet down to the exact model that fired it. They undoubtedly checked the gun shops and dealers for a list of people who'd recently bought one.

"They'll undoubtedly be checking with Stan, too," I added.

"Oh, that'll go over big!" Jake said. "After all the battles Stan has had with the bureaucracy dragging their feet on the AIDS problem, he doesn't look kindly on authority figures. But even so, with my gun missing, I've got a pretty good idea who the police will move up to the top of their suspect list."

I did, too, but didn't say so.

"Well, there's no point wasting your time worrying abut that right now," I said. "Did you tell the police about the guys from the Male Call being over?"

"No. I couldn't see any point to dragging them into it, since for all I know the gun might very well have been gone before they were even here. These guys talk tough, but I can't imagine that any of them could actually steal the gun, let alone use it!"

"But they knew you had it," I pointed out.

"Well, yeah. The weekend I got it, we were at the Male Call, and I know I was talking about it then. It's sort of like getting a new car. Okay, so I was doing the old 'mine's bigger than yours' thing. Hey, how many people do you know with a Chief Crazy Horse Commemorative Winchester 94?"

"And you never had any indication that someone had broken into your apartment?"

"Not a clue, but..." He paused, then: "Jeezus, how stupid can I be? I sometimes leave the kitchen window open a crack. Somebody could have gotten in that way—but there's never been any trouble in my building, and I've never even heard of a break-in anywhere in the neighborhood."

"Jared was there when the cops were?"

"Yeah, but he had to leave for Carrington in time to make it to school. They seemed a little reluctant to let him go, and they fingerprinted us both before he left, which I thought was kind of strange."

I did, too, but again didn't say anything.

"They didn't say so," Jake continued, "but I imagine they think Jared has the gun at his place, and I'll bet the minute they left here they called the Carrington police to get a search warrant. They won't find it, of course, but I guess I can understand their thinking. Of all the rotten luck!" He paused for a moment and then said, "I was wondering if maybe you could do us a huge favor and check with your police contacts to see what's going on. We didn't mention that we knew you, by the way."

Well, now that the police were aware—and I was afraid that was a gross understatement—of Jake and Jared I at least didn't have to avoid using their names.

"I can do that," I said. "But tell me what else they said or asked you.'

"They wanted to know if we knew Cal, and of course, we said yes. It would be stupid to deny it. Then they asked if either Jared or I had a grudge against him. I told them that of course, we did—Cal was murdering gay men. They wanted to know if there might be any other reason, and I told them as far as I was concerned, the reason I gave them was reason enough.

"Then they asked if either one of us had AIDS. I told them to check with our doctor.

"I know they thought we were giving them the runaround, but tough! If we'd given them a direct answer that, coupled with the fact my gun's the same kind that shot Cal, we wouldn't stand a chance. We're not about to hand them our heads on a silver tray. If they want us, they're going to have to get us without our help."

"Look," I said, "just try to take it easy. Let me know if you hear anything else from anyone, and I'll do the same. If you have a chance to call me tonight when Jared gets back, please do. I want to know what happened on the Carrington end."

"Okay. And thanks. Hi to Jonathan and Joshua."

I HAD NO SOONER WALKED INTO THE OFFICE AND FILLED THE COFFEEPOT WITH WATER WHEN there was a knock on my door. Through the opaque glass, I saw two silhouettes. I didn't have to see them clearly to know who they were.

"Come on in," I called, and the door opened to reveal Detectives Carpenter and Gresham.

Marty, being the last in, closed the door behind him.

"Detectives," I said. "This is a surprise. Sit down, please."

From the looks on their faces, I knew this wasn't a social call.

"Would you like some coffee?" I asked as they sat. "I was just going to make some."

"No, thanks," Carpenter said.

I replaced the pot on the coffeemaker and went to my desk to sit down.

"We talked to your friends Jake Jacobson and Jared Martinson this morning," Marty said.

A most telling choice of words, I thought, especially since Jake had specifically said they hadn't mentioned my name and I definitely had not mentioned theirs.

"We saw your photo in Jacobson's apartment," Carpenter, apparently reading my mind, explained.

Shit! I'd forgotten that photo.

"Nice looking kid," he added.

I assumed he meant Joshua rather than Jonathan, but I merely said, "Thanks."

"Why didn't you mention Martinson and Jacobson when we asked you about the Male Call?" he continued.

They had me.

"Well, I don't consider them Male Call regulars, which was what you asked me for," I said. "I know that sounds like an evasion and I guess it is, but these guys are my friends. I didn't want to drag them into something I know they had nothing whatever to do with."

"So, you'd call having the same kind of gun as shot Cal Hysong off a twelve-story building nothing?" Carpenter asked.

"Was it the same gun?" I asked. I didn't want to let them know I'd talked to Jake.

"Well, that's another interesting point—we don't know. Jacobson claims his gun was stolen. Pretty convenient, I'd say."

"Not if it's true," I said. "And if Jake says it was stolen, it was stolen."

"Did you know Martinson had a run-in with Hysong shortly before he was killed?"

How in hell could they have known that? I wondered then realized they'd been doing their job on background checks on the Male Call and what went on there.

"Yeah, Jared mentioned it," I said.

"And you knew this wasn't their first encounter? That Martinson was arrested after a fight with Hysong at the Male Call a couple years ago?"

"Yes, and you probably know I was the one who bailed him out. And you forgot to mention that half the bar was involved in that melee, not just Jared."

"Do they have AIDS?" Carpenter asked.

Oh, Jeezus, how do I get around this one?

"Nice non sequitur," I observed. "You'll have to ask them. I'm not a doctor. You saw them. Did they look sick to you?"

"The evasion game's wearing pretty thin," Carpenter said.

"Do either of you guys have any idea what AIDS is doing to the gay community?" I asked. "Nobody knows who's got it and who doesn't. You're healthy one day, and you're dead the next. Our acquaintances and friends and partners are dying all around us, and no one knows for sure how or why or when it will be our turn. It's scary as hell. The straight world, and too many gays, treat AIDS like leprosy—people hear you have it and they run in the other direction. Did you know some doctors and nurses—and hospitals—won't treat you if they even think you have it? So, am I going to point to someone and say 'He's got AIDS?' Not likely!"

Marty's face reflected his empathy. "Look, Dick, I do understand. But having AIDS is also not a justification for murder."

"Of course not," I agreed. "But as I said, I know these guys, and it is inconceivable to me that either of them could be capable of killing anyone."

I believed that. I really did. But in some far corner of my mind something shameful lurked—could I kill someone who deliberately gave me AIDS? I would sincerely like to think not. Could I kill someone who deliberately gave Jonathan AIDS? In a heartbeat.

"Well, loyalty to friends is an admirable trait," Carpenter said, "but we can't afford that luxury in a murder investigation. We've asked the Carrington police to get a search warrant for Jared Martinson's home. If Jacobson owns the same make and model gun as killed Hysong and it isn't at his place, the next logical place to look is Martinson's."

"You're wasting your time," I said. "As I said, if Jake says the gun was stolen, it was stolen."

Carpenter gave a small smile. "Perhaps. But some coincidences are easier to go along with than others."

"You know Jacobson's brother is an immunologist working with AIDS patients?" Marty asked.

"Yeah, I know that. And if he was an obstetrician that wouldn't mean Jake or Jared was pregnant."

"We asked him for a list of his AIDS patients, and he wouldn't give it to us."

"Like you expected him to?" I said. "You knew damned well he wouldn't, and no other doctor or hospital would, either."

"It would make our jobs a lot easier," Marty observed, "We might be able to track some of the cases back to Hysong and broaden our suspect base. This *is* a murder case, after all."

When he said "broaden our suspect base" I knew "beyond Jared and Jake" was implied, but there was nothing I could say or do about it.

"I don't suppose you know anything else about either Martinson or Jacobson you'd care to tell us?" Carpenter asked.

Jeezus!

"Like what?" I asked. "Look, guys, you know I've always done everything I can to work with the police. I want you to catch whoever killed Hysong, and I know you will. Believe me, if I thought for one second Jake or Jared might have been involved and I knew something that might prove it, I'd tell you. But please don't put me in the position of trying to dig up dirt on my friends when I know they're innocent."

I was thinking specifically of the fact that Jared had been a sniper in Special Forces while in the military. I knew the police would add that to a list of circumstantial evidence, and while they very well might find out about it, they were just going to have to do it on their own.

Marty sighed. "Well, I wish I had a friend like you," he said.

"You do," I replied, and he grinned.

"Touché."

XV

THEY LEFT SHORTLY THEREAFTER, AND I WENT DOWNSTAIRS TO THE COFFEE SHOP IN THE lobby for lunch, though after my talk with Marty and Carpenter I didn't have much of an appetite. I sincerely hoped they were paying as much attention to the many other potential suspects as they were to Jake and Jared, but considering the issue of Jake's missing gun, I tended to seriously doubt it.

THAT EVENING, JUST AS I CAME OUT OF THE BATHROOM WITH A FRESHLY SCRUBBED AND pajama-ed Joshua, headed for the bedroom and Story Time, the phone rang. Jonathan answered, talked quietly a moment then held the phone out to me.

"It's Jared."

"Start without me," I said as he handed me the receiver and went off to collect Joshua, who'd run into the kitchen to say goodnight to his fish.

"So, what happened?" I asked without preamble.

"Thanks to the cops showing up here at Jake's and asking eighteen thousand questions, I was nearly late for my first class. I didn't have a chance to stop at the house. And when I drove into the parking lot at school, a squad car with two cops pulled up right behind me. One of them got out and asked if I was Jared Martinson. When I said yes, he handed me a search warrant and asked me to come with them to the house to let them in.

"I said I had a class from nine until nine-fifty, but my second class wasn't until eleven, so I asked if I could meet them at the house at a little after ten. He went back to the squad car to talk to his partner—it turned out I have the partner's daughter in my nine o'clock. They talked a minute and then the first one came back and said okay, but he made it pretty clear they were going out of their way to oblige me.

"They were nice enough about it all, but I was pretty pissed, just on general principles. And of course, they didn't find a damned thing, though there were a couple of raised eyebrows when they came across some of my leather gear and toys.

"Luckily, the warrant specified it was for a Winchester Model 94 Chief Crazy Horse Commemorative rifle 'and/or any other firearms on the property, including outbuildings,' so they went through the garage, too. They did a good job of rummaging through everything. But if I hear one word at school about any of my personal stuff, I swear I'll sue their asses off! My private life is none of their fucking business!"

"Well," I said, "I wouldn't worry so much about that. They were just doing their job."

"They'd asked us this morning where we were when Cal was killed, and we told him we were coming back from my cabin up in Fenton County. They wanted to know how long a drive it was. I told them."

"Ah, yes, the cabin," I said. "Did anybody see you up there?"

"Nobody that I can think of. It's a pretty isolated area—that's what I like about it. We left here just before dark Friday night, drove straight up and headed back home Monday morning around ten."

"So, you don't have any real proof you were there?" I asked.

"Well, we stopped for gas on the way home. I got a receipt."

"What time was that?"

"Around ten forty-five, I think. I'm sure it's on the receipt. I gave it to the cops."

"And it's how long a drive between the cabin and Jake's?"

"Like I told the cops, it's almost exactly three hours."

"So, you were back in town around one o'clock."

"No, we didn't get in until two-thirty."

I was puzzled. "How's that? Did you stop somewhere between there and here? Somewhere you might have been seen?"

I heard a sigh, then: "No, like I said, we stopped for gas about forty-five minutes after we left the cabin, and we hadn't gone a quarter of a mile from the station before I realized I hadn't locked the shed where I keep the three-wheeler—we'd had it out for a ride after breakfast that morning. So, we had to turn around and drive back. That added an hour and a half."

I instantly realized that, depending on when Cal was killed, that could be a problem. If the gas station receipt was stamped at ten forty-five, theoretically they should have been back in town by one o'clock—they had no proof of turning around and returning to the cabin.

"Did you stop for lunch? Maybe get a receipt there? Or talk to someone who would remember you?"

"No, we still had some stuff in the big cooler we'd taken up with us. We just finished that off on the way back."

So, everything depended on when Cal was killed. Before one o'clock and the ticket exonerated them; between one and two-thirty, it could be used against them. After two-thirty, it was worthless. So, what time did Cal Hysong die? I was sure Tim would know, since he did the autopsy.

"This whole thing sucks!" Jared said, bringing me back to the moment. "Jake doesn't need this hassle, though having that bastard Cal dead almost makes some of it worthwhile. I wish I did know who did it—I'd like to pin a medal on him."

"Maybe they won't bother with a search warrant for the cabin," I said. "After all, the shooting took place after you left there."

But I knew that wouldn't stop them from looking. It was only a two-hour drive from Jared's place in Carrington. They might figure he could have taken the rifle to the cabin after the shooting to hide it.

"Well, look," I said, "I'll give Tim a call right now and see if he can find out Hysong's time of death. With the gas receipt, that could let you off the hook."

"Thanks, Dick. We really appreciate it."

"Hey, that's what friends are for," I said. "All you can do right now is hang tight. The thing is, you didn't do it, and that's all that counts."

"No," he said, "proving it's what counts."

We said our goodbyes and hung up with me thinking of all the innocent people rotting away in prison for crimes they didn't commit.

I PAUSED ONLY LONG ENOUGH TO FILL JONATHAN IN ON THE CONVERSATION THEN DIALED Tim and Phil's number.

I recognized Tim's "Hello."

"Hi, handsome," I said. "How are things going?"

"Pretty good," he said. "I'm thinking of filing for divorce, but otherwise…"

"Uh-oh," I said. "What's Phil done now?'

"He's going to Hawaii for three days," he said, "which is bad enough, but he's not taking me, which is worse."

"Ah, a photo shoot?"

"Spartan is coming out with a line of swimsuits and he's going to be on the cover of the catalog. You know—him striding out of the surf, hair matted back, buff and sexy as all hell, glistening drops of water coursing down his golden-brown body, Diamond Head in the background…

"Did I mention he's not taking me along?"

"Uh, yeah, you did. But it's a work trip, not a play trip."

"It's Hawaii!"

"Well, I'm sure it might be a little much to expect him to go up to his boss and say, 'Oh, and my lover wants to come along—is that okay?'"

"You always did like him more than me."

Luckily, I knew this was simply Tim being Tim and he didn't mean a word of it.

"Okay," I said. "You're right. And if you get a divorce, you can have custody of the fish and Phil can move in with us. three guys in one bed might be a little crowded, but it sure as hell would be fun."

"Okay," Tim said, laughing. "Cancel the divorce. So, what's up with you guys?"

"I was wondering if you could do me a favor," I said.

"If I can. What do you need?"

"I need to know the exact time Cal Hysong was shot off the I-beam. And I don't imagine you would know where the shot came from?"

"I can check out the time for you first thing Monday," he said, "but as to where the shot came from, my best guess would be from the roof of the parking garage across Evans. The angle of the entry wound indicated the shot most likely came from only slightly below. Hysong was on the twelfth floor, the parking garage is eight stories, and there's a two-story service and equipment tower on top of that. Like I say, it's just a guess, but I'll check the notes that came in with him to see if there's anything more specific."

"I'd really appreciate that."

"You're not working on the case, are you?" he asked.

"Not officially, no," I admitted. "But the cops did ask if I could keep my eyes and ears open in the community, and I said I would."

Needless to say, I didn't want to go anywhere near the issue of Jake and Jared's suspected involvement.

"Who's Uncle Dick talking to?" Joshua asked Jonathan.

"Uncle Tim," Jonathan replied.

"I wanna say hi!" he declared, running over to me.

"Do you have a second to talk to Joshua?" I asked.

"Always," Tim said. "Put him on."

I handed the phone over.

"Hi, Uncle Tim! How's Oscar? You got any more new fish?"

It took me a minute to remember he was referring to the new addition to Tim and Phil's aquarium he'd seen when we were last there for dinner—a bright pink specimen with the word *oscar* in its species name.

Apparently, assured that Oscar and the other fish were fine, Joshua abruptly handed the phone to Jonathan.

"Here," he said then dashed over to join me on the couch to watch TV.

"Be sure to wish Phil a good trip for me," I called to Jonathan.

When he got off the phone, he had an oddly sad look on his face. He came over and sat on the other side of Joshua, putting his arm around the boy, who leaned into him. He didn't say anything, but I knew it was the mention of Phil's going to Hawaii that had triggered the memory of the death of his brother Samuel and sister-in-law Sheryl. Joshua's parents had been killed in a head-on car crash while returning from a vacation in Hawaii. The anniversary of their death was coming up, and I knew not a day had gone by that Jonathan had not thought of them and grieved for their loss.

THE WEEKEND PASSED, AS ALL WEEKENDS TEND TO PASS, FAR TOO QUICKLY. IN ADDITION TO the endless weekend chores, we managed to take Joshua to a local park for a couple of hours, and on Sunday afternoon we went to a concert by the Gay Men's Chorus at the MCC. I must admit, I was pretty impressed, and Jonathan, who had sung in his church choir back in Wisconsin, was so enthralled he announced he'd like to think about trying out for it. Where he'd find the time, I didn't know, but I didn't discourage him.

True to his word, Tim called during his coffee break Monday morning to report Hysong's death had occurred at one-thirty. Jared and Jake hadn't gotten back to the city until after two-thirty. The question of whether the time-stamped gas receipt would help or hurt them was resolved—and not in their favor. If only they'd stopped for lunch, or...

Yeah, well, thinking about *if only* was a waste of time.

The missing gun, Jared's past history with Hysong, Hysong's having given Jake AIDS, Jared's having been a sniper in the service and now the gas receipt.

Jeezus!

I put in a call to Marty at the City Annex. I didn't expect him to be in and he wasn't, so I left a message asking him to call. Less than ten minutes later, he did.

"Meet me at the fountain in Warman Park around twelve-fifteen," he said. "We can grab something to eat from one of the carts, if that's okay."

"That's fine." It was obvious from traffic sounds in the background he was calling from a pay phone and that he didn't have much time to talk.

"See you then," he said and hung up.

I TOOK THE BUS TO WARMAN PARK AND GOT THERE SHORTLY AFTER NOON. IT WAS A NICE day, and since school had started the usual crowd of noisy kids racing around and either splashing around in or trying to climb into the fountain was absent. Just office workers and a few tourists milling about or seated on the benches by the fountain having lunch.

I waited until I saw Marty coming across the street from the direction of the City Annex then vectored in to meet him at one of the vendors' carts. We each got a Polish dog with the works, a soda and chips then found our way to an empty bench on one of the side paths.

"Dan had a dentist's appointment," he explained as we sat down. "Otherwise, I probably couldn't have met you."

"I gather I've slipped from grace with the department."

He took a large bite, chewed and swallowed before answering.

"Not really, no. We all—well, Lt. Richman and I especially, since we've known you longer—understand your position, but admittedly it does create some problems for us as far as our being able to rely on you for information. I know that sounds harsh, and it is, but that's just the way it is. It's awkward for all of us that two friends of yours are involved in a murder investigation."

I knew he was right.

"Yeah," I said, "but God knows you shouldn't have any lack of possible suspects. Every single guy who knew what Hysong was doing had a damned good motive."

"True," Marty said. "But not all of them owns a commemorative issue Winchester Model 94 which just happens to have been 'stolen.' And the only person we've heard of to have taken Hysong on—twice—is Martinson. And if either he or Jacobson has AIDS and got it from Hysong, that amps up the motive aspect by a factor of ten. Plus, though they claim not to have been in town when Hysong was shot, we have a time-stamped gas receipt which all but proves they were."

"No," I corrected, "it indicates they could have been. Why would they have bothered to give it to you if they thought it would point a finger at them?"

"Good point, I suppose," Marty agreed, taking a sip from his soda. "Maybe they just hoped we'd buy their story of returning to the cabin after getting the gas. But we have to go on evidence, not on somebody's word, and unfortunately that's all we have here. With no solid evidence to back them up…"

I brushed a lapfull of potato chip crumbs off my pants before saying, "Yeah, I can understand your position, too. But I couldn't be more sure that you're wasting your time with Jake and Jared."

"Well, we got a search warrant for Martinson's cabin in Fenton County. If the gun should show up there…"

"It won't," I said, taking a bite of my Polish sausage and licking mustard off my thumb.

We sat in relative silence, finishing our lunch. We talked a bit about Marty's daughter, who had just turned two, and Joshua and the joys and traumas of having a kid around twenty-four hours a day.

"Maybe we can set the two of them up together when they get older," Marty said, grinning. "Unless Joshua turns out to prefer guys, that is."

I returned the grin. "Or unless she turns out to prefer girls," I said. "The odds are just as likely."

After another couple minutes of talk, Marty looked at his watch. "Ah…time to be getting back"

We got up, dumped our garbage in a trash barrel and continued to the street, where we shook hands and went our separate ways. I was greatly relieved to know Marty didn't hold my evasiveness against me.

THE FIRST THING I DID WHEN I RETURNED TO THE OFFICE WAS TO CALL BOTH JAKE'S AND Jared's numbers, though I knew they'd both be at work, leaving a message on both machines. I'd have preferred to call Jared at the college to alert him to the search warrant for his cabin, but I didn't have a number for him there. I just hoped he'd stop home before he drove down to the city and get the message, in case he wanted to go up and check on it.

I didn't know if he—or most people, for that matter—was aware that if the occupant of a property wasn't home when the police came to execute a search warrant, they had the right to enter the premises any way they could, including breaking the door down. And since they are not obligated to lock the place up when they leave, I knew Jared would want to do so before somebody had a chance to walk in and ransack the place.

XVI

JAKE CALLED JUST AS WE WERE SITTING DOWN TO DINNER TO SAY HE'D GOTTEN HOME early, received my message and managed to reach Jared before he headed for the city.

"He's on his way to the cabin now. He asked me to call you to say thanks for letting him know."

"Well, keep me posted," I said.

"You know it," Jake replied.

"I've been thinking about the Gay Men's Chorus," Jonathan said as I returned to the kitchen and sat back down. "I really would like to try out for it, but with school and everything to do around here and Joshua and…"

"Well, school's a separate issue, but as far as Joshua and I are concerned, we can manage if you can," I assured him. "If you'd really like to try out, do. It would be good for you to do something you really enjoy."

"I'll try out, too," Joshua volunteered.

Jonathan reached out and tousled his hair. "Maybe in a couple years," he said then turned back to me. "It would be fun," he said. "But we'll see."

WHEN I DIDN'T HEAR FROM JARED TUESDAY NIGHT, I ASSUMED EVERYTHING HAD GONE without incident at the cabin. I hoped I was putting way too much emphasis on the whole thing, but experience has taught me that anything is possible and it is better to consider everything than be caught by surprise.

I was tempted to call Jake and Jared but thought better of it. The poor guys had enough to deal with—I didn't want to keep reminding them of the cloud of suspicion they were under.

When the phone rang shortly after I walked into the office Thursday morning I was surprised to hear the voice of Lt. Mark Richman.

"Are you free for lunch today?" he asked without preliminaries.

"Uh, yeah," I replied, both puzzled and just a bit suspicious. "When and where?"

"The usual?"

By "the usual" I knew he meant twelve-fifteen at Sandler's Cafe, a restaurant several blocks from the City Annex where we had met for lunch several times, though not in a long while, when I was working on various cases with the department.

"Okay. See you there."

I knew full well it had something to do with Jake and Jared and Hysong's murder and that whatever he had to say I probably wasn't going to like.

AS I SAID, I'D NOT BEEN TO SANDLER'S IN A WHILE, BUT IT HADN'T CHANGED MUCH. A waiter I hadn't seen before met me at the "Please Wait to be Seated" podium. I'd already looked around the room and not seen the good lieutenant so asked for a table for two. The place was full, but the waiter found a small table near the rear.

I'd no sooner been seated and ordered coffee when I saw Richman enter. He was, somewhat surprisingly, not in uniform, but he still cut an exceptionally attractive figure. Spotting me, he came directly over without waiting to be shown.

We shook hands, and he took the seat opposite me. The waiter brought my coffee and two menus then left to get another cup of coffee for the lieutenant. The fact that I was thinking of him as "the lieutanant" instead of "Mark" reaffirmed my premonition this wasn't a social get-together.

Never one to waste words, he headed directly toward the point, though from a slightly oblique angle.

"I wanted to thank you and Jonathan for everything you've done for Craig. He really looks up to you both, and of course, he's crazy about Joshua. I couldn't have asked for better gay role models for my son and I really appreciate it.

"And you know I appreciate all your help to the department over the years. But this current situation with your friends Martinson and Jacobson is putting us all on thin ice. Strictly between you and me, our new DA is a real throwback to the bad old days. He's charted out his political course, and he sees convictions as the surest way to win the upcoming election. He's been riding the force hard to get them. He also is not particularly fond of gays, which makes this Hysong case particularly touchy. He wants to nail someone for this without 'wasting a lot of time and taxpayers' money.'"

We paused to order when the waiter returned. When he'd gone, I noticed Richman staring at me. I raised an eyebrow in question.

"Were you aware that Jared Martinson was a sniper in Army Special Forces?" he asked.

I knew he was referring to the question in his office as to whether or not I knew anything about Jake or Jared the police should know.

I was also well aware he was trying to tell me something but couldn't say it directly.

"I assume they're in trouble," I said.

He just looked at me. "How's Glen O'Banyon doing these days?"

AS SOON AS I RETURNED TO THE OFFICE, I CALLED BOTH JAKE'S AND JARED'S NUMBERS AND left messages for them to call me as soon as they could. I was sorely tempted to call Glen, too, but thought better of it. I wanted to advise Jared and Jake to talk to a lawyer and would certainly recommend Glen strongly as the best criminal lawyer in the city, but I didn't want to give anyone the impression I was trying to run things. I'd never heard Jake or Jared mention having a lawyer, but they might. And aside from the fact that hiring a top criminal lawyer at this stage might be overkill, Glen's services did not come cheap.

I simply could not believe, even with all the fingers pointing toward Jake and Jared, that they had to worry about being arrested and formally charged. No matter how gung-ho the new DA was, there simply was no concrete evidence on which to build a case, and any defense lawyer worth his salt could blow him out of the water. He would never be dumb enough to try it.

Then the phone rang. It was Jake.

"They found my gun," he said. "I've been arrested."

"Arrested?" I couldn't believe it.

"Yeah. Suspicion of murder."

My mind was working fast. "Have you been arraigned?"

"Not yet, but they're taking me down shortly. I wondered if you knew of a good bail bondsman."

"Of course. Where's Jared?"

"He's at Mountjoy. That's why I called you. I hope you don't mind."

"Mind? I'd have minded if you hadn't called me. Let me give the bail bondsman a call, and I'll come down to the court and give you a ride home."

"So, you think they'll set bail?" he asked.

"I'll bet on it. I'll be down as soon as I can, and in the meantime, just hang in there."

"I have a choice?" he asked. "And thanks!"

When we hung up, I hurriedly called a bail bondsman I'd dealt with in the past who had an office directly across the street from the City Annex. He told me to call him as soon as bail was set and he'd come right over. I managed to make it there in record time.

Criminal court was in the Annex, civil court in the City Building next door. I found the in-session courtroom and got there just as Jake was being brought in. Since he hadn't had time to arrange for a lawyer, he was represented by a young public defender. I didn't catch the name of the assistant district attorney who represented the prosecution, but when the issue of bail came up, he requested it be denied.

I have to hand it to the public defender—he still had a lot of his altruism left, and he convinced the judge that Jake was a respected businessman, had never had so much as a parking ticket and was certainly no flight risk. The ADA then asked for a bail amount that had even the judge raising an eyebrow. It was obvious the DA's office was operating on the principle of "a bird in the hand" and was taking full advantage of it to make an example of how tough the new DA was on crime.

Finally, the judge set an amount I thought was still exorbitantly high but not totally prohibitive, and I went out into the hall to find a pay phone to call the bail bondsman.

I'll spare you a step-by-step trek through the wilds of the criminal court system and simply say that Jake was released within the hour.

As I sat there waiting for him, I realized that Lt. Richman had to have known about the gun and the arrest when we had lunch and was preparing me for it as we ate. Of course, he couldn't have just come out and told me, but I appreciated the telegraphed punch.

Since Jake had been brought in by squad car I'd offered him a ride home when he'd called me. Now he protested he could just as easily take a bus. At last he agreed but asked if I could drop him off at his current construction site instead.

"It's about the same distance," he said, as if it would matter if it weren't.

"You're going back to work?" I asked.

He grinned. "Well, sure. No point just sitting around the apartment twiddling my thumbs."

We walked to my car in the Warman Park underground garage without saying much. I asked where the gun had been found and Jake said all he knew was that it had been found—they didn't tell him anything of the circumstances of finding it.

As we pulled out of the garage, I asked, "What about finding a lawyer?"

"Jared and I had been talking about it," he said, "but we were really hoping we wouldn't need one." He sighed. "I guess we were wrong. From the questions the cops were asking—they're not very big on subtlety—I suspect the DA's trying to figure out some way to charge Jared with something, too. I'll talk it over with him when he comes back to the city tonight."

"But you have one in mind?" I asked.

"Yeah, we were thinking about Glen O'Banyon. We've met him and we know how busy he is, but we know he's the best and I hope he might fit us in." He was silent for a moment, then said, "I hate to ask you, but I know you've worked pretty closely with him in the past and I was wondering if you would mind if we mentioned your name?"

"By all means," I said. "As a matter of fact, I can put in a call to him, too, if you'd like."

"I don't want to drag you any further into this than we already have."

"You're not dragging me anywhere. If there's anything at all I can do to help you get through this mess, you know I will."

EVEN THOUGH IT WAS GETTING CLOSE TO QUITTING TIME, I RETURNED TO THE OFFICE AFTER dropping Jake. I put in a call to Glen's office and talked to Donna, his secretary, asking her to have Glen call me either at work or at home as soon as he could.

I was tempted to call the City Annex to try to talk to either Mark Richman or Marty Gresham to see if I could find out anything at all about the circumstances surrounding the discovery of the rifle, but I realized Mark had already gone as far out of his way as he could by letting me know that Jake and Jared might need a lawyer. Marty might be able to give me the information I needed, but I didn't want Mark to feel I was trying to do an end run around him by immediately going to Marty. I decided it could wait until I found out whether or not Glen would take the case. I knew I'd feel a lot more comfortable if I was sure he would.

I WAS IN THE BATHROOM AS THE EVENING NEWS CAME ON AND I HEARD JONATHAN CALL OUT, "Dick! You'd better come see this!"

I got to the set just in time to catch a glimpse of District Attorney St. John at the main entrance of the City Building, announcing that an arrest had been made in the Tower Shooter case, thanks entirely to the diligent efforts of his office to remove criminal elements from decent society, etc. ad nauseam.

He deliberately held off mentioning Jake's name until several reporters fell over themselves asking for it, then revealed that the suspect—and his careful pause before and after the word left little doubt as to what he actually meant —was one "Jacob 'Jake' Jacobson, of this city." I was rather surprised he didn't give out Jake's address and phone number.

He, of course, added somberly that, under our great system of justice, a man was assumed innocent—though obviously not by St. John—until proven guilty. I knew damned well he only added that last part by way of covering his ass against a false arrest charge further down the line when Jake was proven innocent.

Joshua and I were just finishing doing the dishes while Jonathan studied for his horticulture class when the phone rang. Jonathan got up to answer it as I handed the last plate to Joshua to dry.

"Dick, it's for you. It's Mr. O'Banyon."

I quickly dried my hands and went to the phone.

"Hi, Glen," I said. "Thanks for returning my call."

"No problem," he replied. "And please tell Jonathan it's perfectly all right for him to call me Glen."

"I've told him that before," I said, "but I'm afraid he's still a little bit in awe of you."

Again, even as I said it, I was aware that even I usually thought of him as *O'Banyon* rather than *Glen*.

"So, what can I do for you?" he asked.

"You're familiar with the Tower Shooter case, I assume?"

"Who isn't?"

"Did you know that Cal Hysong, the guy who got shot, is the one everybody thinks—rightly, I'm convinced—had been going around deliberately spreading AIDS?"

"Yes," he said. "I gather you're involved somehow?"

"Unfortunately, yes, I'm afraid so. You'll probably be getting a call from my friends Jake Jacobson and Jared Martinson." I then outlined the situation, albeit not mentioning Jake's AIDS. I knew it was a crucial element to the story, but did not feel it was my place to violate Jake and Jared's confidence. I was sure they would mention it—though knowing how sharp Glen was, I also knew he undoubtedly had deduced it just from what I'd said.

"Well, I'm just wrapping up a case, but it's probably going to the jury tomorrow, so I'll do whatever I can if they decide to call me."

"I owe you yet again," I said.

"Nonsense," he protested. "I'm just doing my job."

As soon as we'd hung up, I dialed Jake's number to tell him I'd talked with Glen. I knew I was, as I so often do, inserting myself into other people's lives and problems without being asked, but this damned protector complex is just part of who I am.

I tried at least a dozen times to get through to Jake but always got a busy signal. I knew he was likely being inundated by calls from the press, who were also undoubtedly banging on his door.

PHIL HAD LEFT FOR HIS HAWAII PHOTO SHOOT THURSDAY, SO WE TOOK TIM OUT TO DINNER on Friday night to a newly opened Red Lobster restaurant—the city's first. The people at Cap'n Rooney's Fish Shack, which had something of a lock on local seafood sales and had some clout at City Hall, had fought tooth and nail to keep them out and were, I was sure, far from pleased when their efforts failed.

Joshua was intrigued by the large tank of live lobsters, which he'd never seen before. Luckily, he did not make the connection between the green creatures wandering around the bottom of the tank and the bright red split shells surrounded by parsley and a little cup of drawn butter shown in the menu.

When Jonathan and Joshua returned from church on Sunday, Joshua and I settled down to "read" the paper—primarily the comics section, which I always held off looking at until he got home—while Jonathan called a number he'd found on the church bulletin board to see about auditioning for the Gay Men's Chorus. This led to his setting up a meeting with the director for Tuesday at seven o'clock, just before the general chorus rehearsal.

Monday evening I got a call from Jared, filling me in on everything that had happened since I dropped Jake off at work the previous Thursday.

"Sorry we didn't get back to you over the weekend," he said, "but we went up to the cabin. We just had to step back and calm down for a few days. Besides, there was nothing we could do about anything until we had a chance to see whether Glen O'Banyon would take the case. We met with him this morning."

"And he's taking it, I hope." I said.

"Thank God, yes. Probably thanks to you—he said you'd talked to him, and we really appreciate that. We'd called him first thing Friday morning, but he was in court. His secretary called us back Friday afternoon and said he could see us this morning. I had to cut another day of classes, but it was worth it."

"Well, I don't think my call had anything to do with it, but I'm glad, in any event. What did Glen have to say, if I can ask?"

"He said he was sure we could beat it, but that the DA has his eye on the governor's office and is out to add as many scalps to his belt as he can. He's apparently a real prick and a homophobe. I gather O'Banyon's had several run-ins with him, and he says St. John's next step is bound to be to convene a grand jury to give the impression he's just doing what the public demands."

"Well, you can be sure Glen won't let him get away with a witch hunt."

"We got that," he said. "He did warn us to be prepared for anything. But we still feel a lot better now that we've talked to him."

"Great," I said and meant it sincerely. "And please keep me posted and let me know if there's anything I can do."

"You know we will."

TUESDAY PASSED UNEVENTFULLY. KNOWING JONATHAN WOULD BE CHECKING OUT THE GAY Men's Chorus at seven, I left work a little early to take some of the lasagna Tim had given us out of the freezer and thaw it. I had it warming in the oven by the time Jonathan and Joshua got home.

After Jonathan left, Joshua and I did the dishes then spent the rest of the evening "playing cards." It's amazing how much fun a five-year-old can have with a deck of playing cards. While regular card games were still a little beyond him, we found a lot of variations that kept us both happy, like my shuffling the deck and having Joshua first put them into the four suits then putting each suit in numerical order after we'd removed the face cards and set them aside. I loved watching him as he gave his full attention to each card and carefully put it in the right place.

Then we played a game of "who wins?" I'd shuffled the cards and had him "deal" them out—one for him, one for me, etc. Then we'd each turn one card over, and whoever had the highest number "won." The relative values of the face cards took him a while, but he soon caught on. He wanted to learn how to shuffle, but that pretty much led to the next game being fifty-two pick-up.

I think I enjoyed it every bit as much as he did.

Jonathan got home shortly before ten, obviously on top of the world.

"I gather you're in?" I said after our hug.

"Yeah!" he said as we walked to the couch and sat down. "One of the members just moved away, so they needed another tenor and I walked in at just the right time. All the guys are friendly, and I recognized a couple of them from church. I really think I'm going to love it." His expression suddenly changed, as though he felt guilty for being too happy. "How did it go tonight?" he asked. "I'm really sorry to put everything on you two nights in a row—I'd almost forgotten about school tomorrow."

I put my hand on his leg. "Don't worry about it," I said. "We manage just fine. I'm just glad that you're happy."

He put his hand over mine and smiled. "I really am lucky," he said. "I have you and Joshua and our friends and school and now the chorus. What more could I ask?"

"How about a game of 'The Very Lucky Guy and His Horny Partner?'" I asked.

He immediately got up from the couch, pulling me up with him.

"Let the games begin," he said with a grin, leading me toward the bedroom.

XVII

WEDNESDAY MORNING I GOT A CALL FROM GLEN ASKING IF I'D LIKE TO JOIN HIM FOR lunch at Etheridge's, directly across the street from the City Building. Etheridge's—and occasionally Hughie's—was our non-office meeting place just as Sandler's was for my meetings with Mark Richman, and an invitation from either of them was almost never just for the purpose of socializing.

I arrived exactly at noon and was shown to what I came to think of as "O'Banyon's booth," since it always seemed to be reserved for him. Glen wasn't there yet, but I was pleased to see that Alex was still working as a waiter. I'd hit on Alex one time before I'd met Jonathan and always appreciated his diplomatic way of informing me that, while he appreciated the offer, he was afraid his partner wouldn't approve. Graceful let-downs are becoming a lost art.

I was about halfway through my first cup of coffee and had already looked at the menu when Glen slid into the booth opposite me.

"Glad you could make it," he said as we reached across the table to shake hands. "I wan—" He stopped as Alex appeared to pour his coffee.

"Would you like a few minutes?" Alex asked.

"Just a BLT for me," Glen said. "I've got to get back to court."

"Make it two," I said, and Alex nodded and moved off.

"I wanted to talk to you about this Hysong murder case," Glen said.

"I was hoping you would. And I wanted to thank you for taking Jake and Jared on as clients. Is there anything I can do?"

He took a sip of his coffee before answering. "Well, as you—and everybody else in the county who reads a newspaper or watches television or listens to the radio—know, Mr. St. John has anointed himself defender of small children, Mom, apple pie and the American flag. There's nothing he loves

111

better than a juicy high-profile case, and this one is right up his alley. It has all the elements for high drama and maximum pontificating, especially considering the background of the case.

"He's empaneling a grand jury to give him at least the appearance of having a stronger case than he actually does. Prosecutors love grand juries because they very seldom refuse to find there is not enough evidence to bring a case to trial."

"But does he sincerely think he can win? The evidence is totally circumstantial unless they have something up their sleeve."

Glen grinned. "St. John always has something up his sleeve. When he first got out of law school, he was a junior assistant counsel to Senator Joseph McCarthy—remember him? St. John learned from the master when it comes to convincing juries that circumstantial evidence is indisputable fact."

"Jeezus!" I said. "What are you going to do?"

Alex brought our food and refilled our coffee then left.

"Well," Glen continued, "since we know Jake didn't do it—and I truly believe that—we have to figure out a way to find out who did. Which is one of the reasons we're here. Jake and Jared have asked me to hire you."

I'm sure my puzzlement showed on my face. "*They* asked *you* to hire me? Why in the hell didn't they just ask me themselves? They're my friends—nobody has to hire me to help them."

Glen raised his hand to cut me off. "Yes, that's precisely the point. They knew if they asked you'd wouldn't hesitate and that you wouldn't charge them. We all know you have a penchant for taking on cases you don't get paid for, and they didn't want that. This way, it's strictly a business transaction. I've hired you before. I'm simply hiring you again."

I thought that over for a moment and realized that while he was, of course, correct, the prospect made me uncomfortable somehow. When I figured out what it was that bothered me, I voiced it.

"Yeah, you've hired me before, but never on a case involving my friends. I've got my own way of working on things, my own patterns and methods. I really don't know if I can put up with being told what to do next."

He smiled. "I don't have any intention of telling you how to do your job. I can't see much change in anything. You've worked on murder cases before, and you've done various other kinds of work for me before. We'll just be combining the two, albeit staying more closely in contact than usual."

We sat in silence while he took a bite of his sandwich, chewed, swallowed and washed it down with a sip of coffee. When he set his cup down he looked at me.

"Deal?"

I still had reservations, but…

"Deal," I said.

"Good. Now, whatever you need from me, just let me know."

I took a bite of my sandwich. "What do you know about how the cops found the gun?"

He dabbed the corner of his mouth with a napkin before saying, "I don't have all the details yet, but apparently some kids found it in a clump of bushes in Barnes Park. Jake's prints were on it."

"Well, of course they'd be on it," I said. "It's his gun." I wondered, though, how they could have known the fingerprints were Jake's, and then I remembered Jared saying they'd both been printed when the police came to Jake's apartment. I had thought that was very strange at the time, and I still did.

"Anybody else's prints on it?" I asked.

Glen shook his head. "Apparently not. Whoever took it and used it probably wore gloves."

"Were Jake's prints on the trigger?" I asked.

He raised an eyebrow. "We think alike," he said. "I didn't see any specifics on where the prints were, but I've asked for them."

His glance at his watch told me it was time to wrap it up. We finished our coffee and Alex brought the check, which I grabbed.

"You'll be paying for it indirectly," I said, and Glen grinned.

As we got up from the booth and headed for the door, Glen said, "So, what's your first step?"

"I'll be calling Jake and Jared for the names of everybody who was at that meeting of guys from the Male Call." I paused. "They did tell you about that, didn't they?"

He nodded.

"Chances are it was one of them who stole the gun," I continued. "And whoever stole it probably is the one who used it."

I paid the bill, and we left the restaurant, exchanged a quick handshake on the sidewalk in front and went on our separate ways.

IT BEING JONATHAN'S CLASS NIGHT, WE DECIDED TO GRAB DINNER OUT, AND JOSHUA announced he wanted to go to "see the fish." So, even though we'd just had seafood the Friday before, we headed to our local Cap'n Rooney's Fish Shack, where Joshua endeared himself to the management by asking loudly, "Where's the lobsters?"

As usual when we went out for dinner on a class night, we brought both cars, and after Jonathan left for class, it was still sufficiently light for Joshua and I to go to a nearby kids' park for a while. Watching him racing from the swings to the slide to the teeter-totter to the monkey bars made me wish I were five again.

As soon as we got home, I called Jake. Jared got on the other line as I asked for the names, addresses and phone numbers of the Male Call regulars who had come over to talk about Hysong before Jake realized his gun was missing. I figured, again, that they were the most likely suspects.

None of us mentioned Glen's having hired me. It was just mutually understood and spared me from going into the issue of my being paid for something I would gladly have done for nothing. I knew they knew that. It was just easier for all of us not to even mention it.

There had been six guys there other than Jared and Jake, none of whom I knew—Don Gleason, Chuck Fells, Steve Morse, Butch Reed, Tom Spinoza and Art Manners. Apparently, only Jared, Art Manners and Don Gleason had not had sex with Hysong. The rest—with, I hated to think, perhaps the exception of Jake—showed no visible signs of infection.

Gleason had lost a younger brother to AIDS after the brother had had sex with Hysong, one of Manners's close friends had just died, and Morse and Fells had friends who were currently in and out of the hospital. They all knew at least some of the Male Call's dead.

"And they never zeroed in on Hysong as the source?" I asked.

"Not really," Jake said. "Most of the guys who go to the Male Call are pretty active and don't keep track of who they sleep with and when. So, when AIDS really started sweeping through the community, no one was sure where they got it. Then the rumors started concentrating on Cal, and Carl eighty-sixed him, and everybody started putting two and two together."

"Can you tell me anything at all about any of them that might make them stand out in any way as a possible suspect?"

I heard a sigh, then Jake's voice: "Look, Dick, we really don't feel comfortable pointing the finger at any of these guys and—"

I interrupted to say, "I understand. But somebody killed Hysong, and if anyone is going to go to trial for it, I'd just as soon it not be you. We've got to take a close look at everybody, like it or not."

"Yeah, you're right," Jared agreed. "But the fact is, we're really not all that close with any of these guys. Our contacts have been almost exclusively limited to talking with them at the Male Call or running into them somewhere else and having been to a couple of parties with some of them. As to their personal lives, I don't think we know anything at all except the basics. Right, Jake?"

"Right," Jake verified.

"But you do have their phone numbers, right?" I asked.

"Phone numbers, yeah," Jake said. "Hold on a second while I get them for you."

I heard the sound of one of the receivers being set down. Neither Jared nor I said anything in the interim and a minute later, Jake was back.

"Got a pencil?" he asked.

When I said yes, he read off the names of the six guys and their numbers.

"Many thanks," I said. "So, given that all of them had reason to hate Hysong, did any one of them feel particularly strong about it?"

There was a moment of silence while they thought, then Jake said, "I can't imagine anyone could have a stronger reason to hate Cal than Don Gleason. His brother's death really devastated him. As a matter of fact, Don didn't even show up at the Male Call for at least three months after his brother died. He started coming back just about the time the rumors about Cal started circulating."

"Did he ever confront Cal about it?"

"No. Nobody ever confronted Cal about anything, except my boy, here, of course. Don just kept it all inside, but I could tell from the way he looked at Cal that he wanted to."

"He wasn't the only one," Jared added. "Art Manners did confront Cal once a couple years ago. Art likes to think of himself as a tough guy—and he is— but the one time he tried standing up to Cal, Cal beat the crap out of him. Art never tried it again. He never forgot it, though, and he's been bad-mouthing Cal behind his back ever since."

"Well," I said, "I'll have a talk with him…with all of them. Do you know if any of these guys might be home during the day?"

"Butch Reed's a fireman," Jared said. "He works three on and one off, but I don't know his exact schedule. And Don Gleason is an artist—metal sculptures. I think he has a studio in his home. I'm not sure about the rest of them. You, Jake?"

"No. Just nine-to-fives, I think."

"I'll just try calling until I get them," I said. "Thanks for your help. And if you think of anything at all, please let me know right away."

"You know we will," Jake said. "So, give Joshua a hug from both of us and give Jonathan a nice slow grope and tell him it's from me."

"He'll love that," I said, grinning. "I can just see him blushing now. We'll talk again soon. Take care."

"You, too," they said in unison, and we hung up.

THAT JAKE AND JARED HAD NUMBERS FOR ALL SIX OF THE GUYS WHO CAME TO THE MEETING saved me quite a bit of hassle with the phone book, and I started calling them first thing Thursday morning after my coffee/newspaper/crossword ritual. Not knowing what days Reed might have off, I tried his number first and got a machine. I then moved on to Manners, Fells, Morse and Spinoza. I didn't expect them to be home, and they weren't. Fells and Spinoza also had answering machines, on which I left messages, including both my office and home numbers. With both Morse and Manners, I let their phones ring at least eight times before I hung up. I'd try them from home that evening.

I'd been toying with the idea of getting a separate phone at home for business calls but had hesitated about incurring the extra expense. Now, though, with Joshua getting to the age where we frequently had to race him to the phone when it rang, I figured it might be time to reconsider.

Don Gleason was the one I most wanted to talk to, so I saved him for last. Jared had said he was a metal sculptor with a studio in his home, so chances were good I'd be able to catch him. Sure enough, after hearing three rings, I heard a deep-voiced "Hello?"

"Don Gleason?" I asked.

"Yes."

I introduced myself and told him the purpose of my call.

"I heard Jake had been arrested," he said. "He should get a medal. If you're collecting for his defense fund, I'll be glad to contribute."

"No," I corrected, "I'm calling because I'd like to talk to you about the meeting you attended at Jake's house shortly before Hysong was killed."

"How did you know about that?"

"Well, that's the joy of being a detective," I said. "I was hired to prove they arrested the wrong guy and find out who really did it. I've been checking on guys who might had a special reason to want to see Hysong dead. Jake and Jared are friends of mine, and when I heard about the meeting, I realized everyone there qualified. Do you suppose we might meet in person for a talk? I know you're busy, but it really might help me figure out who to zero in on."

"Like me, for example?"

"That's my point—I don't have any idea. Right now, everybody's a potential suspect, but it will help if I can start eliminating some of them."

He didn't hesitate. "Sure. You want to come over now?"

"I can do that," I said. "You'd better give me your address, though."

He did, we said our goodbyes, and I headed out the door to meet him.

THE ADDRESS WAS IN ONE OF THE OLDER AND MORE RUNDOWN COMMERCIAL AREAS OF town, dotted with warehouses and closed factories. Gleason's building had apparently in its heyday, around 1920, been a combination garage and gas station, set just far enough back off of the street to allow a car to pll in front of the pumps without blocking the large garage door. It was of concrete block and two stories high—I assumed Gleason lived on the second floor.

I found a parking place easily enough and walked back. Closed Venetian blinds, mottled with dust and age, covered the large window and there was no indication that anyone was in the place. I went up to the front door and peered in. I could see a car and a motorcycle parked just inside the garage doors. The building was quite deep, and a single hanging fluorescent light fixture in the back provided the only interior illumination. That and the small, searingly bright blue flame of an acetylene torch sending out occasional sprays of sparks.

The entire place was filled with hard-to-discern shapes, some of them reaching to the ceiling. I assumed they were Gleason's sculptures.

I knocked loudly on the door, not sure if he would be able to hear me or not. He did, for the torch went out, and a moment later I saw someone walking toward me. He opened the door, his welder's visor pushed back atop his head.

"That was quick," he said, standing back to let me enter. Then he grinned. "Or it could be that I just lost track of time again. I do that a lot."

He removed his helmet and set it on an old desk under the front window then undid his protective apron, slid it over his head and laid it on the back of the desk chair. As he did so, I realized he looked familiar, though I couldn't place where I might have seen him—in the bars, probably.

"Let's go upstairs," he said, pointing to a plain wooden stairway along the side wall closest to the desk.

I followed him up, and he opened a door off the landing at the top to lead me into his living quarters. Unlike the downstairs, which was murky and cluttered, bright light from the curtainless windows illuminated a neat and surprisingly comfortable apartment. With no surrounding residences, I guess he figured curtains and blinds weren't necessary to protect his privacy.

"Have a seat," he said, and I did, choosing a high-backed padded armchair. He sat in a wooden rocker opposite me and leaned back, staring at me. After a moment, he broke into a grin.

"You don't remember me, do you?"

I felt a flush of embarrassment. So, I did know him. I frantically searched my mind and drew a blank. I shook my head slowly.

"I do recognize you," I said, "but I'll be damned if I can remember where from."

"That's okay," he said. "My hair's shorter now, and I've been working out."

And then the light came on.

"Of course!" I said. "We met one night at the Easy Pickin's. But that place has been closed for a couple of years now. You've got a great memory, and I apologize for not having made the connection immediately."

We'd picked each other up just before closing one night—long before I met Jonathan—and had gone to my place.

"You're not an easy guy to forget," he said, still smiling, rocking the chair slowly.

I wasn't quite sure how to respond to that one. I also remembered why we hadn't had a rematch. He was pretty good sex, but then he wanted to get into an area I've never been comfortable with. I went along with it, but when I realized how much he was into it, I knew it was going to have to be a one-night stand.

"Well, again, I apologize," I said. "You're looking great."

"Thanks," he said. "I was always sort of hoping we'd run into one another again."

Dodge ball time, I thought. "Yeah, it has been a long time. I've got a partner now; we've been together a couple years already. It sure goes by fast!"

Obviously, he got the message. "I'm glad for you," he said. "Monogamous?"

"Yep," I said then decided to segue right to the subject that had brought me to him in the first place. "We figure, in today's climate, it's the safest way to go." I paused only for a second before saying, "I was very sorry to hear about your brother, by the way."

He stopped rocking, and it was as though an invisible cloud had swept across his face, though I could clearly see its reflection in his eyes.

He sighed then said, "Thanks."

"You think Hysong gave it to him?"

"I know damned well he did," he said bitterly.

"Can I ask how you can be so sure?"

He leaned forward, both hands on the arms of his chair.

"You had to know Paul. He was eight years younger than me, and I was his Big Brother. He always wanted to be just like me, do everything I did. I turned out to be a sculptor, but Paul's big dream was to be an architect and he would have been a terrific one.

"He moved out here from Duluth a year and a half ago to go to Greer, which is one of the best architectural design schools in the country. Naturally, I said he could live with me while he went to school. When he found out I was into leather, he wanted to do it, too. I tried to explain to him that it wasn't that simple, that for me it wasn't just a game. It's part of who I am.

"It wasn't who he was, but he wanted it to be. I tried to keep as close an eye on him as I could. I wouldn't let him go to the Male Call without me. I had to protect him. He was my kid brother, for Christ's sake!

"He went home with a couple of the guys there, but he always checked with me first so I'd know who he was with. If I said no, he didn't go. And I told him never to go into the back room. Going home with someone was one thing, but the back room was strictly off limits. He didn't belong there—it would be like tossing chum into a shark tank.

"Then one night I was busy talking to someone, and the next thing I know, I see Paul coming out of the back room. I had a shit fit, but he swore he'd just gone to look in to see what was going on. He said he hadn't done anything, so I believed him, but I was still pissed.

"Then, a couple months later he started getting sick. Then he got sicker. And sicker. And I..." He leaped from his chair and said, "Excuse me, I've gotta take a piss."

He hurried out of the room. A minute or so later, I heard the toilet flush, and he returned and sat back down in the rocker, picking up his story.

"Just before he died, he told me he'd lied to me. That he had gone into the back room that night and he'd had sex. He said Cal had been cruising him all night, and when I got distracted talking, Cal motioned for Paul to follow him into the back room and he did. He asked me to forgive him for lying to me."

For a moment, he clamped his lips together, and his face looked as though it was going to break into pieces and crumble off his skull. My gut ached for him.

"Can you imagine that?" he said, pulling himself together. "He's dying, and he asks *me* to forgive *him*! Two days later, we both died."

All I could do was shake my head. "God, Don, I'm so sorry," I finally managed to say. "Did you do anything about Hysong after you found out he'd given it to Paul?"

He took a very deep breath and resumed his rocking. "When he told me, I was more concerned with him and with being with him. I couldn't have left him even for a minute, and I didn't. But the day after I got back from the funeral in Duluth, I bought a gun and I went down to the Male Call that night to wait for Cal. I was going to kill him the minute he walked in the door.

"I had it all planned. Six bullets. I'd shoot him in each knee first then blow his balls off then shoot him in the stomach, then the chest just below the heart, then in the head. I wanted him to know exactly what was happening to him and why."

"But you didn't," I said.

"Only because Cal didn't come in that night. And because Carl had been watching me every second and knew what I was going to do. I don't know how he knew—I probably had it written across my forehead. But he came over and took me back to his office and sat me down and talked to me for three hours. He convinced me the worst thing I could do for Paul would be to rot in jail for the rest of my life for a piece of shit like Cal.

"He told me that if Cal had given it to Paul, that meant he had it himself and that he was bound to die the way Paul had died and that shooting him would just put him out of his misery quickly. That he'd suffer a lot more dying the way Paul had."

"What happened to the gun?" I asked.

"I gave it to Carl. He locked it in his safe. I guess it's still there. I stayed away from the Male Call for a couple of months just because I didn't want to have to face Cal."

"But you did start going back," I said.

He nodded. "Yeah. I really like the Male Call—it's the only place in town where I feel really comfortable, and I was becoming a hermit. So, I started going back and kept as far away from Cal as I could. I didn't even look at him if I could avoid it. I tried to warn everybody I could about him, until I was sure he'd come after me, but he didn't."

Obviously, I'd just found one of the major sources of the rumors.

"So, why did you go to the meeting at Jake's?" I asked.

"Because I thought the guys were going to talk about killing Cal, and I wanted to tell them what Carl had told me. But we ended up just talking about ways we could make Cal's life as miserable as he'd made ours. And you know, even though shooting Cal was too good for him, I'm glad somebody took him out."

"Yeah," I said. "But the cops arrested the wrong man. That's why I'm trying to find out who really did it."

Gleason simply shrugged. "Good luck," he said.

I LEFT SHORTLY THEREAFTER AND HEADED BACK TO THE OFFICE, HOPING ONE OF THE OTHER guys from the meeting might have gotten my message and called.

On the way, I went over my conversation with Gleason. I really felt sorry for him—it was clear he felt responsible for his brother's death. And he'd been open about wanting to kill Cal, something I don't imagine he'd have admitted to if he really had done it.

I found it very interesting that Carl Brewer had talked him out of it. I'd had Carl on my list of potential suspects, but if he'd killed Hysong, why would he risk getting caught stealing Jake's gun when he had Gleason's right there in his safe? So, on the one hand, that might remove them both as suspects. On the other hand, Gleason may have been counting on my being thrown off-track, and Carl Brewer might not have wanted to have the murder weapon traced back to a gun in his safe.

Shit! Why can't life be easy?

No messages on my machine, and I was just turning around to go back downstairs to grab something for lunch when the phone rang.

"Hardesty Investigations."

"This is Frank Reed, returning your call."

Frank Reed? I realized I hadn't heard his real name before—Jared had referred to him as "Butch."

"I'm glad you called," I said. "I wanted to talk to you about Cal Hysong's death."

"What about it? I heard they think Jake did it, and I'd like to shake his hand. Why are you calling me about it?"

"Well, it's kind of complicated," I said. "I've been hired to look into the circumstances leading up to Hysong's death, and I understand you and several other guys from the Male Call had a meeting shortly before he was killed."

"So?" he demanded. "Does that mean I had something to do with his death?"

"I wasn't implying that it did," I said, calmly. "This is all just part of the information-gathering process, and I'd really appreciate it if we could meet face to face for a few minutes to talk."

There was a long pause, then: "I suppose, but I don't know what you're looking for or what I can possibly tell you."

"That's what private investigators do—we look at bits of seemingly unimportant or unrelated information and see if they might fit into a bigger picture. Sometimes, the pieces fit, sometimes they don't. So, when would you be free? We can meet wherever's convenient for you."

Another pause. "There's a coffee shop near me, on the corner of High and Gibraltar—Alexander's. You know it?"

"I know where it is, yeah."

"I can meet you in front of the place today at two-thirty."

"Great. I'll see you there. Thanks."

GERTRUDE STEIN SAID "A ROSE IS A ROSE IS A ROSE." SHE COULD JUST AS EASILY HAVE SAID "A coffee shop is a coffee shop is a coffee shop." Alexanders was...uh...a coffee shop. Large windows faced both streets, covered with mostly raised Venetian blinds. There was a recessed doorway with a menu posted on the window beside it, a long counter along the inside wall with maybe a dozen round stools, orange-plastic-upholstered booths along the outer walls and under the windows and four or five tables, with red-and-white checkerboard plastic tablecloths, in the middle. High ceilings with ceiling fans making a half-hearted effort to stir the air—you know the place.

I got there about 2:25, having driven around looking for a parking place on the side street where there were no meters. I spotted Reed half a block away, though I'd never seen him before. One thing about leather men—when they're not in leather, they tend to look just like everybody else. But for some reason, the second I saw Reed approaching, I thought, *Fireman.* Don't ask me why; I long ago gave up trying to figure how my mind comes up with these things.

Nice-looking guy, about my height and build, probably a couple years younger. I'd noticed recently that more and more people seemed to be "a couple years younger" than me, and while I chose not to dwell on it, I was very much aware of it.

"Dick Hardesty?" he asked as he came up to me.

I extended my hand. "That's me," I said as we shook. "Do you prefer Frank or Butch...or Mr. Reed?" I added with a grin.

"Butch," he said. "It has nothing to do with leather—my dad started calling me that when I was four."

"Obvious prescience," I said, and he returned the grin.

"Or wishful thinking," he replied.

We entered the coffee shop and took a booth under the side window. There were only five other people in the place, including the waitress.

"Menus?" she called from behind the counter.

"What kind of pie you got today, Janice?" Reed asked.

"Cherry, coconut creme, blueberry and apple."

"Cherry," he ordered. "And coffee."

Both he and the waitress—Janice, unless Reed was into making up names—looked at me.

"Coconut creme and coffee," I said, raising my voice just loud enough to cover the fifteen feet between us.

Reed and I small-talked while waiting for our orders.

"Your day off, I gather?"

He nodded.

"I was out running when you called," he said. "I was really surprised to get your message. Still am, as a matter of fact. What's this all about?"

Janice was approaching with a coffeepot and two paper placemats in one hand, and two small plates of pie in the other. How waitresses manage to do that without dropping things all over the floor always amazes me.

The coffee cups were already on the table, inverted on their saucers. She pulled two paper-napkin-wrapped silverware sets out of her apron pocket and got everything set up for us.

"Cream and sugar's over there," she said to me, indicating the ubiquitous array of condiments lined against the wall as though awaiting a firing squad.

"Thanks," I said.

"You need anything else, just let me know," she said pleasantly but without smiling, and then returned to her station behind the counter.

When she'd gone, I got to the business at hand. "You heard an arrest was made in the Hysong shooting?"

He nodded. "Yeah, I heard."

"Well," I said, "Jake didn't do it, that's for sure. I've been hired to find out who really did it."

"Isn't that what the police are for?"

"The DA has pretty much tied the police's hands. He's more interested in chalking up another conviction than in making sure they arrested the right guy. And when it comes to a dead gay guy, one fag's as good as another to pin it on. No point wasting the taxpayers' money on trying to make sure you have the right one."

"So, how did you find out about the meeting?" he asked after washing down a forkful of pie with a large swig of coffee.

"I've been contacting guys from the Male Call, and Jared and Jake are good friends of mine," I explained. "They mentioned it. One of those seemingly insignificant facts I like to collect. I understand everybody there had it in for Hysong."

"You could say that," he acknowledged.

"Anybody there with a particularly strong grudge?"

He set down his fork and looked at me. "That's all pretty relative," he said. "Every guy there had damned good reason to kill that bastard."

"Including you."

"Including me," he agreed. "But I didn't. And I can't imagine that any of the other guys did, either."

"But you did talk about killing him," I said.

He picked up his fork to scoop another bite of pie into his mouth then followed up with more coffee.

"The subject did come up, sure," he said. "How couldn't it? Hysong deserved what he got. But that's all it was—just talk. Don Gleason said that if Hysong gave AIDS to others, that meant he had it himself and it was a lot more fitting for him to die the way the guys he infected had died, and he was right.

"What we mostly talked about was our forming up teams of two guys to take turns following Hysong everywhere he went and not giving him the chance to give it to anybody else."

"And what happened with that idea?" I asked.

He shrugged. "Not much, I'm afraid. We talked about getting together again that weekend, but Jake and Jared were going out of town and Cal was killed that following Monday. That sort of settled the matter."

Although I knew the answer before I asked the question, it was an obvious one.

"And what, precisely, did you have against Hysong?"

"I had sex with him," he said.

I looked at him. "So did a lot of guys, apparently. They weren't all at the meeting."

He shrugged, but I sensed there was something he wasn't saying.

"Something you're not telling me?" I pursued. "Did you have sex with him more than once?"

He shook his head strongly. "No way, and I wouldn't have had sex with him the one time I did if..."

The waitress appeared with more coffee, and Reed said nothing more.

When she'd left he didn't pick up where he'd left off until I said, "If what?"

"I'd known Cal for a long time," he said. "We got along okay, and sex was never an issue. He knew me well enough to know he wasn't my type, physically. But that one night he made it clear he it was time we got it on—without actually coming out and saying anything.

"I just sort of shined him on, so he started buying me drinks. That should have been a clue right there—Cal never bought drinks for anybody but himself. And he didn't start doing it until he saw I had my eye on somebody else. Then, he deliberately stood so he was blocking my view. I'd edge over a bit, and Cal'd edge over a bit. All very subtle.

"And all the time Cal's talking to me. He bought me that drink, and then every time I'd start to make a move toward the other guy, he would buy me another drink and keep on talking. Finally, somebody else moved in on the other guy, and not more than two minutes later they left together.

"So, there I am, getting progressively more drunk and more frustrated—not to mention horny, since booze does that to me—by the minute, so when Cal told me to follow him into the back room, I did. He knew damned well what he was doing every minute, and I was too damned drunk and stupid enough not to realize it. He knew I never would have gone with him sober."

As he talked, it occurred to me that being in effect taken advantage of was bad enough, but the realization that Hysong undoubtedly knew he had AIDS when he did it was totally unconscionable—and a damned good motive to kill the sonofabitch. And I was sure every other guy who Hysong had used at the Male Call felt exactly the same way.

"Were you in the service, by any chance?" I asked.

He nodded. "Navy."

"Do you know much about guns?"

He gave me a small smile. "A little. I did a lot of skeet shooting when I was a teenager, and I've got a Colt .38 police pistol around somewhere. It belonged to my dad, and I haven't seen it in years. Why? Am I a suspect?"

I shook my head. "In my job, everybody's a potential suspect, but I wouldn't worry about it. So, when you were at the meeting at Jake's and talking...hypothetically...about killing Hysong, did anybody mention shooting him?"

"No. Like I said, the conversation never really got that far. Besides, I don't know of anybody there who has a gun, other than me...and Jake, of course. He's got a whole display case full of them."

"Antiques," I said, just to see if he might mention the Winchester.

Sure enough. "I know he just spent a fortune on a new hunting rifle not too long ago. I didn't see it, though, and Jake didn't mention it at the meeting."

So, he knew about Jake's rifle. But so, probably, did everyone else there. Jake had said he'd talked about it at the Male Call when he first got it.

"Which one of the guys there would you say might have had a particularly strong grudge against Hysong?"

He shook his head. "Jeezus, we all did! That's why we got together. Who can say who hated him more? Don lost his brother, Art just lost his best friend, Steve and Chuck have good buddies who are dying. Any of us who had sex with Cal could be next."

No argument there. The thing was, somebody's hatred was stronger, or Hysong would still be alive.

This was not, I realized again, going to be an easy case to solve.

XVIII

I DON'T KNOW WHICH IS WORSE—WORKING ON A CASE WHERE THE MURDERER IS LIKE something you scrape off the bottom of your shoe, or on a case where I actually empathize with the killer. I've had both, and this one definitely was the latter.

On my way back to the office I thought about Don Gleason and Butch Reed and their stories, and I really could understand how good, decent people might be moved to murder. But I also know that murder is never excusable. I empathized totally with both of these guys and was pretty sure I'd empathize equally strongly with everyone I interviewed on this case. And I know from experience that having to turn in someone I knew and liked was probably the hardest part of this job.

There were still no messages waiting for me at the office so I wrote up some notes for Glen and tried to think of whom else I would want to talk to after I'd gotten in touch with the other four guys from the meeting. I'd want to talk to Carl Brewer again, since he knew just about everything that went on at the Male Call and I was sure that whatever had led to Hysong's death had originated there. I also made a note to talk to the guys Hysong worked with at the construction company and maybe check with some of his neighbors. From what little I knew of him, I sincerely doubted anyone would have anything helpful to contribute.

WE WERE JUST FINISHING DINNER WHEN THE PHONE RANG. JOSHUA SLID OFF HIS CHAIR AND raced for the living room.

"I'll get it!" he called, but Jonathan got up quickly for an interception, scooping him up in mid-run.

"Thank you, Joshua, but I'll get it this time," he said, holding the boy in one arm while reaching for the phone with the other.

A slight pause after his "Hello?" then: "Dick, it's for you."

Joshua raced back into the kitchen as I got up.

"It's for you!" he said.

I tousled his hair as I passed on my way to the phone.

"Hi, this is Dick," I said, after Jonathan handed me the receiver and headed back toward the kitchen.

"Yeah. This is Chuck Fells. I got your message. What did you want?" The voice was one I'd associate with a Male Call hardcore regular—no-nonsense butch.

"I'm looking into Cal Hysong's death," I said, "and was hoping I could meet with you for a few minutes to talk about it."

"Hysong was a worthless piece of shit, and I'm not going to waste a minute of my time meeting with anybody about him. Anything you want to know, ask me now."

Nice guy.

"I understand you were at a meeting to talk about Hysong's spreading AIDS to guys at the Male Call."

"Yeah? So?"

"Well, the guys at the meeting all seemed to have a special grudge against Hysong. I was wondering what yours was." I knew he had a friend or friends Hysong had probably infected but wanted to see what he'd say.

"That's none of your business. They arrested the guy who shot him. What difference does it make?"

"For one thing, I don't think they arrested the right guy."

There was only a slight pause before: "And you think I'm the right guy?"

"That's not what I'm saying. I'm saying I don't think either one of us wants to see someone going to prison for something he didn't do, and I can use your help in finding out who did."

Another pause, a bit longer, then: "So, what do you want from me?"

"You know what goes on at the Male Call. Who would you think would have the best reason for killing Hysong?"

"There is no best reason. Hysong was an asshole who deserved to die. I'm just sorry he died so quick—he deserved to suffer."

"Did you ever hear anyone talk about killing him?"

"Shit, yeah. Just about everybody after they found out what he was doing."

"And how did they find out?" Another question to which I already knew the answer but wanted to see what he said.

"Carl eighty-sixed him."

"That isn't solid evidence it was Hysong," I observed.

"Who the hell's side are you on, anyway?" he demanded.

"I'm not on anybody's side. I'm just trying to do my job. A guy was murdered. I'm trying to find out who did it. Period. I can't let my personal feelings get in the way."

When Fells said nothing, I continued. "Do you know any of the guys who were infected through the Male Call?"

"Yeah. We all do."

"Did they specifically say they'd gotten it from Hysong?"

"Every one of them had sex with him, that much I know. It doesn't take a rocket scientist to do the math."

"You're right," I said. "But even though it isn't any of my business, why were *you* at that meeting?"

Again a pause, and I was afraid he wasn't going to say anything. But finally he said, "I've got two buddies I ride with from the Spike. They hung out there more than at the Male Call. Both of them are sick now, and both of them had sex with Hysong in the Male Call's back room. They're gonna die soon. They know it and I know it. Johnny's back in the hospital now, and they don't think he'll make it out. I went to the meeting because I owed it to them to do whatever I could to see to it that bastard paid for what he did before they died."

"Well, he paid," I said.

"Not enough."

We hung up shortly thereafter, and I returned to the kitchen.

AFTER DINNER, WHILE JONATHAN STUDIED FOR HIS HORTICULTURE CLASS, JOSHUA AND I had a little quality roughhouse time until I begged off to try to call Art Manners and Steve Morse. There was no answer at Manners's, but Morse's phone was picked up on the second ring. I introduced myself and explained the reason for the call.

He mainly verified what I'd learned from Gleason, Reed and Fells until I asked him my usual question whether he knew of anyone at the Male Call who might have had a special grudge against Hysong.

"Well, just between you and me, I can't imagine anyone having more of a reason than Carl."

"Carl Brewer?" I'd more or less shifted him to a side burner as a serious suspect in my concentration on the guys at the meeting, mainly because I was trying to figure out who had stolen Jake's gun—and Carl hadn't attended.

Besides, I'd talked to him, and while I recognized his right to be angry, he didn't come across as its being a major issue.

"Well, with the Male Call up for sale..."

Now, that was something of a bombshell.

"Where did you hear that?" I asked, hoping my surprise wasn't reflected in my voice.

"Art told me."

"Art Manners?" I asked, sounding, I'm sure, like a not-too-bright parrot.

"Yeah. It might just be a rumor, but Art heard it from Pete Reardon at the Spike. Art and Pete are pretty close."

"But Art still hangs out at the Male Call? I thought the two bars were arch rivals."

"I know. Reardon and Carl hate each other, but a lot of guys go to both places. And I kind of suspect Art might just keep Pete posted on what's going on at the Male Call. Art told me about the sale a while ago but asked me not to say anything. I didn't, until now."

"And why now?" I wondered aloud.

"I'm not stupid," he said. "There's no way in hell you can call every single guy who goes to the Male Call, so that means you called me for a reason. You figure if I was at that meeting that makes me a prime suspect and I don't want you wasting your time thinking I really had anything to with it, much as I hated Cal Hysong's guts."

"Can I ask when you heard about the sale? Before or after Hysong was killed?"

"Before, I'm pretty sure. Carl's business really took a dive when the rumors started circulating. I know he tried to get a loan from the bank, but they turned him down because of the rumors."

"And how did you know that?" I asked. "Did Manners tell you?"

"No, I got that from the loan officer at Carl's bank. He goes to the Male Call sometimes, and we get together every now and then."

"So much for gays supporting gays," I said.

"Yeah, well, business trumps sexual orientation every time."

He was right, of course.

"And what was your special grudge against Hysong? I assume you had one."

"One of my best friends, Danny Popko, died this past week."

I remembered Popko's name from the list of the Male Call's sick Brewer had given me.

"I'm really sorry to hear that," I said.

"Yeah, well, Cal killed him as sure as if he'd put a gun to his head and pulled the trigger—only it would have been a lot better for Danny if he had. I guess you might call that a grudge. But I wouldn't waste a bullet on that prick—I wanted to see Cal die like Danny and all the others did. Still, I'm glad he's dead."

BY THE TIME I'D FINISHED TALKING WITH MORSE, IT WAS TIME TO START GETTING JOSHUA ready for bed, so I put off trying to call Art Manners until the next day. He and Spinoza were the only two from the meeting at Jake's I'd not talked to, and I determined to try to reach them from the office. I'd leave another message for Spinoza, if necessary, and if I hadn't heard from him by evening, I'd call both of them from home

Morse's revelation that Carl Brewer had put the Male Call up for sale, assuming it wasn't just a rumor—and I'd definitely check it out—would put Brewer back on the suspect list...and pretty close to the top. When I'd talked with him Hysong was still alive; and while it was clear Carl was understandably unhappy with him and that the rumors about him spreading AIDS were responsible for the sharp decline in the Male Call's business, I had no idea it might have driven him to sell the business he'd had for twenty-plus years.

It then occurred to me—albeit belatedly—that while Brewer had not been at the meeting, he knew about it, and he'd known about Jake's having the gun. Could he have taken advantage of the fact that suspicion for stealing the gun would logically fall on one of the guys at the meeting? Again, he could have used the one he took from Don Gleason, but that would have been a little too easy to trace.

I didn't really have a chance to go over my other conversations of the day until after Joshua was safely tucked in for the night. While Jonathan sat beside me on the sofa, still studying, and I ostensibly stared at the TV—I haven't a clue what was on—I went back over my talk with Fells. I finally identified the muffled alarm bells that had gone off in my head while we'd talked.

Fells had said he wanted his two sick friends to see Hysong pay before they died, and that's exactly what happened. Despite both his and Morse's protestations they wanted Hysong to suffer, it wasn't inconceivable that either of them had chosen instead to give their friends the satisfaction of knowing Hysong had paid for what he'd done before they died.

Okay, so Fells and Morse were definite suspects. Add Reed and Gleason, who had their own solid motives. I'd probably find out, when I talked to

Spinoza and Manners, that they did, too. And if Carl Brewer did have the Male Call up for sale, he'd be right there with them. All of them were aware Jake had the gun, and any one of them could have stolen and used it.

Momentarily distracted by a TV commercial featuring a shirtless hunk demonstrating a new 32-blade shaver—"For the closest shave ever!"—that got even Jonathan's attention, my mind again sank back into speculation. Why did I always seem to get cases with multiple suspects? Two is fine. Maybe even three. But this one had at least seven that I knew of—and how many others that I didn't?

Then, there was the element of motive. This case wasn't about greed or power or secrets. This, except perhaps for Carl Brewer's losing his business, was totally about emotions. All these men had lost or were losing something that can't be assigned a pricetag. Who can possibly accurately determine which human being's emotions are stronger than another's?

I noticed Jonathan had closed his book and was staring at me.

"Figure it out yet?" he asked.

I shook my head and laid one hand on his thigh. "Nope," I said. "Too many suspects."

He grinned. "Can I be one?" he asked.

"Sure, why not?" I said. "But why would you want to be?"

"Well, I was thinking we might play a game of The Tough PI and the Stubborn Suspect. You know, maybe rough him up a little bit. Maybe even a full-body search…"

"Sounds good to me," I said, getting up. Reaching to pull him up with me, I led him toward the bedroom.

NO MESSAGES ON MY OFFICE ANSWERING MACHINE WHEN I GOT IN FRIDAY. I WAITED UNTIL after my morning ritual before trying to reach Manners and Spinoza. Again no answer on either phone, and I left another message for Spinoza, telling him it was important I talk to him and again leaving both my office and home phone numbers.

I then dialed Carl Brewer's home number to try to set up an appointment to talk with him in person. I wanted to know if the rumor about his selling the Male Call was true, and I preferred to do it face to face so I could better gauge his reactions.

The phone rang twice before I heard the receiver being lifted. "Brewer."

"Mr. Brewer, this is Dick Hardesty. I was wondering if you'd have a couple of minutes today to talk to me."

"About what? Didn't you get my check?"

"Yes, I got it, and thanks. But I had a couple of questions about Cal Hysong's death."

"That book's closed as far as I'm concerned," he said. "The bastard's dead. Good riddance. End of story."

"Well, not quite," I said. "That's why I'd like to talk to you in person."

There was a rather long pause, which clearly conveyed the idea he'd just as soon not be bothered.

"Today's not a good day. I've got some business to take care of, and I have to go in to work early to do some paperwork."

"Could I come by the bar for a few minutes when you first get there? I won't take up much of your time."

His sigh underscored his earlier pause. "I suppose. We open at four."

I'd been hoping to talk to him alone, not only because of the nature of my questions but to avoid the distractions of other people being nearby. But I didn't want to push it.

"Thanks," I said. "I really appreciate it. See you then."

I called Jonathan's work to leave a message I might be a few minutes late getting home.

I ARRIVED AT THE MALE CALL SHORTLY AFTER FOUR AND IMMEDIATELY SAW I NEEDN'T HAVE worried about distractions. The place was empty—no sign of a customer or of Carl Brewer. It was so quiet I could have heard a cockroach belch.

I walked to the bar and sat down. After what was probably a minute but seemed much longer, I called out, "Hello?"

The door to Brewer's office opened, and he emerged carrying a case of beer, which he brought up to the bar without a word and began to unpack into a slide-top cooler.

"On time again," he said, glancing at me for the first time. When he'd put the last of the bottles into the cooler, he set the empty box on the ledge behind him and turned to me. "What'll it be?"

"A Bud," I said, and he reached into another cooler and plunged his hand into a mound of ice to retrieve a bottle, which he uncapped and set in front of me.

I reached into my pocket for my wallet, but he waved me off.

"On the house."

"Thanks," I said and took a long swig.

By this time it had dawned on me that, though the bar was officially open, there was no bartender, and the lack of any other customers clearly explained why.

"So, what did you need to know?" he asked, idly running a damp rag over the highly polished rail on his side of the counter.

"I've heard you've got the Male Call up for sale," I said and saw the muscles in his jaw clench, though he kept his face impassive.

"Yeah, I do. It's time. I've been thinking about it for a couple of years, now. And then when I do decide, the roof falls in. Talk about lousy timing. First those fucking AIDS rumors, and now everbody's assuming there's a murderer running around here."

"You put a hell of a lot of work into this place," I said.

"Twenty years. But everything's got to end sometime." He leaned forward, resting his arms on the bar.

"Any offers yet?" I asked, though I knew it wasn't any of my damned business and I expected him to tell me so.

"Pete Reardon made a half-assed offer on it," he said casually, "though the Spike's just hanging on by a thread itself. It's been doing better since guys stopped coming here, but I know he couldn't afford it even if I'd consider selling to him. And he knows I'd burn the place to the ground before that happened."

Reardon wanted it? That was an interesting bit of news.

"He's already got the Spike. Why would he want the Male Call, too?"

Brewer looked at me. "Because it's mine. He's been out to destroy me ever since the Dog Collar fire."

"I'm curious," I said, after taking another swig of beer. "If this Hysong thing hadn't come along, would you still be selling?"

"Like I said, I've been thinking about it for awhile," he repeated, and I didn't believe him. "Cal was just the final push."

"It must be really tough to give up something that's been so big a part of your life for all this time. And it must have been hard to see your business drop off so sharply."

He shook his head. "I don't blame the guys for staying away when those AIDS rumors started. They were scared—and they had every reason to be." He paused a minute, then said, "So, what's your interest in all this?"

"I've been hired to try to find out who killed Hysong," I said.

He gave a short snort of disgust. "Why bother? Who cares who killed him?"

"Well, the guy they arrested for it, for one."

"Oh, right—Jake Jacobson. I was surprised to hear it, but I'll buy him a beer next time I see him, by way of thanks."

"Yeah, well, Jake didn't do it."

Brewer just shrugged.

The front door opened, and two guys came in. Brewer pushed away from the bar.

"Well," he said, "I've gotta get to work."

"Sure," I said. "Thanks for the beer."

Already walking toward the two guys, now seated at the far end of the bar, he merely gave a wave over his shoulder in response.

I PULLED INTO THE APARTMENT GARAGE JUST AS JONATHAN AND JOSHUA TURNED INTO THE driveway. I opened his garage door for him and waited until they got out of the car and joined me.

"Piggyback!" Joshua demanded, running up to me, and I obligingly knelt down so he could climb on. If I had any doubts of the rate of his growth, carrying him up a flight of stairs resolved it.

The minute we finished dinner, I went to the phone to call Tom Spinoza and Art Manners. I'd already left two messages on Spinoza's answering machine in as many days without a reply. It was possible he was out of town or for some reason didn't get them. It was also possible he got them and chose to ignore them, which is why I called him first.

The phone rang three times before I heard it being picked up, followed by "Yeah?"

Whatever happened to hello?, I wondered.

"This is Dick Hardesty calling," I said. "I left a couple of messages on your machine."

"I know. I got them."

That's it? He got them? And...?

"I was hoping to hear from you," I said.

"I been busy," he said. "What do you want?"

"I'm trying to find out who killed Cal Hysong," I said.

"I heard they arrested Jake Jacobson for it," he said. "I think they should pin a medal on him."

"I understand you had sex with Hysong after he knew he had AIDS. You must have been really pissed when you found out."

"Pissed?" he said. "Pissed?" His voice dripped with sarcasm dipped in hatred. "Yeah, you might say that!"

"But you're okay?"

"Sure, I'm fine. For now. You ever have a fucking hand grenade shoved up your ass and you don't know whether the pin's been pulled or not? Yeah, I'm pissed. I wish that sonofabitch would come back to life just long enough so I could have a chance at killing him again."

Again? I thought. *An interesting choice of words.*

"I was wondering if we could get together for a few minutes to talk about who might have stolen Jake's gun—it was the one that killed Hysong, and you were at Jake's with a bunch of other guys just before Cal was killed. Maybe you could give me an idea of who to look at."

"No, we can't get together. I'm not going to waste one more second thinking of that bastard. He's dead. I don't know who killed him, and I don't give a shit. All that matters is that he's dead, and I hope he rots in hell!" There was a very brief pause, then: "I've got work to do."

And with that there was the click of the receiver being hung up.

Well, if Spinoza had killed Hysong, it certainly hadn't brought him much closure.

Again I thought of how hatred was undoubtedly the primary motive in Hysong's death. The problem remained in trying to determine whose hatred was strong enough to pull the trigger of Jake's gun.

Without setting the phone back on the cradle, I dialed Art Manners's number, hoping both that he would be home and also a bit more cooperative than Tom Spinoza.

I was pleasantly surprised when the phone was picked up on the second ring.

"Hello?"

"Art Manners?" I asked, not sure he might not have a roommate.

"Yeah?"

Assured I had the right guy, I went into my by-now-standard introduction, reason for calling, etc.

The entire conversation followed the usual pattern. As Jared had told me, Manners had lost a close friend to AIDS within months after the guy's having had sex with Hysong in the back room of the Male Call. Except for the possible lingering grudge against Hysong for having beaten him up in a fight, I didn't get any indication his hatred for Hysong was any greater than anyone else's who'd been at the meeting at Jake's. I was glad when he agreed to meet with me after he got off work Monday night and suggested Happy Hour at the Nightingale, which I gathered was close by for him. I was somewhat relieved he hadn't mentioned either the Spike or the Male Call.

When we'd hung up, I glanced over at Jonathan, on the couch with Joshua lying with his head in his lap. Joshua had been uncharacteristically quiet ever since I got home. He'd complained of a stomach ache during dinner and hadn't eaten much. Jonathan motioned me over with a jerk of his head.

"Feel Joshua's forehead," he said. "I think he's got a fever."

I knelt down in front of Jonathan's legs and put my hand on Joshua's forehead. It felt warm to me.

"Let me get the thermometer," I said, getting up to go into the bathroom.

"My stomach hurts," Joshua declared as I brought the thermometer to him and had him sit up as I put it in his mouth, instructing him to put it under his tongue.

Sure enough, he had a temperature of just above 100.

"Tell you what, Joshua," I said, "why don't we go get you ready for bed and then we'll have time to read an extra story."

"It's not time to go to bed," he complained. "I wanna stay up!"

Since it was still fairly early, we agreed he could stay up until the end of the TV show he and Jonathan were watching, and he lay back down with his head in Jonathan's lap. My mother always used to say she could tell how I was feeling from my eyes, and I realized she was right. I could tell from Joshua's expression he was *not* feeling well.

After a couple of minutes, he sat up and said, "I think I'm gonna throw up!"

I scooped him off the couch and carried him to the bathroom, where we made it to the toilet just in time. Jonathan came in with us and held his head.

Having a kid around isn't always fun, and we had to stand around helplessly until he was reduced to the dry heaves. We cleaned him up and took him into the bedroom to change into his pajamas. His stomach pains seemed to be getting worse.

"Maybe we should take him to the ER," Jonathan said, concern all over his face. A quick glance in the mirror showed I wasn't exactly a picture of calm myself.

"Let's wait for about half an hour," I said. "If he's not feeling any better then, we'll go."

HALF AN HOUR PASSED. HE WASN'T AND WE DID.

Part of the paperwork asked for the name of our family doctor, and we realized we didn't have one. Well, that would have to change pretty quickly. We also didn't have any insurance. Jonathan had health insurance through his work, but we didn't know if Joshua would be covered under it, since he wasn't Jonathan's biological son. I'd been playing Russian roulette with my health for years and had never taken out insurance. Stupid, I know.

We filled out the paperwork as best we could, turned it in then waited impatiently for Joshua to be seen by a doctor. Joshua was pale, definitely had a fever and had tried to vomit several times on our way to the hospital. I did my best to do my protective butch number, but I don't think I pulled it off very well.

At last we were taken into an examination room, where we waited for what seemed another eternity until a doctor came in.

I don't know if he was a pediatrician, but he was very good with Joshua who, to his credit, was really pretty terrific through it all. There were only a few crying spells, during which either Jonathan and I would do our best to comfort him. When the doctor pressed the area around Joshua's bellybutton, the boy yelped with pain, and the doctor looked up at Jonathan, apparently assuming because of their strong resemblance he was Joshua's father.

"It looks like appendicitis," he said. "Not at all uncommon for kids Joshua's age. We'll admit him and do a few more tests, then probably schedule surgery for tomorrow morning. I think he'll be fine until then."

"Can we stay with him?" Jonathan asked.

The doctor looked back and forth between Jonathan and me then smiled.

"Both of you?" he asked.

"Well, one at a time, at least," Jonathan said.

"Sure," he said, "though I don't have to tell you it won't be necessary. We'll give him something to help him sleep and he'll be pretty much out till morning."

"Still, we should be with him," Jonathan insisted.

"Okay," the doctor said, walking toward the door. "Let's see about getting him a bed."

XIX

JONATHAN INSISTED ON TAKING THE FIRST SHIFT, SO AFTER JOSHUA WAS SAFELY IN BED AND asleep I headed on home. I was back at the hospital by seven-thirty, bringing Bunny, Joshua's favorite toy, and several of his story and coloring books. Both Jonathan and Joshua were still asleep, Jonathan in a chair beside Joshua's bed. I wasn't going to wake either of them, but when Jonathan opened his eyes and gave me a small smile I motioned for him to get up, then told him to go down to the cafeteria and get some coffee and something to eat. He was reluctant to leave, but I insisted. He was back in ten minutes with two cups of coffee and a couple sweet rolls.

The doctor came in around eight and said surgery was scheduled for nine-thirty.

"I'm sure you're anxious to get it over with," he said, and we both nodded. He checked on Joshua, who was still pretty much out of it, then left.

EVERYTHING WENT SMOOTHLY, THOUGH BOTH JONATHAN AND I TRIED TO HIDE OUR nervousness from one another until they brought Joshua up from recovery. I've always admired Jonathan for not being as concerned as I am about not showing emotions, though he tried admirably.

The hardest part, though, was when Joshua first woke up. He looked around the room, still groggy, and said, "Where's my mommy?"

Jonathan and I glanced at one another then away, but not before I saw the pain in his eyes.

We stayed with Joshua until a little after noon, when I insisted that Jonathan go home and get some sleep.

"I'm not tired," he said. "I slept most of the night."

"In the chair. Right," I said. "At least go home, take a shower and lie down for a while. Joshua's not going anywhere, and he'll probably be asleep most of the time, anyway." I reached into my pocket for the keys to the car and the parking stub. "You okay to drive?"

"Sure," he said, taking the keys and ticket. "I told you I'm not tired." But his bloodshot eyes said different.

It wasn't exactly the most comfortable of weekends; neither one of us got as much sleep as we needed. Jonathan wanted to spend Saturday night at the hospital, too, but I insisted on taking my turn so he could sleep in a real bed. At least one of us was always with Joshua who, ham that he was, took full advantage of his situation to con us into buying some new toys and new books to keep him occupied.

Jonathan had brought his schoolwork to the hospital, and I watched a lot of TV and called Glen O'Banyon's office to let him know what was going on. I spoke to Donna, and she expressed her empathy, adding that her own daughter had gone through the same thing at just about the same age.

Jonathan and I had plenty of time, sitting there during Joshua's frequent naps, to arrange a schedule for Joshua's recover period. Since my schedule was much more flexible than his, I would take as much of the week off as I could. It would undoubtedly mean I'd lose out on some business, but since I was my own boss, I could manage where we couldn't expect Jonathan's employer to be as accommodating. And if I had to go somewhere during the day, Jonathan was sure he could take off work, though we both hoped that wouldn't be necessary—Joshua's hospital bills were going to be a major financial setback, though Jonathan hoped his insurance from work might cover them.

Joshua was set to be released on Thursday. The doctor said he was making an excellent recovery, but said he felt we should keep him home for two weeks to be safe. I wasn't pleased with that prospect, but we had no choice.

When Monday afternoon rolled around I was actually looking forward to my appointment with Art Manners at the Nightingale. I was more than ready for a Happy Hour.

I had to leave the hospital before Jonathan arrived from work, but Joshua took my departure totally in stride, hardly looking up from his coloring book as I hugged him goodbye and left.

It occurred to me as I got to the Nightingale I hadn't a clue as to what Art Manners looked like. It was 5:20, and there were only five guys in the place, including the bartender. They all looked up as I came in but then went back to their drinks and conversations.

The bartender, who must have weighed close to three hundred pounds and barely fit in the space between the bar and the back bar, came over to take my order.

"A Manhattan," I said and he merely nodded and went off to make it.

While he was gone, I looked around. The Nightingale was a typical small neighborhood bar, comfortably nondescript. The only attempt at individuality was a metal birdcage suspended from the ceiling in a small alcove set into the back bar, in which was a dusty stuffed bird on a perch. Since I was never very good at ornithology, I took a wild guess that it was supposed to be a nightingale.

I took my drink to a small table against one wall—I knew it might get pretty crowded at the bar, and I wanted a little privacy for my talk with Manners. As I took my fourth or fifth swallow of my Manhattan, the door opened and a short, stocky guy in a crewcut came in. As he approached the bar, I saw that he wasn't so much stocky as a compact mass of muscle. He looked in my direction then continued to the bar. I heard the bartender say, "Hi, Art," thereby confirming my assumption.

Manners ordered a beer, paid for it and came over to me. I gather I was the only unfamiliar face in the place.

"Are you Dick Hardesty?" he asked.

I nodded and extended my hand, which he took with a very strong grip then pulled up a stool and sat down opposite me. A really nice-looking guy, I determined, his outstanding feature being green eyes that contrasted with his medium-brown hair. Sexy.

Down, boy!

Our conversation went pretty much like the other ones I'd had. Manners had lost a close friend shortly before the meeting and blamed both Hysong and himself.

"Drew never went to the Male Call," he said. "I met him through work. He wasn't really into leather all that much, but we had other…common interests, you might call them. One night I talked him into coming with me to the Male Call, and Hysong latched onto him so fast I didn't have time to warn him not to go with that bastard. Six months later he was dead."

"You can't blame yourself," I said.

He looked at me. "Yeah, I can. If I hadn't taken him to the Male Call, he wouldn't have gone with Cal and I'm sure he'd still be alive. And I blame Carl, too."

"Carl Brewer? Why?"

"He knew the rumors. He should have eighty-sixed Cal as soon as he heard them. Instead, he held off until too late. I don't know how many other guys Cal got to between the time Carl should have done it and the time he did."

"I understand you're a friend of Pete Reardon," I said, deciding it was time to take the conversation in another direction.

"Yeah, I ride with him from time to time. What about it?"

"I've heard talk about the Male Call being up for sale and that Reardon is interested in buying it. Do you know anything about it?"

"I've heard," he said.

"Why would Reardon want it? He already has the Spike."

"The Male Call's bigger," he said. "And it belongs to Carl."

"I know they don't get along, but..."

Manners's grin cut me off in mid-sentence.

"'Don't get along' doesn't come close. Pete still swears Carl had something to do with fire-bombing the Dog Collar and his being sent to jail."

"As I understand it, Reardon went to jail because the Dog Collar was a firetrap and a disaster just waiting to happen. It did, and twenty-nine guys died."

He shrugged. "Whatever."

It was clear I had crossed the line in suggesting maybe Reardon might have richly earned his jail time.

"Sorry," I said. "I shouldn't of brought that up."

He looked at me. "No, you shouldn't," he said. "Pete Reardon is a great guy, and he's bailed me out of a couple of scrapes. I owe him."

"I'm a little curious," I said. "Knowing how Reardon feels about Carl Brewer and the Male Call, why do you go there?"

He took a long swig of his beer. "I said I owe Pete. He doesn't own me. I go where I want to go." He then polished off the rest of his beer and got up from his stool. "I've gotta get home," he said and walked out without a backward glance.

Well, that certainly went well, I thought. At least I'd gotten some interesting information from him. Exactly what it meant I had no idea at the moment. Sometimes my mind is like a cow's stomach, with one chamber for ruminating and another for digesting.

I MADE IT BACK TO THE HOSPITAL BY SIX-THIRTY TO FIND JONATHAN SITTING BESIDE

Joshua's bed, writing in a notebook.

"Hi, guys," I said, going over to give each a hug. "Whatcha doin'?"

"Joshua's been telling me stories, and I've been writing them down for him," Jonathan said. I noticed he had several pages of the notebook folded over.

"Can I read one?" I asked.

"Sure," Joshua said before Jonathan had a chance to. I'd noted immediately he was looking and feeling much better and was anxious to go home.

Jonathan flipped the pages to the first one and handed it to me. It appeared to be an epic saga involving a cowboy who is taking his sick horse to the hospital when he is captured by pirates and then thrown overboard from the pirate ship and is saved by his trusty horse. Not exactly what one could call a linear story—more stream-of-five-year-old-boy consciousness—but it was definitely creative.

"Wow, Joshua!" I said. "This is good! I'll bet you're going to be a writer when you grow up."

He nodded solemnly, though he was obviously pleased by the praise.

"Got time for a break, Jonathan?" I asked. "I can take over while you run down to the cafeteria."

He got up from the chair and handed me the pen. "Yeah, I am pretty hungry."

"Me, too!" Joshua said. "I want some ice cream."

"You had your dinner, remember?" Jonathan reminded him. "We'll talk to the nurse when she comes back. I won't be long," he said, tousling Joshua's hair.

"Bring me some ice cream!" Joshua called after him as he left the room.

AFTER A GREAT DEAL OF PERSUASION, I CONVINCED JONATHAN IT WOULD BE ALL RIGHT IF WE both went home after Joshua was asleep.

"We've been here every night. He'll be fine," I said.

"I know, but..."

"He sleeps straight through anyway. At least he did last night. I asked."

"Well, yeah, but he wakes up whenever the nurses come in to check him and..."

"And he goes right back to sleep, right?"

"Yeah."

"And I don't think he even knows we're there when he does wake up for those few seconds."

"Uh, maybe not. He's too sleepy."

"Exactly. And look, babe, he's five years old, and we can't be hovering over him every minute. He'll be fine. This way, you can go right to work in the morning. I'll come back first thing then go in to work myself and come by a couple times during the day. He's got the TV and his books, and the nurses will keep an eye on him."

"I should be here."

"He'll be fine," I repeated. "And I can bring him home without any help, I'm sure." I thought it was time to pull out my trump card. "Besides," I said, "we have not had one single night alone in over a year. I think we deserve one, don't you?"

"I suppose," he allowed. Then his face broke into that sexy, slow grin and he said, "You can bellow. I miss your bellowing."

"I never bellow!" I protested.

"Uh-huh."

The nurse assured us Joshua would be fine and told us to go home and not worry.

After Joshua was soundly asleep, we left.

Oh, and Jonathan was right. I guess I do bellow. A little.

AS WE WERE GETTING DRESSED TUESDAY MORNING I REMINDED JONATHAN IT WAS rehearsal night for the Gay Men's Chorus.

"Of course you're going," I said, "It wouldn't look good for you not to show up—this is only your second rehearsal. I'll stay at the hospital until he goes to sleep, and there's no real reason you can't go and enjoy yourself."

After a little more persuading, he reluctantly agreed.

Thursday finally arrived, and I got Joshua home safely at around two o'clock. He didn't want to go to bed, so I put several pillows on the couch, so he could lie there and watch TV, and covered him with a light blanket. The excitement of getting out of the hospital and being back home had worn him out, and he soon fell asleep, Bunny on the floor beside him.

Since I'd gotten precious little work done since he went to the hospital, I took the opportunity to start writing up some case progress notes for Glen O'Banyon.

Jonathan called around four, waking Joshua up from another nap, asking me if I could start dinner—he suggested macaroni and cheese and hot dogs by way of celebrating Joshua's return.

"Let me say a quick hi to Joshua," he said before hanging up, and I carried the phone over to the couch.

"Hi, Uncle Jonathan!" he said. "I'm home!" He listened for a few seconds then said, "Okay. Bye." and handed the receiver back to me. "We're having macaroni and cheese and hot dogs tonight," he announced happily.

After dinner, which we made into an impromptu picnic on Joshua's bed—the only way we could talk him into getting into his pajamas and under the covers so early—Jonathan left for the chorus and Joshua and I spent some time "playing cards." When he decided he wanted to color, I went into the living room to call our friends, to whom we'd not talked since Joshua'd gone to the hospital, to let them know what was going on.

Bob and Mario were already at work, so I left a short message on their machine. Phil and Tim expressed surprise and said they'd like to come over and see Joshua the next night. I reminded them that Wednesday was Jonathan's class night, so we switched it to Thursday. Since Jonathan had made a huge pot of chili a week or so before and the containers had left little room in the freezer for anything else, I suggested they join us and they agreed.

Not sure whether Jared was still commuting to Mountjoy from Jake's during the week, I called Jake's number after making a quick check-in on Joshua. I felt I owed it to Jake and Jared to let them know what was going on with the case, too, so was glad to find Jake home. Jared, I learned, was back to spending the work week at Mountjoy.

I first told Jake about Joshua's trip to the hospital, and like Tim and Phil, he expressed surprise and concern.

"Jared'll be here Friday night…maybe we can come by and see him. Is there anything we can bring him?"

"Thanks," I said, "but he's already spoiled rotten. He's got enough toys and books to last him until he goes off to college. He'll just be glad to see you."

Jake brought up the case before I had a chance to. "So, how's your investigation going, if I can ask?"

"Of course, you can ask!" I said and gave him a quick rundown of my conversations with the guys from the meeting.

"You still think it was one of them, then?" he asked.

"Well, they all knew you had the gun, and they're the most likely to have figured out where it was. Your bathroom has two doors, right?"

"Yeah, from the hall and from the bedroom, but I always keep the bedroom door closed."

"But someone could get from the bathroom into the bedroom to look for the gun, right? Especially if the hall door to the bedroom was closed, they wouldn't be seen."

There was a pause. "Yeah, I guess you're right. That never occurred to me."

"Do you remember who went to the bathroom that night?"

He laughed. "I have a hard enough time remembering what I had for breakfast this morning," he said. "Remembering who might have gone to the bathroom weeks ago...sorry."

"No problem," I said.

"So, anybody stand out as a prime suspect?"

"Not really. They all had a damned good motive. You don't run into someone like Hysong very often, thank God." I paused while my mind did a quick flashback through my conversations.

"What do you know about Tom Spinoza and Art Manners?" I asked.

"Good question," Jake said. "Tom likes to play hard-ass, but I think his bark's worse than his bite. I think he gets a kick out of ticking people off."

"Yeah, well, he succeeded with me," I said, and he laughed.

"I'm not surprised," he said, "but Tom's basically okay. As for Art, he's a good-enough guy, but there's something...I don't know. It's hard to put my finger on. I understand he's really close to Pete Reardon, and I always wondered why he spends so much time at the Male Call, considering the bad blood between Pete and Carl Brewer. Not that guys don't go to both places, but..."

"I was wondering the same thing. You suppose he might be keeping tabs on the Male Call for Reardon?"

"Hmmmm, that never occurred to me, but I wouldn't be surprised. It seemed like he was always up on the latest rumors, though I don't remember that he particularly went out of his way to spread them."

"How does Manners get along with Carl?"

"Okay, I guess. I know they speak, but I've never saw them having much of a conversation. I'm sure Carl knows about Art's being close to Pete. But again, you have to remember we've never been what either of us would consider regulars at the Male Call. All we really know is what we pick up when we do go there."

"Understood," I said.

We talked for a few more minutes then said our goodbyes. I returned to Joshua's bedroom just in time for Story Time.

JONATHAN GOT HOME AROUND TEN, AND BY THE TIME I'D FILLED HIM IN ON MY PHONE conversations and our busy weekend, it was time for bed. My mind wouldn't let me sleep, though. It kept replaying my conversations with the guys from the meeting. Again, any one of them could very well have done it. They all had a solid motive and they all were angry, but for some reason, Spinoza and Manners's anger seemed to have an element of—What? Defensiveness?—in it. True, with Manners I'd undoubtedly provoked it, but still...

Once again, the gun was the pivotal element in this whole case. Whoever had stolen it had killed Hysong, and while there were probably an untold number of guys out there he had infected and who but for the gun might also have been prime suspects, not all of them knew about Jake's gun and only one person had taken it.

I'd never given much thought to "Why Jake's gun?" It was clearly a matter of opportunity. Most people don't have guns of their own, and to buy one for the purpose of killing someone, as Don Gleason had done, would be a slam dunk for the police when it came to tracing the murder weapon to the killer. So, knowing someone else had a gun that could be stolen—and particularly a rifle with the power and range of Jake's...

So, though I might be wrong—it's been known to happen—I was pretty much staking everything on its being one of the guys at the meeting. If I was wrong, well...

I'm not sure what time I finally did get to sleep, but it seemed as though I'd just dozed off when I felt Jonathan move my arm from over his chest as he got up, and I cracked one eye open to see that it was morning. Damn! I hate when that happens.

The next thing I knew, I heard the shower running and was aware of someone standing beside the bed, not two feet from my face. I opened my eyes to see Joshua, his pajama top pulled up with one hand.

"You wanna see my scar?" he asked.

Apparently, the bandage I'd put on after changing it before Story Time the night before had come off during the night, showing a bright red scar about two inches long.

"That's a very nice scar, Joshua," I said. "Thank you for showing it to me. I'll get you a new bandage in a minute."

"That's okay," he said, dropping his pajama top back in place and turning to pad out of the room toward the kitchen.

I got up quickly, threw on my robe and followed him; as I'd suspected, he was dragging a chair over to the cupboard preparatory to climbing up on it to reach into the cabinet for the cereal. I didn't want him to do any stretching just yet, so I hurried over and said, "I'll get it, Joshua. You can get the milk out of the refrigerator for me."

I got the cereal, a bowl and a large and small glass out of the cupboard and set them on the table as he came over with the milk. Rather than let him scramble up on the chair as he normally did, I lifted him onto the thick cushion that enabled him to reach the table then went to get him some juice from the refrigerator.

"As soon as you finish your cereal, we'll put on a new bandage," I said.

"Can I go to school today?" he asked, splashing milk over the mound of cereal in his bowl.

"Not for a while yet," I said. "We want to make sure you're ready."

"I'm ready," he said, munching a mouthful of cereal. "I want to show them my scar."

"It'll still be there," I said, pouring water into the coffeemaker. "Trust me."

Jonathan came into the kitchen, toweling his hair.

"Hi, Uncle Jonathan!" Joshua said, pulling up his pajama top. "You wanna see my scar?"

Jonathan shot me a look, and I said, "His bandage must have come off during the night. I told him I'd put a new one on as soon as he finishes his cereal."

"You put the one on that came off," he noted in an interestingly constructed sentence. "I'll do it."

I just shrugged and continued getting the coffee ready.

AT TEN O'CLOCK, GLEN O'BANYON CALLED.

"I was sorry to hear about Joshua," he said. "How's he doing?"

"He's doing fine, thanks," I said. "We're keeping him home for another week, if I can last that long," I said.

He laughed. "Kids are a lot of fun, I understand," he said.

"Most of the time," I conceded.

"The reason I'm calling is that I just heard St. John has convened the grand jury for this afternoon and was wondering if you've found out anything that might help us. I'm pretty sure he'll get his indictment. He wouldn't have convened it if he didn't think he would. Oh, and I also found out that while Jake's prints were on the gun, there were no prints on the trigger."

"Jeezus," I said. "Doesn't that pretty much invalidate the other prints? I mean, if Jake left his prints on the gun but not on the trigger…"

"You'd think so and I'd think so, but neither one of us is Victor St. John. I suspect he sees some karmic significance in his first name."

I sighed. "True. Well, I've been writing up my notes for you, but I can give you a quick rundown, if it might help."

"Shoot," he said, and I outlined everything I'd done to date.

"Not much in the way of hard evidence," I said, "but my money's resting pretty heavily on either Spinoza or Manners."

"Now all we have to do is prove it," he said.

"I'll do what I can."

AS I HUNG UP THE PHONE, I HAD AN IDEA—AS SO OFTEN HAPPENS, ONE I SHOULD HAVE had when I first heard Jake had discovered his gun missing. He'd said something about leaving his kitchen window open a crack.

I wanted to talk to Marty Gresham and had just picked up the phone to call the City Annex when Joshua came up to me and said, "Can I go outside and play?"

I suddenly felt guilty, realizing the poor kid must have a major case of cabin fever, having not been outside, other than to go to and from the hospital, for more than a week. A week is like forever to a five-year-old boy. And living in a large city in a twelve-unit apartment building where he was the only kid his age couldn't be easy for him.

"Sure," I said. "Why don't we go down to the park for awhile?"

"Okay," he said, immediately heading to the door.

"JUST REMEMBER," I SAID AS WE WALKED THE TWO BLOCKS TO OUR LOCAL PARK, "YOU'VE got to take it easy. The swings and the slide and the merry-go-round are okay, but no monkey bars and no jumping around. Understand?"

"Okay," he said, making it perfectly clear I was talking to a brick wall. The minute we reached the park, I took his hand to keep him from taking off like a shot toward the monkey bars.

He tried to free himself from my grip, but I persisted and led him over to the swings.

"Let's swing first," I said, and released his hand so he could sit down.

"Push me high!" he urged.

We then did the slide and the merry-go-around, which was one of his favorites—mine, too, if truth be told. I would run it around until it reached a pretty good clip then jump on with him.

We both had fun, though he frequently got frustrated when I kept him from doing everything he wanted to. I knew he would have done a lot more running and jumping than was good for him at the moment, but I was concerned that he not risk loosening his stitches.

By the time we returned to the apartment, I could tell he was pretty tired, and I hoped he hadn't overdone it. I put him on the couch with his coloring book while I went into the kitchen to fix lunch. I'd opened a can of tomato soup and was getting bread, butter and cheese from the refrigerator for grilled cheese sandwiches when I glanced into the living room to find him sound asleep, coloring book still in his lap.

I decided lunch could wait a bit.

IT WAS TWO O'CLOCK BEFORE I HAD A CHANCE TO CALL THE CITY ANNEX AND ASK TO SPEAK TO Detective Gresham. I wasn't surprised to hear he wasn't in, but I left a message for him to call me at home and about three he did.

"Hi, Dick. What's up?"

"I need a favor," I asked.

"On the Hysong case?"

"Yeah.'

"I heard the grand jury's convening today. The DA is really pushing it."

"Unfortunately, yes, and they'll almost surely vote to indict. That's why I called."

"What do you need?"

"Well, I should have thought of this a long time ago, but Jake thinks whoever stole the gun got in through his kitchen window. Since Jake's were the only prints on the gun, whoever stole it probably wore gloves, but it wouldn't hurt to check. I got a fingerprint kit right after I got my PI license, but I've never had occasion to use it. I could dust the window myself, but to head off any possible charges of impeding an investigation—and I sincerely hope there will be an investigation—I was wondering if you could find the time to do it? It's pretty much a no-brainer that whoever stole the gun killed Hysong."

There was a slight pause, then: "Well, we're not officially on the case," he said, "and a fingerprint is a fingerprint, but what I can do is stop over there on my own time—maybe on my way to work in the morning—and do it. I'll bring a camera, too, to make sure there's no doubt as to where the prints came from. It might be a long shot, but I agree it's worth taking."

"How about getting fingerprints of all the guys who were at that meeting at Jake's?" I asked. "I still think chances are pretty good one of them did it."

"Well, like I said," Marty repeated, "a fingerprint's a fingerprint. They can be taken from anywhere. I don't think I can justify trying to get them without an okay from higher up, but if you want to put your fingerprint kit to use, by all means feel free. But why don't you give me the guys' names, and I'll run a check to see if we have any already on record. If so, if they might match."

I gave him all six names, slowly.

'Thanks, Marty," I said when I'd finished. "I owe you. Jake's coming over tonight so I'll let him know you'll be by."

"He doesn't even have to be there," Marty said. "I can come up the back steps. Just ask him to leave the window open so I can dust the whole lower frame and the sill."

"Will do. Thanks again! Let me know when you're available for lunch."

"I will. Ah, another call's coming in. Talk to you later."

"Okay. So long," I said.

SINCE WEDNESDAY WAS JONATHAN'S CLASS NIGHT, I FIXED DINNER. WELL, I THAWED OUT A meatloaf and put it in the oven with some baking potatoes. Domesticity has never been my strong suit.

When Jonathan left for class, Joshua and I did the dishes and I called Jake to let him know about Marty's coming over in the morning.

"Great!" he said. "I never would have thought about fingerprints."

"I should have earlier," I admitted. "Let's just hope that if Marty finds any, we're able to match them to someone. I gave him the guys' names and he's going to check the files, but it's kind of unlikely any of them would have their prints on record. If not, I'll have to try to get them myself."

We talked a few minutes more, confirmed their coming over on Friday night—Jake asked again if they could bring something for Joshua, and I heartily discouraged the idea with thanks—and hung up.

It occurred to me, as I sat there watching TV—or rather, staring in the direction of screen—that in addition to the guys at the meeting, I really should pay a little more attention to Carl Brewer as a potential suspect. Despite his claim it was his idea to sell the Male Call, I didn't believe him. Hysong had, in effect, robbed him of a business in which he had invested twenty years of hard work. While he may not have had as intense a direct emotional motive as some of the others, it could not be overlooked. Perhaps Don Gleason's having come into the bar to kill Hysong had given him the idea.

It occurred to me now that he had been pretty elusive in the brief conversation I'd had with him about guns.

Well, I'd find out.

Joshua had crawled up on the couch beside me with a copy of *Life* that had come in that day's mail.

"Let's read," he said. I grinned at him, flipped off the TV and turned the first page.

I REALIZED THURSDAY MORNING THAT WHILE I WANTED TO TALK TO CARL BREWER AS SOON as possible I couldn't really do it until at least Saturday. Tim and Phil were coming over Thursday night, and Jake and Jared were coming Friday. Bob and Mario had called Wednesday to asked if we'd like to come over for brunch on Sunday, if Joshua was up to it. So, Saturday was the first chance I'd have to really do much on the case.

Marty called around eleven, saying he'd been over to Jake's to do the dusting for fingerprints on the kitchen window.

"Any luck?" I asked.

"Well, there were no prints on the outside of the window frame, or on the sill. I assumed at first that meant either there hadn't been any or you were right when you suggested whoever it was might have worn gloves.

"But then I checked the inside lower frame and found four perfect prints—whoever had opened the window might have put on gloves once he got into the apartment, but he thought he'd wiped everything off when he left. He didn't realize he'd hooked his hands around the frame to lift it, leaving prints on the inside edge. I took a couple of photos, too.

"I've already compared the prints to Jacobson and Martinson's we took the day the gun was discovered missing. No match, so I ran the names you gave me to see if any of them might have an arrest record. Found a couple speeding tickets, one or two disturbing-the-peace charges, but nothing that would have necessitated their being fingerprinted. We can tap into the military's files if we have to, but that would start to involve other people, and I'd just as soon avoid making waves if we can avoid it. So, let's see what you can come up with first."

"Okay. Thanks for everything, Marty."

"No problem."

Glen called at one-thirty to say the grand jury had issued an indictment against Jake and that he was awaiting news on a date for trial, which turned up the heat considerably. I told him of my plans to try to see Carl Brewer over the weekend and of the discovery of the fingerprints and my intention to get more, and he seemed encouraged

"If we can get a match on the prints," he said, "I'll press the police for a full investigation, and we might be able to blow St. John out of the water before he gets around to wasting any more of the taxpayer's money on a trial he's bound to lose anyway."

JONATHAN STOPPED ON THE WAY HOME FROM WORK TO PICK UP A LOAF OF GARLIC BREAD and a banana creme pie for dessert, and I had already defrosted a couple large containers of chili so that all we had to do was heat it up when Tim and Phil arrived, which they did at seven o'clock sharp, carrying a large gift-wrapped box.

Spotting them and the box, Joshua ran over, arms flung wide like the Norman Rockwell painting of a mother running to met her boys, home from the war. Phil set the package down to kneel and give him a hug. Normally, he'd have picked him up and tossed him in the air, but probably figured—rightly—that it might not be a good idea so close after an operation. Joshua, of course, never took his eyes off the box.

"Is that for me?" he asked, obviously exerting all his five-year-old willpower to resist ripping the wrapping off.

Tim's "Yep" had hardly left his mouth than Joshua was on his knees, scraps of wrapping paper flying every which way.

Unwrapped, the package proved to contain a large set of Lincoln Logs. Since the cardboard of the box proved more difficult to remove than the wrapping paper had, Phil helped, and Joshua began removing all the pieces, repeating "Wow!" every couple of seconds.

"What do you say, Joshua?" Jonathan prompted.

"Wow!" Joshua said.

"No, not 'wow.' Aren't you going to say 'thank you?'"

As though he'd been caught with his hand in the cookie jar, Joshua scrambled to his feet and went to hug first Phil, then Tim.

"Thank you, Uncle Phil! Thank you, Uncle Tim." He then immediately returned to the box.

While I very much appreciated their thoughtfulness, I rather wished they hadn't done it—not only because we'd be tripping over Lincoln Logs for weeks, but because Jonathan and I had had more than one conversation in which we determined we would really try not to spoil Joshua any more rotten than we already had.

While I went into the kitchen to fix drinks, Phil and Joshua sat in the middle of the floor building a log cabin.

WHILE MY FIRST WEEK—WELL, PARTIAL WEEK—OF FULL-TIME BABYSITTING HAD, OVERALL, not been too bad, the prospect of another full week of it, and the realization that I wasn't doing a damned thing on the case, started to get to me, though I tried not to show it, especially to Jonathan. He had sensed it, though, and announced his boss would let him take three of his vacation days starting Monday so I could get back to work.

Joshua spent the day playing with his new Lincoln Log set, and as I'd predicted, they soon were scattered all over the apartment, including one found beside the cereal box in the kitchen cupboard and another, inexplicably, floating in the fish tank.

I devoted my time to typing up my notes for Glen. I couldn't complete them until I went by the Male Call again Saturday afternoon to talk to Carl Brewer. I planned to drop the full set of notes off at Glen's office first thing Monday morning, and I called to leave a message with Donna telling him so.

Around eleven, Marty Gresham called to say he'd run the prints from the window through the complete police files and had not come up with a match. I hadn't really expected he would, but I'd hoped. So, now I had to figure out a way to get prints from everyone who'd been to the meeting.

The simplest and most logical way was just to ask. That would pretty well rule out those who agreed to it, though I expected some wouldn't just on general principles, and in a way, I couldn't blame them. I wasn't sure I'd be too happy about volunteering *my* prints. Still, if they had nothing to hide…

XX

JAKE AND JARED ARRIVED ABOUT SEVEN-THIRTY. JOSHUA AND I HAD JUST FINISHED A heated battle over the necessity of picking up his toys that were scattered all over the living room and put them away. Jonathan wisely stayed out of it for the most part, simply saying "Listen to Uncle Dick" when Joshua went tearily running to him for moral support. As a result, I was temporarily removed from Joshua's "favorite people" list.

The guys, of course, made a big fuss over him and were, as Tim and Phil had been, dutifully impressed by his scar, which he insisted on showing them. The showing was accompanied by a lengthy and dramatic recounting of his trip to and adventures at the hospital.

We had cake and coffee—milk for Joshua—and talked for a bit, by mutual unspoken agreement avoiding mention of the case, the grand jury indictment or Cal Hysong until Jonathan excused himself to get Joshua ready for bed.

There wasn't really much more I could tell them I'd not already mentioned to Jake when we'd talked, but I did ask them if they might have a chance to think of anything more about the meeting, the guys there or who might have taken the rifle. They hadn't.

When Jonathan and Joshua emerged from the bathroom Joshua, obviously still holding a grudge for my making him put his things away, announced that he wanted Uncle Jake to read him his bedtime story.

SATURDAY BEING CHORE DAY, I VOLUNTEERED TO DO MOST OF THEM WHILE JONATHAN stayed home with Joshua. I love the kid dearly, but after nearly twenty-four hours a day for more than a week, it was nice just to be on my own for a bit.

I headed out for the Male Call at about three-forty-five. I found a parking spot two doors down and noticed, as I headed for the bar, that every telephone pole seemed to have a flier on it. They were for a bike run for AIDS the following Sunday, sponsored by the Spike. Interesting, and undoubtedly plastering them all over the area around the Male Call was another of Reardon's little jabs at Brewer. Sort of like one tiger marking another's territory.

When I walked in, I saw there were two customers—better than the last time I'd been in—but still no bartender; Brewer was behind the bar. He gave me a heads-up nod of recognition when I walked in and took a seat at the far end.

The two guys got up and carried their beers over to the pool table as Brewer came over to take my order. When he brought it, he took the bill I'd set on the bar.

"Social call or business?" he asked.

"Mostly business, I'm afraid."

"Figured," he said.

"Did you know Cal was killed with Jake's gun?" I asked, getting right to the point.

He didn't bat an eye. "No. I know he's got several, but I thought they were all antiques."

"Not his new hunting rifle. That's the one that was used to kill Hysong."

"Oh, yeah, I forgot about that one. I do remember him bragging about it in here when he first got it. It's a nice gun."

"You know much about guns?" I asked.

Oh, subtle, Hardesty! a mind-voice said.

He looked at me and gave me a slow smile. "Yeah, I know about guns," he said. "I know they kill people and that I don't want anything to do with them."

Well, since I was batting a thousand in the subtlety department, I thought I might as well go for broke.

"You ever been over to Jake's place?" I asked.

Again the smile. "You got me! I went over there and stole his damned gun and used it to shoot Cal and then took it back, right?"

I hadn't meant to be that obvious, though the part about taking the gun back could either mean he didn't know it had been stolen or that he was throwing me a clever curve.

But he could have said "took" rather than "stole."

He could have, but he didn't. Enough with the semantics, already!

"That's not what I was getting at," I said unconvincingly. "I just thought that if you'd been there you might have some idea about how whoever stole it might have gotten in—there was no sign of forced entry." I wasn't quite sure what I was fishing for with that one, unless to see if Brewer knew about the back porch.

"Can't help you," he said. "I know where he lives—a friend of mine lives just down the block from him—but I've never been to Jake's."

"The cops found fingerprints they're pretty sure belong to the guy who stole the gun. Now we just have to figure out who they belong to."

Brewer gave me that smile again, bent down below the counter and came up with an empty beer bottle, which he wiped carefully with a towel. He then wrapped both hands around it and set it down in front of me.

"Here you go," he said. "I'll save you the trouble of trying to get mine."

Now that was unexpected. I didn't pick it up, but fully intended to take it with me when I left.

"Damn," I said, "You take all the fun out of it!" And returned his grin. "I'm afraid not everyone I'll be checking on will be so cooperative." I rattled off the names of the six from the meeting. "I know all those guys have been at Jake's. Anything you know about them that might help me out?"

He thought a minute, then shook his head. "Nope, not really," he said. "Except maybe Art. I don't trust him."

Obviously, he was aware that Manners and Pete Reardon were close.

"Any specific reason?" I asked.

Again the head shake. "I think Reardon uses him to spy on what's going on over here. I've heard a rumor Art thinks that if Reardon got his hands on the Male Call, he'd have Art run it for him. I think he's just blowing smoke out his ass, and if he's waiting for me to sell to Reardon, he's got a long wait."

One of the guys from the pool table came over to the bar with two empty bottles, and Brewer moved off to get two more. He didn't seem in any great hurry to come back and talk, busying himself instead with something in one of the coolers, so I took my time finishing my beer, set the empty on the bar, used a napkin to pick up the bottle with his prints and got up to leave. I walked over to where he was still busy doing whatever he was doing.

"Thanks for talking with me," I said, making a small gesture with the empty bottle. "I hope you didn't take my questioning personally."

Brewer shrugged. "Hey," he said, "that's your job. I wish you luck in getting Jake off the hook—though I'd hate to see anybody go to jail for doing a public service in getting rid of Cal."

WELL, SO MUCH FOR BREWER BEING A VIABLE SUSPECT. THAT HE HAD SO QUICKLY volunteered his fingerprints had really surprised me, and my suspicious nature wondered if there might have been a reason.

Oh, come on, Hardesty! a mind voice—the one in charge of skepticism— said, a bit impatiently. *What reason could there be? There doesn't have to be a sinister motive behind every single human action.*

It was right, of course. I did have something of a tendency to second-, third- and fourth-guess myself, which was both frustrating and counterproductive.

But Brewer had made a comment in there somewhere that had rung a bell. What the hell was it? Ah, yes, the rumor that Art Manners thought he was going to be managing the Male Call when—and if, both equally unlikely— Brewer sold to Reardon. I had no idea where that one had come from and should have asked, though Brewer probably hadn't a clue either. Rumors are rather like mushrooms in that they just spring up out of a pile of shit. I hadn't been aware that Manners had any sort of bar managing background—if, indeed, he did.

My thoughts were luckily sidetracked when I pulled into the garage and headed up for the apartment and dinner.

SUNDAY BRUNCH AT BOB AND MARIO'S WAS JUST WHAT I NEEDED—NOT ONE SINGLE WORD from anybody about the case. I knew it wasn't because they weren't interested or curious, but that they, like good friends often do, intuitively knew I'd fill them in when I was ready.

Butch and Pancake, the two no-longer-kittens, kept Joshua totally occupied playing with or harassing them—depending on whether you were seeing it from Joshua's or the cats' perspective. The cats took it all in good stride until Joshua did something I didn't see which elicited an ears-back hiss and a quick claws-extended swipe at his hand from Butch, at which point Jonathan called Joshua over to join us at the table. Mario suggested we take our coffee into the backyard so Joshua could play while we grown-ups continued catching up on each others' lives and activities. Both Bob and Mario were great storytellers, and we as usual had a lot of laughs.

MONDAY MORNING FIRST THING I CALLED THE CITY ANNEX TO LEAVE A MESSAGE FOR MARTY Gresham and was surprised to find him in.

"Not out chasing the bad guys?" I asked.

"Not today. Dan's in court on a case that's been hanging on since before we partnered up, and I'm doing paperwork."

"Can I buy you lunch?" I asked.

"I never pass up a free meal," he said. "Warman Park?"

"Nah, let's splurge and go to a real restaurant. How about Sandler's around twelve-fifteen?"

"See you there," he said.

Because I wanted to start collecting fingerprints from the guys at the meeting, I dug out my old fingerprint kit and checked it to be sure it was still okay by taking my own prints. Noting that everything seemed in order, I then took the beer bottle Carl Brewer had given me and used the kit's brush, iron shavings and wide clear tape to lift his prints, putting the tape into a glassine envelope.

So far, so good. Now all I had to do was remember to keep the kit nearby everywhere I went.

Since I knew Don Gleason lived above his shop, I called him first. The phone rang several times, and I was just about ready to hang up when I heard the receiver being picked up.

"Hello?"

"Don, hi. This is Dick Hardesty." I explained that the police had found the gun that had killed Cal Hysong and had traced to Jake, who swore it had been stolen.

"Jake was the one they'd arrested?" he asked, though I had assumed he already knew.

"Afraid so," I said, "though, as I say, I'd stake my life he didn't do it." I then told him that fingerprint evidence had been found at Jake's apartment to back up his claim, and that I was collecting fingerprints from everyone who had been at the meeting in order to eliminate them as suspects and asked if I could get his.

"Sure," he said. "I don't have anything to hide."

Exactly, my mind voice agreed, mentally crossing Gleason off the suspects list. *It's the ones who won't be willing to give them you'll have to concentrate on.*

Still, having asked, I'd have to take them. Better safe than sorry.

"I'll stop by around eleven, if you're going to be there," I said.

"Yeah," he said. "I've got an appointment with a client at one, so eleven should be fine. I'll leave the door open, and if I'm not in the shop, come on upstairs—I'll be either in or just getting out of the shower."

"Okay, thanks. I'll see you then."

I tried the other five numbers and got no answer. I didn't want to leave a message for those who had machines. Asking them to voluntarily give me their fingerprints was imposition enough; I didn't want to ask them to call me back for the privilege.

I GOT TO GLEASON'S A FEW MINUTES BEFORE ELEVEN. PEERING IN THROUGH THE WINDOW, I couldn't see either him or the glow of the acetylene torch, so I tried the knob and it was, as he'd said, open.

I noticed that his motorcycle, sitting just inside the door, seemed to have been recently buffed to a high shine. I then wandered toward the back in case he might be busy back there and took my first real look at his sculptures.

I'm not really big on modern art, I'm afraid. If I see a statue titled *Nude Whistling* I expect to see something I can say "Yeah, that's a nude whistling." Gleason's art was mostly free-form, but I could appreciate it for what it was, and many of the pieces created strong impressions of power, or grace. The largest went from floor to just short of the ceiling—a writhing, twisting collage of metal giving the effect of debris caught in a tornado. It exuded an almost tangible sense of power. Others were deceptively simple—even delicate, if you can say that about metal—and there were two mobiles that looked as though they were somehow defying gravity. I was impressed.

Not finding him on the ground floor, I made my way up the wooden stairs to his apartment. The door at the top was open, and I went in.

"Don?" I called. I could hear water running, which stopped at my call.

"I'm in here," he said from what I assumed to be the bedroom. "Come on back." I followed his voice to where I could look through the open door to the bathroom. Don as out of sight but then stepped into view, drying his hair.

Nude *not* whistling, I thought, though I was tempted to do some whistling of my own. He looked like something Michelangelo might have done on one of his better days. I found it kind of ironic that Don Gleason had been one of the last guys I'd had sex with before I met Jonathan, and seeing him again now brought back strong memories of what my crotch-voice still occasionally insisted on referring to as "the good old days."

But I forced my mind away from such thoughts by dragging out the scale of what I would gain from another romp with Don or anyone else against what I would lose in destroying my relationship with Jonathan. No contest.

Wimp! My crotch-voice muttered.

Gleason wrapped the towel around his waist and padded into the room, going to the dresser to rummage around for underwear and socks. He dropped his towel to step into his shorts, reminding me once again just why I turned out gay rather than straight.

"Still can't get over the idea that Jake's gun killed Cal, or that he's been arrested for the murder," he said, turning toward me and sitting on the edge of the bed to put on his socks.

"Right," I said, "but as I said, he didn't do it."

"Right," he echoed.

Having put on his socks, Gleason stood up, giving me yet another chance to reflect on my decision for monogamy. He indicated the fingerprint kit I hadn't realized I was still holding.

"So, that's for the prints?" he asked.

"Yeah. Since the DA sort of tied the hands of the police when it came to looking at other possibilities once Jake was arrested, I decided to do some of their work for them. They can't initiate an investigation at this point, but they'll compare all the prints I bring them to those they found at Jake's."

I moved to the dresser and set the kit on top of it, opening it. Gleason came over to stand beside me. A little too close, I thought, but, hey...

"Which fingers do you want?" he asked as I took out a print card with little labeled squares for each finger.

"We probably should do them all," I said.

"Okay," he said amicably, offering me his left hand.

I took it and one finger at a time rolled the tips over the pad, transferring each to the appropriate space.

"You're pretty good at this," he said with a sexy smile.

"Years of practice," I said, trying to channel my full concentration into what I was doing.

When I'd finished, he made no effort to back away. I reached for the solvent and one of the paper towels I'd put in the kit.

"These should get rid of the ink," I said, noticing with mild discomfort that he was staring at me. He took the wet towel from my hands with probably a little more contact than was necessary.

"So, you've got a partner, huh?" he said.

"Yep."

"No fooling around?" He flexed his impressively muscled pecs just in case I might not have gotten what he was asking.

I sighed. "I'm afraid not."

He smiled and shrugged. "You don't know what you're missing," he said.

Oh, yes, I do! all my mind voices chorused.

"You're probably right," I said, though recalling we hadn't really been on the same page sexually the one time we'd gotten together made it easier.

Looking for a way to change the subject, I remembered his motorcycle and the posters for the AIDS ride I'd seen on the street near the Male Call.

"So, are you going on the Spike's bike ride this Sunday? I hear it might rain."

"Yeah. We'll be running up to Neelyville. Should be a good group, and a little rain won't hurt anybody. I've been helping Pete with the registrations— we've got forty guys and a contingent of fifteen women from Dykes on Bikes so far."

"That's great!" I said. "Any of the guys from the meeting at Jake's going?"

"Chuck Fells and Art, for sure," he said.

His mention of Art Manners reminded me.

"You and Art are good friends?" I asked.

"Not good friends, no. He's okay, and we ride together with Pete's group. But we don't hang around together much otherwise."

"I've heard he and Pete are pretty close."

"From what I know, yeah. I've heard they're fuck-buddies. Art tries to hide it, but I know he'd do anything for Pete."

Interesting.

"You know anything more about Manners?" I asked.

"I know he comes from a lot of money, though he tries not to show it. I hear his old man is Richard Manners of Tri-State Industries."

Tri-State Industries was one of the city's largest employers.

We talked while he finished getting dressed, until a glance at my watch told me I had to get going if I was going to make it to Sandler's in time to meet Marty.

"I'd better get going," I said. "I appreciate your cooperation, Don, you've been a big help."

"Any time," he said. "And tell Jake I'm rooting for him."

"Will do," I replied, picking up my bag to leave. "Have a good time on Sunday."

THE FIRST THING I NOTICED WHEN MARTY WALKED INTO THE RESTAURANT WAS HOW attractive he was. Coming so close as it did after my encounter with a naked Don Gleason, I determined that Jonathan and I—okay, especially I—needed a little quality fantasy playtime. Luckily, mindreading is not one of Marty's abilities. He came over to the table I'd taken, we shook hands and he sat down.

We talked a bit about what was going on in our private lives; Marty announced his wife was pregnant with their second child.

Lucky her! a mind voice—my crotch, obviously—observed.

Watch it, Hardesty! the other voices cautioned—totally unnecessarily, I might add.

I told him about Joshua's appendicitis, at which he expressed empathy, and my week-long stint as watchdog, comfort giver and toy picker-upper, at which he just smiled.

"At least you never had to do dirty-diaper duty," he said. "Consider yourself blessed."

As a matter of fact, I did.

After we'd ordered, I picked up the paper bag beside me.

"I brought you a few things," I said. "A couple sets of fingerprints I'm almost positive won't match those on the window ledge, since they were given voluntarily. I've got another five sets to collect. I really hope you don't mind doing this for me."

"Not at all," he said. "I wouldn't want the DA to know what we're doing, but if you're right and Jacobson didn't shoot Hysong, we'd just have to do all this ourselves. You're saving us some time, and the taxpayers some money."

"Glad you see it that way," I said.

Since Marty wasn't privy to what new information the DA's office might have on the case, we just concentrated on our lunch and casual conversation.

AS SOON AS I RETURNED TO THE OFFICE, I TRIED CALLING THE GUYS ON THE MEETING LIST again. I'd rather hoped I might catch Butch Reed on his day off but left a message on his machine asking him to call me.

Right after dinner that night, while Jonathan and Joshua watered the plants and fed the fish, I sat down with the phone and began redialing the numbers. I subconsciously put Manners and Spinoza at the bottom of the list, since I figured they were the most likely to give me a hard time and I wanted to put off any hard times as long as I could.

I tried Steve Morse first and was lucky enough to catch him in. When I explained what I wanted and why I wanted it, he seemed a bit hesitant.

"I don't know, Dick," he said. "While I want to help you, I've got pretty firm convictions about the right to privacy. Being fingerprinted is just one more erosion of that privacy."

"I can appreciate your position, Steve," I said, "but this involves a murder. I'm convinced the police will be expanding their investigation soon, and if we can show them the prints they have aren't yours, it can save you them having to hassle you. Once they start looking into it, they might—however wrongly—take the refusal to give prints as an indication of possible guilt. If we can eliminate you right off the bat, why not do it?"

There was a rather long pause, then: "Well, I..."

Sensing he was reconsidering, I said, "Look, it will only take a few minutes. I can meet you on your lunch hour, or right after work, or whenever and wherever is convenient for you."

Another pause, followed by a sigh. "Well, I usually take my lunch to work and eat in Barnes Park. I suppose if you want to meet me there between noon and one..."

"That'll be great," I said. "Any particular part of the park?"

He laughed. "Yeah, there are some benches within easy sight of the men's room. I like the view."

"A man of exquisite taste," I said, also laughing. "I'll see you there, then. And thanks."

It occurred to me as I hung up that I had no idea what he looked like. I've never understood why these things always come to me after I've hung up, but...I'd find him.

And again I thought about how kind of stupid it was to actually take fingerprints from someone willing to give them. The fact they were willing all but ruled them out as a suspect, as far as I was concerned. Still, I'd learned never to underestimate the power of a devious mind. So, far better safe than sorry.

I next tried Chuck Fells's number and immediately recognized the butch-voice.

"Hello?"

"Chuck, this is Dick Hardesty," I said, beginning my spiel. "I'm sorry to bother you, but something's come up in the Hysong shooting and I need your help."

Before he had a chance to object, I went on to explain about the gun being tied to Jake, Jake's arrest, my certainty he was innocent and the fingerprint evidence found at Jake's. As I'd done with Morse, I went out of my way to try to phrase my comments to emphasize the "eliminating you as a possible suspect when the police expand their investigation" angle. The fact I had absolutely no real guarantee the police ever would do any such thing was beside the point. If the guys I talked to thought they would, that's what mattered.

"I don't like being hassled," he said.

"I don't blame you," I assured him. "I don't either. But with the fingerprints, it's either a matter of me taking five minutes of your time to get them or your dealing with the police. All I want is your prints. They'd probably want to give you that whole 'you're a potential suspect' routine, and I guarantee that'll take up more time than I will."

"Okay, okay!" he said. "I get off work at five. You can come over at five-thirty. You've got five minutes, not six, got it?"

"Got it," I said, holding my temper in check. I glanced at the address I had written on my notepad with his phone number. "Sixty-two-sixty-three Cherry, right?"

"Right."

"All right, I'll see you at five-thirty sharp. Thanks." I hung up before he had chance to.

Because I dreaded calling Manners and Spinoza—I'd had a hard enough time holding my temper with Morse—I took a break to join Jonathan and Joshua, who were on the floor. Joshua, with a number of toy soldiers, was bravely defending the Lincoln Log fort against a combined force of Indians and pirates—for whom he'd apparently suddenly developed quite a fascination, I noticed—represented by Jonathan with identical toy soldiers.

"How's it going, guys?" I asked.

"Looks like Joshua's got me on the run," Jonathan said. "Of course, we're playing by his rules, which are kind of flexible."

I went into the kitchen for a glass of water then returned to the phone to try Art Manners.

He picked up on the third ring. I again went into my spiel but didn't get very far. I did make it all the way to mentioning the prints found at Jake's when he broke in.

"Look," he said, "I can't be bothered with all this shit. I didn't do it, I'm not about to give anybody my fingerprints without a warrant and if Jake didn't do it he'll be acquitted. I gotta go."

And he hung up.

Charmer, I thought, as I replaced the receiver onto the cradle.

Reluctantly, I dialed Spinoza's number. No answer, but I left a message on his machine, knowing even as I did so it was probably an exercise in futility.

BARNES PARK, LOCATED AS IT WAS ABOUT TWO BLOCKS OFF BEECH, THE MAIN COMMERCIAL street of the gay community, had a reputation as being one of the cruisiest parks in the city at night, and had a large gay/lesbian contingent any time of day. A last-minute phone call from a prospective new client had delayed my departure from the office, so I didn't arrive there until nearly twelve-twenty. Fingerprint kit in hand, I headed in the direction of the public restrooms. As Morse had said, there were several benches within a hundred feet or so, and several of them were already occupied with people—mostly guys—eating lunch or reading. If any of them were there specifically to keep an eye on who entered or left the restrooms it certainly wasn't obvious.

Having absolutely no idea which of the half-dozen or so guys might be Morse, I took a chance on just walking slowly by and trying to make a guess. This proved to be not the most scientific of approaches, and I still hadn't a clue as I approached the last bench.

"Dick Hardesty?" the man on it asked. Morse, obviously, though I would never have picked him out unless he'd said something. He was wearing a dress shirt and tie, with his suit coat folded neatly beside him, on which sat a brown paper bag apparently containing his lunch. He'd been reading a book, which he set down next to the bag.

"Yeah," I said, walking over as though I'd known it was him all along. "Sorry I'm late."

We shook hands, and I sat down beside him, on the side opposite his coat, lunch and book.

"I figured it was you when I saw the kit. It's obviously not a lunch box," he said, grinning.

"I really appreciate your meeting me."

"Not a problem."

"Don't let me interrupt your lunch," I said, noting he'd set a half-eaten sandwich aside when I'd approached.

"Thanks," he said, picking it up.

We talked in generalities for a few minutes while he ate. A nice guy, I determined. He mentioned he was an actuary for a large insurance company nearby, and I found it a little hard envisioning him as a leather bar regular—which just goes to prove...what?

I asked him, as casually as I could, what he knew about the other guys from the meeting.

"Not all that much, really," he said.

"Are you and Art Manners close?" I asked, remembering it was he who had reported Manners's saying the Male Call was for sale.

He crumpled up his sandwich wrapper and replaced it in the bag, taking out a large peach.

"Not really," he said, taking a large onomatopoetic—love that word—bite.

"We talk quite a bit when we run into one another at the Spike or the Male Call, but we don't hang out together other than there. He's into bikes big time, and I don't have one."

"I understand he's pretty close to Pete Reardon," I said.

Morse grinned. "Yeah, you could say that. They both try to keep it quiet—they don't want to tarnish their butch image—but everybody knows they've got something going on."

A thought popped into my head, which I immediately latched on to and put it in my "mull it over later" file.

Finishing his peach, he glanced at his watch. "I've got to be getting back in a few minutes," he said. "You want to do this fingerprint thing now?"

"Sure," I said, scooting a bit farther from him to put the kit down on the bench between us. I took his prints as surreptitiously as possible, though we did get quite a pause-and-stare from a hunky guy passing on his way to the restroom.

While I put everything back into the kit and closed it, Morse wiped the ink from his hands then got up to leave.

"Good luck in finding who did it," he said, extending his right hand while holding his empty lunch bag in his left.

"Thanks," I said. "And I really appreciate your cooperation."

He smiled, nodded and moved off in one direction as I headed in the other.

Since Jonathan had to leave for chorus practice by six-thirty, I'd told him he and Joshua should just go ahead and eat, and I'd eat when I got home. No messages on my machine when I returned to the office, so I spent the rest of the afternoon puttering, organizing my notes for Glen and going over yet again everything I'd learned thus far.

There was something Morse had said that had rung a bell, about Reardon and Manners having something going on. Was it possible, I wondered, that Manners might have decided to settle his grudge against Hysong and help his buddy get even with Carl Brewer by forcing him to sell the Male Call? The bar's business was already sliding because of the AIDS rumors and killing Hysong would finish the job. Plus, Manners had ample reasons of his own to want to see Hysong dead—having "the crap beat out of him" by Hysong, as Jake had related, must have been humiliating.

But first, I'd have to prove he stole Jake's gun, and I couldn't do that without getting his prints, which he wasn't about to give me.

If worse came to worst, I figured, I could try going over to his place and rooting through his garbage for something with his prints on it. Definitely a last-resort move, but I'd do it if I had to. I'd probably end up with the same option with Spinoza, too, since I was pretty sure he'd also refuse to give his prints voluntarily.

Oh, well.

XXI

F ELLS'S APARTMENT WAS IN A LARGE OLD APARTMENT BUILDING NOT FAR FROM THE river. I rang the bell to Apartment 503 at exactly five-thirty and was buzzed in. Fells let me in without either a smile or the offer of a handshake. He proved to be tall, lanky to the point of being skeletal, with his hair cropped almost to his skull. His apartment, from what I saw of it, was in no danger of being visited by photographers from *House Beautiful* anytime soon. *Utilitarian* would probably describe it best and most charitably. It made Jonathan's and my place almost palatial by comparison.

He was wearing a blue work shirt with a white patch with an embroidered "Fells" on the pocket, and from some oily smudges on his blue work pants, I assumed he must be a mechanic of some sort.

"Let's get this over with," he said, indicating a TV tray set up in front of a recliner on one side of the living room. I hadn't said a word yet but walked over and set the kit on the tray, opening it.

"I appreciate your doing this, Chuck," I said, and he shrugged. He held out his right hand and I took it. "Relax," I said when he splayed his hand, his fingers rigid. "Just let me roll them."

It took some effort, but eventually, he got the idea and the left-hand printing went much easier.

"You're going on the AIDS ride this Sunday?" I asked, though Don Gleason had already told me he was.

"Yeah. You ride?"

"No," I admitted. "I've never been around bikes much."

As he wiped off his fingers, I said, "Do you have any idea who might have stolen Jake's gun. Your giving me your prints pretty much rules you out."

"Not a clue," he said, wadding up the paper towel and laying it on the TV

169

tray.

"What do you know about Art Manners and Tom Spinoza?" I asked.

"Why them?"

"No special reason, except that I haven't gotten their prints yet, and I know they both had a good reason to want to see Hysong dead."

He shrugged again. "We all did. Both Art and Tony have had it in for Cal for a long time, way before this AIDS thing ever came up."

"What was Spinosa's beef?" I asked, taking my time to put everything back in the kit and close it.

"Cal was always on his case," he said. "Any time Tom'd start zeroing in on somebody, Cal would barge in and snap the guy up. One time, Tom and a guy were in the back room and in the middle of getting it on when Cal just pulled Tom off the guy and took over. Tom didn't have the guts to fight him.'

"I gather most guys didn't," I said.

"True."

"One last question," I said. "I understand Spinoza had sex with Hysong once."

I was totally surprised when he actually laughed. "Once? Cal used to screw him at least once a month. It was his way of showing Tom who was boss."

Then, as though suddenly thinking he'd said too much, he glanced into the kitchen, where I could see a bag of groceries sitting on the plain wooden table.

"I just got home, and I've got stuff to do. And your five minutes is up."

"Right," I said, though I'd gotten the impression he was more bluster than bite, which took away some of my irritation with him. "Well, thanks again."

I deliberately extended my hand. A flash of mild surprise crossed his face, but he took it and we shook.

"You ought to get yourself a bike," he said, which I took as an oddly out-of-left-field compliment.

"Have a good ride Sunday," I said, walking to the door.

INTERESTING BIT OF INFORMATION ABOUT SPINOZA, I THOUGHT ON MY DRIVE HOME. I'VE often said that I never really understood the leather scene or what motivates guys who are into it. My problem, not theirs. But I do know that if somebody used me like a blow-up doll whenever he felt like it, I'd be a little more than mildly resentful. And to then find out the guy was doing it even though he knew he had AIDS...

I got home a little after six and joined Jonathan and Joshua near the end of their dinner. Though Joshua almost always hopped out of his chair and ran into the living room to play as soon as he was finished eating, he'd apparently been in the middle of a long dissertation on his day at "school" when I arrived and, for my benefit, started over from the beginning. Jonathan excused himself to get ready for practice, but Joshua sat with me until both his story and most of my dinner were more or less finished—it's a little hard to tell with Joshua's stories sometimes.

Jonathan left on time, and after we did the dishes, Joshua brought over the latest issue of *Life* for us to "read." We'd no sooner sat down when the phone rang. I got up quickly to answer it.

"Dick, it's Butch Reed. You left me a message?"

"Yeah, Butch, I did. Thanks for getting back to me," I said and then went into my story and request.

"Sure," he replied. "Though my prints are on record with the department, and you can get them there if you want."

"Thanks, Butch, but the police aren't officially involved yet. I'm just laying the groundwork for when they are."

"Ah, okay," he said, sounding a little confused. I certainly couldn't blame him. "Your office is downtown, isn't it?"

"Yeah," I said, giving him my address.

"I've got some business downtown tomorrow," he said. "Do you want me to stop by your office? Say ten-thirty?"

"That'd be great!" I said. "I'm on the sixth floor—six-thirty-three. I'll see you there, then."

"Right," he said and hung up, and I returned to Joshua and *Life*.

I'd gotten so I really enjoyed my time with Joshua. Sometimes, I'd just watch him while he played and reflect on how much he'd grown since he first came to us. He was a terrific kid. I understood how difficult it must be for him to have lost his mother and father at so young an age, and he still talked of them in terms that implied he expected them to come back, though he was old enough now to realize they couldn't. But despite his occasional testing, Jonathan and I did our best to let him know he was loved, and I think he realized it.

AT EXACTLY TEN-THIRTY WEDNESDAY MORNING, THERE WAS A KNOCK AT MY OFFICE DOOR and Butch Reed entered.

"Wow, you're prompt!" I said as I stood up and moved around my desk to shake hands.

He grinned. "Hey, we try never to be late for fires, either," he said.

I gestured him to a seat and asked if he'd like coffee, which he declined.

As long as I was up, I figured we might as well get the prints out of the way, so I took the kit from the file cabinet drawer where I'd put it earlier and set it on my desk closest to him.

"I've been wondering," I said as I opened it and took out a blank card and the fingerprinting materials. "What do you know about Tom Spinoza? I hear Hysong almost singled him out for harassing."

"Yeah, that was Cal for you. I just had that one incident with him. With Tom it was a regular thing. If it had been me, the second time Cal tried to pull his bullshit, I'd just have found myself somewhere else to hang out. But Tom kept coming back for more."

"You think he liked it?" I asked, and Reed shrugged.

"I really don't know Tom all that well. I don't think he did," he said, "and I don't think he thinks he did. But who knows how somebody else's mind works? I have a hard enough time figuring out my own sometimes."

We accomplished the fingerprinting without breaking our conversation.

"And Tom isn't exactly the friendliest guy in the world," he continued, wiping his fingers. "He's fine when you get to know him, but he likes to hold most people off at arm's length. He's like a lot of guys in figuring that the best defense is a good offense."

"Well, he does a great job of that," I said. "I've only talked to him once, and I don't think I'd recommend him for a job as a maitre'd at the Imperator. I fully expect that when I ask him for his prints he'll tell me to go fuck myself. The whole idea of getting the prints is to rule people out, and it's pretty evident that anyone giving them willingly didn't steal the gun. Anybody who won't give them goes to the top of my suspects list, and so far Art and Tom are right up there."

"Well, I wish you luck," he said. "And if that offer for coffee still stands, I think maybe I would like half a cup."

As I got up to go to the coffeemaker, I had a thought. "Do you know where Tom works, by any chance?"

"Yeah, he works for the phone company—repairman. Why?"

"Just curious," I said.

I poured for us both, offered him creamer and sugar, then took my cup behind my desk and sat down. We spent the next half-hour just talking, and I decided that, barring some sudden damaging revelation, he was definitely off the suspect list entirely.

After he left, I dialed Spinoza's number again. I assumed he'd be working but wanted to give it a shot, just in case. Answering machine again, so I hung up, determined to keep trying from both the office and home until I got him. The "going through the garbage" option seemed increasingly likely, if no more appealing.

I'D NOT SPOKEN TO GLEN IN SOME TIME SO CALLED HIS OFFICE TO CHECK WITH DONNA TO see when he might be in. I was surprised when she put me directly through to him.

"Hi, Dick," he said. "How's it going?"

I brought him up to date with what I'd been doing and the fact I was still intent on getting Manners's and Spinoza's prints. I asked him if he'd heard anything on Jake's impending trial.

"Got word this morning just before you called. It's set to start three weeks from today, and Judge Ferber has been assigned to it."

"That's good or bad?" I asked.

"Judge Ferber is a man born far after his time. He'd have been a great judge for Dodge City in the 1870s."

"Not good, then, I gather."

"Not good. But we'll deal with him. I just hope we can get some sort of break in the case before trial."

"I promise I'll get those prints somehow by the first of next week," I said. I didn't even mention the possibility of what we might do if none of them matched the ones on Jake's kitchen window.

I TRIED THREE TIMES WEDNESDAY NIGHT TO REACH TOM SPINOZA WITH NO LUCK, AND I didn't even consider leaving another message.

It hadn't occurred to me, when Butch said Spinoza worked for the phone company, to ask if he was a home repairman or a lineman. If he was a lineman, he might well have sporadic hours and/or put in a lot of overtime, accounting for his not being home when I called. Or maybe he just didn't answer his phone.

It wasn't until my second call on Thursday night that I finally heard the receiver lifted, followed by "Yeah?"

"Tom." I usually didn't use first names as a matter of courtesy, but in Spinoza's case courtesy wasn't an issue. "This is Dick Hardesty calling. I wanted to let you know the police found fingerprints at Jake Jacobsen's apartment after determining his stolen gun had been used to kill Cal Hysong."

I rather expected to hear a hang-up, but there was nothing so I continued.

"I'm sure the police will start with the guys at the meeting. I'm trying to spare everybody from an interrogation by collecting everyone's prints to give to the police so they can rule them out without bothering them. However, it's a damned sure bet that anyone whose prints I don't have will be at the top of their suspects list. I just thought I'd spare you the hassle."

"Don't do me any favors," he said. "I told you I don't have the time for this crap, so just leave me the hell alone!"

Then I heard the click of the disconnect.

My mental sigh was accompanied by a physical one.

Ohhh-kay, Hardesty. Now what?

Garbage time, I guess.

Well, garbage time was just going to have to wait until Monday night; garbage was picked up on Tuesday morning in Spinoza's neighborhood, I knew. At least he lived in a single-family house—I'd driven by his place a week or so before when I was in the neighborhood—so I could be fairly certain any garbage at the curb would be just his.

Friday I had to take Joshua to the doctor to check his progress and have his stitches removed. Jonathan wanted to take time off work to go along, but I convinced him it was a very simple procedure, and I could provide sufficient moral support should it be needed.

Everything went smoothly, and Joshua took it far more in stride than I would have at his age. We celebrated his bravery with a hot fudge sundae on the way home.

As an alternative to reading books at Story Time, Jonathan and I had recently begun telling Joshua fairy tales, which totally fascinated him. His favorite, which he insisted on my retelling Friday night for the third time, was one my mother had told me when I was his age, about why the Chinese have very short names.

"Tell me about Time-Bo!" he insisted.

"Not tonight, Joshua," Jonathan said then turned his attention to me. "You know what's going to happen," he warned.

"Yes, please! Tell me Time-Bo!"

Jonathan rolled his eyes to the ceiling but said nothing more.

"Okay," I began. "Do you know why Chinese children have short names?"

"No," he said, wide-eyed, playing along like a pro, though he'd heard the story twice before.

"Well," I continued, "once upon a time, Chinese little boys had very long names, and there was a little boy named…" I paused, giving him the chance to jump in.

"Time-Bo!" Joshua responded.

"Well, not quite," I said. "His name was Rickety-Tickety-Time-Bo-Time-Bo-Meta-Meta-Kibo-Kibo-Blotz."

It was important to the story to say the name as rapidly as possible.

"Yeah!" Joshua replied.

"And one day, Rickety-Tickety-Time-Bo-Time-Bo-Meta-Meta-Kibo-Kibo-Blotz and his sister were out playing in the backyard." I was very glad he never asked what the sister's name was. "And do you know what happened then?"

"He fell down the well!" Joshua exclaimed.

"That's right!" I said. "And his sister ran into the house to tell their mother that Rickety-Tickety-Time-Bo-Time-Bo-Meta-Meta-Kibo-Kibo-Blotz had fallen down the well. But she was so nervous and excited that by the time she was able to say 'Rickety-Tickety-Time-Bo-Time-Bo-Meta-Meta-Kibo-Kibo-Blotz has fallen down the well!' he had drowned."

Joshua looked appropriately crestfallen.

"And that," I concluded, "is why forever after Chinese boys have had short names."

"Rickety-Time-Bo-Kibo-Tickety..." Joshua said, brows knit.

"You'll get it," Jonathan said, reaching out to push him gently down to his pillow and pulling the sheet up to his chin. "But don't worry about it tonight."

"Good night, tiger," I said, getting up from the bed to join Jonathan, who had moved to the door, his hand on the light switch.

"Rickety-Tickety-Kimbo," said Joshua.

"Go to sleep now," Jonathan said, shooting me a dirty look and turning off the light.

ON HIS WAY TO CHORUS PRACTICE ON TUESDAY NIGHT, JONATHAN HAD NOTICED OUR neighborhood movie theater was having a weekend CartoonFest and suggested we might call Craig Richman to ask if he'd like to take Joshua while the two of us went out for a just-us dinner. I'd called Craig Wednesday. He initially hesitated, since he was hoping to get together with his boyfriend Bill, but when I offered to pay for Bill's ticket, too and spring for a before-the-movie pizza here at the apartment, Craig said he'd check with Bill and get right back to me, which he did. Never underestimate the bargaining power of a free pizza and a movie.

As always, Saturday chores took up most of the day. We were able to fit in a half-hour at the park for Joshua, but cut it short when the clouds began moving in, threatening rain.

Craig and Bill arrived, as arranged, promptly at five-forty-five, and the pizza was delivered shortly thereafter. Joshua was obviously still jealous of Bill, and though Bill went out of his way—I suspected partly at Craig's urging—to pay him lots of attention, it was clear where Joshua's affiliations lay. Bill did earn a brownie point or two, however, when upon being shown Joshua's scar he praised him on his bravery in surviving such a grievous wound.

It had not yet rained when it was time to leave for the movie, but even though the theater was within easy walking distance, we drove them over on our way to Napoleon. Jonathan insisted, when giving Craig his house key, that they take an umbrella in case it should be raining when they got out of the theater.

JONATHAN LIKED TO REFER TO OUR TOO-RARE JUST-US EVENINGS AS "DATE NIGHT," AND that's really how we both looked at it, I think. We splurged on a Chateaubriand and had the rare opportunity to concentrate just on each other.

After dinner, we made a quick run out to Ramon's for a drink/Coke and to talk with Bob for a bit. Again, not that I in any way regretted Joshua's presence in our lives, but an occasional "old times" night did me a world of good.

The rain held off until right after Jonathan and Joshua returned from church on Sunday, and then the skies opened up to the point I expected to see pairs of animals heading for the Ark. I thought of the AIDS bike ride to Neeleyville and was reminded once again why motorcycles never had much of an appeal for me. I didn't envy the riders getting drenched, though I hoped they'd have sense enough to pull in somewhere until the rain stopped.

The evening news underscored my hesitations about motorcycles when, reporting on the rain, the announcer mentioned the weather-related death of a motorcyclist killed by a semi just south of Neeleyville. End of report.

Of course, me being me, I was sure it had to have involved someone from the AIDS ride. I immediately looked up Don Gleason's number and dialed. I knew Fells, Manners and Spinoza had also been scheduled to go on the ride, but Don was the only one I felt comfortable enough to call.

When there was no answer, I had a quick sinking sensation in my stomach. Could it have been Gleason who died? Luckily, I was able to snap myself out of it and left a message asking him to call me as soon as he got in, regardless of the time.

I then called Jake's number. I knew he wouldn't have been on the ride but thought perhaps someone might have called him to tell him about the accident.

His answering machine picked up, and I was just starting to ask him to call me, when I heard a click and a breathless "Hello?"

"Jake, hi. I gather I caught you at a bad time?" I said.

"Not really. I just this minute got in the door. Jared and I spent the weekend up at his cabin. We really needed to get away from town for awhile. I left Carrington a little early because of the rain. What's new?"

Obviously, even if he'd heard about the accident on the radio, he wouldn't have had a chance to talk to anyone as to who it might have been who died. I quickly explained my reason for calling and my concern it might have been one of the guys from the AIDS ride.

"Jeez, no, this is the first I've heard of it!" he said. "I know several of the guys who were going—I'll give them a call and see what I can find out."

I didn't mention I already had a call in to Don Gleason. "I'd appreciate that."

We talked for a few more minutes about our respective weekends, but I was in something of a hurry to hang up in case Don might be trying to call.

I stood by the phone for a minute, as though expecting it to ring. When it didn't, I went into the kitchen to help Jonathan with dinner.

THE TEN O'CLOCK NEWS SIMPLY REPLAYED THE EARLIER REPORT, WITH NO NEW DETAILS. I switched channels, but either they didn't mention it or had done so before I switched.

Damn!

No further word from Jake, either.

Just after Jonathan and I had gotten to bed, the phone rang. Jumping up and grabbing my robe—one minor inconvenience of the good chance that a five-year-old will pop out of the woodwork without warning—I hurried to answer.

"Dick? It's Don Gleason. I hesitated about calling you this late, but your message said to call whenever I got in. You heard about Art, I assume."

Art? It was Manners who was killed? For some reason, though I barely knew the guy and didn't particularly like him, I felt a wave of sorrow.

"Yeah," I said. "The news didn't give any details, but I was afraid it might have been someone from the ride. What happened?"

He sighed. "We were in the hills heading back to town and it started raining like hell. Pete had some sort of problem with his bike and dropped back, signaling for the rest of us to go ahead. Art dropped back, too, to see if he could help with whatever the problem was. From what Pete said the light that comes on when the ignition is turned on before the bike starts kept flashing, and he just wanted to check it out. He told Art to go on ahead, but Art said he'd wait. And when they started out again, knowing Pete and Art, they were going a little fast for conditions trying to catch up with the rest of the group.

"Art was just a little ways ahead of Pete when they started around a curve and saw a semi coming toward them. Somehow, Art lost control and his bike went right under the truck. He didn't have a chance."

"How did you find out about it?"

"We were all a couple of miles down the road and realized Pete and Art hadn't caught up with us yet, but we weren't too concerned, because if something had been wrong with Pete's bike, he could have got a lift with Art. But when the police car passed us with its lights and siren on and then an ambulance, we all turned around and headed back.

"They didn't need the ambulance, of course. So, after they took Art away and got the semi driver's and Pete's statements, they told us all to be on our way. We came back to town and went to the Spike for a drink in Art's memory. I just got home. What a rotten way for a end a ride!"

And a life, I thought.

THE FIRST THING I DID MONDAY MORNING AFTER GETTING TO THE OFFICE AND STARTING A pot of coffee was to sit down at my desk and scan quickly through the paper, looking for a report on Manners' death. I found a short article on page four with the heading "Ride for AIDS Ends in Death" that briefly outlined the facts of the incident—that the weekend's bad weather had resulted in the death of one of the motorcyclists participating in a charity Ride for AIDS fundraiser. The dead cyclist was identified as 35-year-old Arthur Manners..."

A quick search of the obituary page found no mention of him. I thought that a little odd, since Don Gleason had mentioned Manners was from a very wealthy family. I assumed it would appear in a later edition.

Again, even though I didn't care for the guy, Manners was someone I'd met and talked to, however briefly. I don't like death, in any way, shape or form, and the death of anyone I have actually met strikes me personally.

The question of getting Manners to give me his fingerprints was now moot, but it occurred to me the coroner's office routinely fingerprinted all bodies passing through their department. Tim might be able to get me a copy of Manners's.

I'd already planned to go to garbage-can-diving at Spinoza's that night, and if I found anything from which I could take his prints I'd then have covered from everyone at the meeting and could get them to Marty maybe as early as the next day.

I immediately picked up the phone and called Tim's work number, leaving a message for him to call me.

Even though I'd told Glen on the phone just about everything I had learned on the case, I spent the remainder of the morning putting it all in writing, going back carefully over every conversation I'd had and including every detail I thought might have any significance.

I held off lunch in the expectation—correct, as it turned out—that Tim would call me on his own lunch hour. My stomach was beginning to growl just as the phone rang.

We kept the call short, since we were both hungry, but Tim agreed to surreptitiously get me a copy of Manners's prints. I always feel a bit guilty when I ask him for a favor of this kind, since I know he's probably violating any number of codes, rules and restrictions in doing so, but he never seemed to mind and I was eternally grateful to him.

I was just about to ask him how and when I could get them when he beat me to it.

"Why don't you and the boys come by tonight after dinner to pick them up?"

"That'd be great!" I said. "We'll have to make it quick, since tomorrow is a 'school' day for Joshua. Say seven, seven-fifteen?"

"Perfect. See you then."

WE GOT HOME FROM PHIL AND TIM'S JUST IN TIME TO GET JOSHUA READY FOR BED. IT WAS Jonathan's turn to do the bath/toothbrush/pajama duties, and I was just thinking about driving over to Spinoza's to check out his garbage—whoever said being a private investigator wasn't a romantic job?—when the phone rang. It was Jake.

"Sorry I didn't get back to you sooner, Dick," he said. "I didn't find out anything at all last night. Most of the guys on the ride were still at the Spike having an impromptu wake for Art. Then I called Jared to tell him, and by the time we were through talking it was too late to get back to you. But I talked to a couple of the guys tonight who were on the ride. They're still shook up."

"Do you know if any of them were very close to Manners?" I asked.

"I don't think anyone was really close to Art," he replied, "except for Arnie Rios, who died from AIDS, which Art swore Arnie got from Hysong. The next

179

closest, probably, would be Pete Reardon. He really took it hard. Well, I sure can't blame him. If I saw a friend of mine getting run over by an eighteen-wheeler..."

"I can't imagine how he must feel."

"Yeah. And especially now, when Pete's trying to get the Male Call."

"What's that got to do with it?"

"Well, Mark Neese—you might not know him, but after Arnie and Pete, Mark was probably as close to Art as anyone—was saying he'd heard Art was going to help Pete finance the deal."

Now, that was an interesting bit of news.

"Why would he do that?" I wondered aloud.

"Not a clue. Art was kind of a strange duck."

Indeed, I thought.

WANTING TO BE SURE SPINOZA HAD ENOUGH TIME TO PUT HIS GARBAGE OUT AND HOPING HE didn't wait until morning to do it, I decided to stick around until after Story Time to leave the apartment. Joshua wanted me to tell him "Time-bo" again, but I said, "Why don't we have Uncle Jonathan tell you a story this time?" I knew he didn't much care who told him a story as long as he got one.

Jonathan opted for "Rumpelstiltskin," to which Joshua listened with his usual rapt attention. Caught up in the story, he was still wide awake when it ended. He wanted to hear another, but Jonathan declined with a promise of tomorrow. Tucking him in and telling him to go to sleep, we left the room, turning out the light and leaving the door open a crack.

Since it still was fairly early, we watched some television until the late news came on, at which point I figured it was time to leave. Giving Jonathan a hug and telling him I'd be back soon but not to wait up, I left.

It took close to twenty minutes to get to Spinoza's. I found a parking place three doors down from his house and was just backing into it when I saw someone coming out from the side of his house carrying a garbage bag. I didn't recognize the guy, but assumed it was Spinoza, whom I don't think I'd ever seen before.

I pulled into the parking spot, turned off the lights and engine and watched as he set the bag down on the curb and went back to the house. I waited a few minutes then got out and hurried over to the bag. Rather than rummage through it on the spot, I picked it up and brought it back to the car, putting it in the trunk.

When I got back home, I pulled into the garage, closed the door from the inside, turned on the light and took out the garbage bag.

Rummaging through other people's garbage is not high on my list of enjoyable pastimes, but I did come up with three beer cans and an empty cranberry juice bottle. Setting them on the floor at the rear of the car, I retied the bag and put in in the garbage bin alongside the building.

Returning to the apartment, I went directly to the bathroom to wash my hands, being as quiet as possible so as not to wake Joshua or Jonathan. I needn't have worried about Jonathan. I walked into the bedroom to find him naked as a jaybird on top of the bed. I also didn't have to use Mae West's old line "Is that a gun in your pocket, or are you just happy to see me."

XXII

TUESDAY MORNING, EVEN BEFORE THE COFFEEMAKER AT WORK STOPPED HISSING AND burbling through its first pot of the day, I got out the fingerprint kit and opened the paper bag in which I'd put the beer cans and bottle of cranberry juice. I took prints from all of them, since I didn't know whether he might have had company and some of the prints not be his. Even if they weren't, chances were good the majority would be, especially on the cranberry juice bottle.

I then called the City Annex and left a message asking for "Detective Gresham"—I still got a kick out of calling him that, since he credits me for helping him make the rank—to call me. I finished typing up my detailed report for Glen, adding the information I'd gotten from Jake the night before. I planned to run it over to Glen's office after I'd gotten the fingerprints to Marty.

Checking the obituary column, I was surprised to find a rather lengthy article on Manners's death, though it was more focused on the fact he was the son of R. D. Manners of Tri-State Industries than on Art himself. The article, of course, skipped totally over any mention that in addition to being the son of a millionaire Art was also a motorcycle-riding leather-man.

As I sat drinking my coffee, my mind kept going back to what Jake had said about Manners's perhaps backing Pete Reardon in his attempt to take over the Male Call. I'd wondered, ever since I first heard that Reardon wanted the bar, how Reardon could possibly swing it financially. I'd imagine he'd been all but wiped out following the firebombing of the Dog Collar and his two-year stint in jail, and the Spike never did nearly the business the Dog Collar had, or that the Male Call did before the AIDS rumors and Hysong's death.

And other than as a form of revenge against Carl Brewer, whom Reardon still suspected of having something to do with the bombing, I couldn't figure out why he would want to take on another failing bar. He'd bring with him the still-lingering albatross of the Dog Collar plus the Male Call's double stigma of the AIDS rumors and Hysong's murder.

While Manners could undoubtedly afford to back Reardon, why would he want to? It strongly suggested the two were far more involved than either let on. And if Reardon and Manners had been more than just friends, I felt another quick flush of empathetic anguish over what it must have been like for Reardon to see Manners die in front of his eyes.

But I forced myself to realize that all this was pure speculation based on yet another rumor.

Further ruminations were cut off by the phone's ringing.

"Hardesty Investigations," I said, picking it up and using my quarter-octave-lower "business" voice.

"Yeah, Dick...Marty. What's up?"

"I have those prints for you," I said. "Can you run them for me? Jake's trial is coming up a lot faster than I'm comfortable with."

"Sure. I'm going to be tied up for a good part of the day, but can you put them in an envelope and drop them off for me? I'll take them right up to processing as soon as I get back."

"Thanks, Marty. I really appreciate it."

"Hey, no problem," he said. "If we can save the taxpayers the cost of trying the wrong person, it's well worth it."

AFTER HANGING UP, I PUT THE FINGERPRINTS IN A LARGE MAILING ENVELOPE, SEALED IT AND wrote "Detective Marty Gresham, Homicide Division" on it in large block letters, put my report for Glen in a slightly smaller envelope and left the office.

Having dropped off the prints, I was waiting for the elevator in Glen's building when I felt a tap on my shoulder and turned to find Glen himself, looking every inch the epitome of a rich and powerful lawyer.

I grinned, and we shook hands.

"Coming to see me, I presume?" he asked.

"Well, I didn't think you'd be in, so I just wanted to drop my report off, but I guess you saved me an elevator ride."

"Not at all," he said. "I've got a few minutes. Let's go up to my office and talk."

At that point, the elevator door opened, and we got on.

I followed him as he swept through the large reception area and down a series of hallways, greeting everyone he encountered pleasantly and by name.

Donna looked up as we entered the antechamber to his office. She smiled when she saw me.

"Hello, Mr. Hardesty," she said warmly. I'd known her for a number of years now, but I was always "Mr. Hardesty." As Glen was the consummate lawyer, Donna was the consummate executive secretary.

Glen looked at me as he reached for the knob on his office door.

"Coffee?" he asked.

I nodded. "If you've got the time."

"I do," he said, then turned to Donna. "Could you get it for us, Donna?"

She arose immediately, smiling.

"Of course," she said as she moved off down the hall. I didn't have to tell her I liked mine black. She never forgot.

As Glen moved around his desk to his seat, I took one of the comfortable leather chairs facing him.

"So," he said, "let's have a look."

I leaned forward to slide the envelope across the desk.

"We went over most of it on the phone," I said as he opened the envelope, took out the several sheets of paper and read through them quickly, nodding from time to time. When he'd finished he set them aside and was just about to say something when Donna rapped on the door and came in with our coffee, setting the cups on the desk in easy reach.

"Thank you, Donna," Glen said, and I echoed.

She smiled and left the room.

"I hadn't realized," he began when the door closed behind her, "until I read today's paper that Art Manners was R.D. Manners's son. I've known the family for years, though I never got to know Art. He was always a rebel and a source of constant embarrassment to his family...particularly to his father, who was never hesitant to let his disappointment show. Finally, from what I understand, Art just totally divorced himself from the family. He didn't have to worry about money, of course—he had a very large trust fund.

"So that he might have been considering backing Reardon in buying the city's largest gay leather bar doesn't surprise me in the least. It would be one more way for Art to take a swipe at his father. That he and Reardon might have had something more going for them does, too, sort of. I don't know, maybe a psychiatrist would make some sort of father-son thing out of it."

He took a long sip of his coffee before saying, "All of which is very interesting but not necessarily relevant to the case against Jake. Finding a match for the prints is. People don't steal high-powered hunting rifles unless they plan to use them, so whoever stole Jake's gun most likely is Hysong's killer. If nothing else, identifying the prints creates a very strong case for reasonable doubt. St. John is so desperate for publicity he's letting his common sense get away from him. He has the typical homophobic mindset in thinking that because both Jake and Hysong are—were, in Hysong's case—gay, a jury won't be overly concerned with the facts.

"I know the jury selection process is going to be fun. St. John will want to stack the panel with people he senses share his own views. He's putting more emphasis on the 'sin of homosexuality' than on the fact this is first and foremost a murder case. That's a big mistake, and he'll pay for it. But I'm still hoping we won't have to go to trial at all."

"Well," I said, "I'm pretty sure that if they get a match on the prints, the police will be willing to step in and pursue it and that will hopefully take the pressure off Jake and lead to the real killer."

There was a soft rap at the door and Donna came in.

"Sorry to interrupt," she said, "but Mr. McPhearson is on the phone and insists he has to talk to you."

Glen sighed, set his coffee down and said, "Okay. Tell him I'll be right with him."

I took that as my cue to gulp down the last of my coffee and set the cup and saucer on the desk. I got up, saying, "I'll let you get back to work, and I'll call you the minute I hear from Marty Gresham."

I reached across the desk to shake hands, turned and left as Glen picked up his phone.

MARTY CALLED FIRST THING WEDNESDAY MORNING, CATCHING ME IN THE MIDDLE OF A crossword puzzle: "Beginning of quote…"

I hate those things.

"We have a match on your prints," he said.

"Great!" I replied. "Whose are they?"

"Art Manning. Isn't he the guy run over by the truck during the AIDS ride? If so, questioning him is sort of moot."

"Shit!" He was right, of course, and though chances were ninety-nine-to-one that since Manning had stolen the gun he'd used it, now we'd never know for sure. He had more than ample motive in the death of his apparently only real friend and in the humiliation of having Hysong mop the floor with him in a fight.

I didn't really know how much stock to put in the domino-effect idea that

Hysong's death would somehow help Reardon ruin the Male Call's business, which would lead to Brewer selling it to Reardon, who then would make Art manager. Hell, if he wanted to go to all that trouble to manage the place, why wouldn't he have just bought it himself? His willingness to finance Reardon indicated a lot more than Art's wanting to manage a bar.

I pulled myself back to the moment.

"Well, thanks for everything, Marty. What's the next step from your point? There's really not too much the police can do now that Manners is dead."

"We can and will provide the information to the DA's office. I hope that might help your friend. And while I can't call Jake's lawyer and volunteer the information, if he were to contact the department and ask for the results of any fingerprint testing..."

"Gotcha," I said, "and I wouldn't be surprised if he just might do that. Frankly, I don't think St. John will pay much attention to it—he's got his sights set on convicting Jake."

"Well, good luck," he said.

"And thanks again, Marty," I said. "You're going to make captain before you reach thirty-five!"

He laughed. "From your mouth to God's ear," he said.

I CALLED GLEN'S OFFICE, ASKING DONNA TO HAVE HIM CALL ME AS SOON AS HE COULD. When I hung up, I debated on finishing off the coffee left in the pot, which had the color and consistency of crankcase oil, or making a new pot, or going downstairs for a cup from the diner in the lobby, or...

Get with it, Hardesty, a mind-voice scolded, and I realized I was experiencing one of my "slamming door" moments when something ends far more abruptly than I'd anticipated. Another anticlimactic moment. I hate anticlimaxes.

The case was over—or at least out of my hands—now, and Jake's fate was totally up to Glen O'Banyon. Art Manners had stolen Jake's rifle and used it to kill Cal Hysong, and now Manners was dead himself and that was it. You can't try a dead man for murder, or have whatever closure or wrap-up value a court trial may have produced. Anticlimactic. Have I mentioned I hate anticlimaxes?

Usually, when I sense that a case is coming to a logical conclusion in a reasonable period of time, my mind is able to shift gears at its own pace. This was sort of like slamming on the brakes of a stick-shift car without first engaging the clutch.

Glen called just as I was chewing on the last bit of coffee in the cup—I'd gone with the what-was-left-in-the-pot option and resented it, though it didn't stop me.

I quickly gave him the information, for which he thanked me, and when I asked if there were anything else I could do, he said, "Well, this puts a lot of new spin into the case, and I'm not exactly sure what tack I'll take with it, so consider yourself still employed until I let you know otherwise, okay?"

"Fine with me," I said.

And so we left it.

THE NEXT WEEK WAS PRETTY QUIET, AND I WAS ABLE TO DO A FEW QUICK RESEARCH JOBS FOR another of my lawyer clients, involving trips to the Hall of Records and the library—nothing he couldn't have hired someone from a temp agency to do, but I was glad he didn't. On Wednesday of the next week, Glen called.

"I think you should have a talk with Pete Reardon," he said. "I'd like to know a little more about his relationship with Art and if he had any idea that Art had been seriously planning to kill Hysong. Whether he mentioned Jake's guns, for example. You might also ask him about their financial arrangement and what Art wanted in exchange for the loan. He may tell you to go take a flying you-know, but it's worth a try. I might decide to put him on the stand if it comes to trial, and it looks like that's where it's headed."

"St. John was unimpressed by the fingerprint evidence, I take it?"

"You take it right. He's apparently going to claim the prints on the window indicate Art opened the window, but not when he did it or that he actually took anything. To him, the only prints that matter are Jake's on the gun."

"But it's Jake's gun, fer chrissake!" I said. "What does he expect?"

"For him, it's not the fact that Jake's prints are on it so much as that nobody else's are."

"Good Lord! The man's never heard of gloves or picking something up with a cloth?"

"Apparently not. But don't underestimate St. John. As I told you, he's got an uncanny talent for skewing facts to his advantage."

"Well, I'll go talk to Reardon and see what I can find. I can't make it tonight—I've got Joshua duty while Jonathan's at school. But I'll do it tomorrow sure, and let you know what he has to say."

I debated, after hanging up, whether I should try to contact Reardon by phone first or just show up at the Spike and hope he'd talk to me. I had no idea if he knew Art probably killed Hysong and if he didn't…well, I was most curious as to what his reaction might be. I decided that, whatever it was, I'd like to see it firsthand.

It was already close to quitting time and I was pretty sure the Spike didn't open until five, but I dialed the number just to be sure. No answer. Okay— later, from home. I also wanted to find out what time Reardon got there.

JONATHAN LEFT FOR CLASS AT HIS USUAL TIME, AND JOSHUA AND I DID THE DISHES, AFTER which he wandered off to his room and I went to the phone to call the Spike.

"Spike," a very butch voice announced on picking up the receiver.

"Two questions," I said. "What time do you open tomorrow and what time does Pete usually get in?"

"We open at four, and Pete usually comes in around five," he said. "He's here now. You want to talk to him?"

"No, that's okay, I'll catch him tomorrow. Thanks." And I hung up.

When Jonathan got home I explained there was an outside chance I might be a little late getting home Thursday and why.

"I should be back in plenty of time before dinner, but if I'm not you go ahead and start without me," I said. "If I'm late I can warm something up."

"We'll wait," he replied.

"Uh, are you sure? I don't want to come home and find Joshua on the verge of starvation."

Jonathan grinned. "We'll wait," he repeated. "If he passes out, I'll just wave a cookie under his nose and that'll bring him to."

I ARRIVED AT THE SPIKE AT FIVE-FIFTEEN THURSDAY AFTERNOON. THREE CUSTOMERS AND A bartender—not Val, who I thought worked days. This guy was only in his late twenties, so I knew it couldn't be Reardon. I took a seat at the far end of the bar and ordered a beer.

"Val off today?" I asked.

"Val's not here anymore," the bartender said.

Ah, the peripatetic life of a bartender.

"Is Pete Reardon here?" I asked as he brought the beer. No glass offered, of course, not that I would have wanted one if it was.

"Yeah. He's in the office. You want to see him?"

"If I could," I said, taking out a bill and handing it to him. He took the bill and reached under the bar for a phone and apparently pressed a button.

"Guy here wants to see you," he said then put the phone back under the bar and moved off to the cash register.

As I waited, I looked around, noticing that Pete's '56 Harley gleamed under the spotlights, though it was facing in the other direction from the last time I saw it. I noticed, too, that it was now almost touching the wall.

I glanced at the bartender just in time to see him looking over my shoulder and indicating me with a nod of his head. I turned to find Pete Reardon towering over me.

"What can I do for you?" he asked.

"I was wondering if we could talk for a few minutes about Art Manners."

I saw a quick facial twitch.

"What about him?" he asked. "And who are you?"

"Sorry," I said, remembering I hadn't introduced myself. "My name's Dick Hardesty and I'm investigating Cal Hysong's death. Did you know Manners stole the gun that killed Hysong?"

He scowled, and his eyes darted around the room as if he feared we could be easily overheard, which I sincerely doubted.

"Let's go into my office," he said, turning abruptly and heading for a door beside the platform on which his motorcycle sat.

I picked up my beer and followed him.

When we got into his office, which was a surprisingly large storeroom, he pointed to a chair and said "Sit" as he pulled another chair out from the desk and turned it around to face me.

"So, Art did what, now?"

"He stole the gun that killed Cal Hysong," I repeated.

"How do you know that?"

"The police found his fingerprints."

"On the gun?"

"No, on Jake's window ledge, which pins Art to stealing the gun, and they figure whoever stole it used it."

Reardon shook his head slowly in a wide arc.

"That stupid son-of-a-bitch!" he said. I wasn't quite sure how he meant that.

"You didn't know anything about it?" I asked.

"He hated Hysong's guts. I knew that."

Was it just me, or did I hear the sound of tapdancing?

"Do you think he could have killed him?"

He looked at me as though the thought had never occurred to him. I wasn't convinced.

"Shit, that sonofabitch was crazy enough to do anything."

Well, that was an interesting response, I thought.

"He could have?" I echoed. "Do you have any reason to suspect he *might* have?"

He stared at me for a minute before answering.

"Look," he said, "I don't feel right talking about Art—him being dead and all…"

"I understand you and Manners were close."

He shrugged. "Neither one of us was exactly the 'close' type, but we got along pretty good. So what?"

"I've heard you're trying to buy the Male Call and that Manners was going to back you financially."

"I've been thinkin' of buyin' the Male Call for a long time, yeah. Brewer's run the place into the ground, but it's got a lot of potential for somebody who hasn't got his head as far up his ass as Brewer does. When Art heard I was thinkin' about it, he offered to help with the financing. Not that I couldn't handle it on my own, but both places need a lot of work and a little extra money would come in handy."

"That was pretty generous of him," I said. "And what did Art want in return?"

"He didn't want anything. Like I said, we were friends and Art had more money than he knew what to do with. But we talked about him maybe managing the Spike while I ran the Male Call."

Interesting, I thought. From what I'd heard, Manners wanted to run the Male Call, which was the bigger bar by far. And I was more than a little skeptical of Reardon's claim he had enough money to buy Brewer out on his own.

"You really need two leather bars?" I asked.

He looked at me as if I were slightly daft. "Why not? This town's been supporting two leather bars for years. Always competing with each other. Why split the profits when you can have them all? Nothin' wrong with a monopoly. I can tell you this—if I don't take over the Male Call, it's gonna fold. Nobody else's willing to touch the place with those AIDS rumors and Cal's death hangin' over it. Who's he going to get to buy it? The shape it's in now? I know the leather scene better'n anybody in town, including Brewer. No, anybody else who tried would fall flat on his face."

"So, why not let the Male Call fold? Then the Spike'd be the only game in town."

"Spike's not big enough," he said. "And guys like to be able to move around—as long as they got more than one place to go, they're happy. They don't give a shit who owns them. And I could save a bundle on volume discounts from the suppliers if I was buyin' for two bars. Split Specials nights between 'em, different events, different nights, no makin' it difficult to choose which bar to go to on which night. That way, neither place gets shortchanged. No, it'll work out great."

Though I didn't say anything, I couldn't quite see how he thought he could overcome the stigma of the AIDS rumors and Hysong's death. Plus, he'd be bringing with him his own stigma of the Dog Collar fire, which he'd never fully overcome.

I realized we'd gotten off my main line of questioning. Reardon obviously knew more than he was saying, and I wanted to find out what it was.

"So, bottom line," I said, "do you think Art killed Hysong?"

He took in a long, deep breath and let it out slowly before nodding.

"Like I say, Art could be pretty crazy sometimes. I remember more than a couple of times him sayin' he wanted to see Cal dead." After another pause, he continued. "I remember, too, that right after he went to a meeting at Jake Jacobson's place to talk about what could be done to stop Cal from spreading AIDS, he was telling me about Jake's collection of rifles. Art said he was thinkin' about borrowing one to go shoot a rat."

Hmmm, I thought. But I was getting tired of the bobbing and weaving.

"So, *do* you think Art killed Hysong?"

Another long, deep sigh, then another head-nod. "I know he did."

"And you know this how?"

"He told me."

Surprise, surprise!

"He told you?" I asked. "When?"

"A couple of days before the ride," he said. "Art had been acting really strange, really depressed. He was always moody, but I'd never seen him so down."

"Did you ask him why?"

He shook his head. "I figured he'd tell me if he wanted me to know."

"But why didn't you tell the police when you found out he'd killed Hysong?"

"I don't rat on my friends," he said simply.

"Well, that's noble of you, but what about Jake? He's going to be tried for a murder he didn't commit."

Reardon shrugged. "If they know Art stole the gun and have his prints, that should let Jake off the hook. And now that Art's dead, if the trial does go on and it looks bad for Jake, I'll step in with what I know."

"So, why not go to the police now and save everyone a hell of a lot of time and effort?"

"Because I don't want to get into trouble for not coming forward the minute I knew Art did it. But don't worry—like I said, if it starts looking like Jake'll be convicted, I'll come forward. But not until then. I've got too much to lose."

And in the meantime, Jake goes through hell and the city spends tons of the taxpayer's money, I thought. Jeezus, what did this guy use for brains? I knew that arguing with him wasn't going to get me anywhere.

The intercom light on his desk phone came on followed by an angry bee-on-steroids buzzing. He picked it up.

"Yeah? Okay, I'll take it." Putting his hand over the mouthpiece he said, "I've got to take this one," and I quickly got up from my chair.

"That's fine," I said. "I think we were about done anyway. Thanks for your time."

We did a fast handshake, and I let myself out.

Actually, I wasn't done: I just needed some time to step back and think some things over.

As I walked through the bar I paused to look at some of the photos on the wall surrounding the platform with Reardon's bike, noting again that the bike was facing in the opposite direction from usual. No big deal, of course, but it's new position meant it had to have been backed up the ramp rather than pushed up. It struck me that it would have been easier to guide it up the ramp from the front end than from the back, but I wasn't exactly an expert on manipulating motorcycles up and down ramps.

I then got distracted looking at the photos. Reardon and his bike were in probably a quarter of them, and in two of them he and his bike were side by side with a guy I recognized as Art Manners on a powerful-looking bright-yellow Harley—I didn't know Harley made yellow bikes and suspected Manners must have customized it, as the elaborate detailing also indicated.

Must be nice to have money, I thought.

FIRST THING FRIDAY MORNING, I CALLED GLEN'S OFFICE, ASKING DONNA TO HAVE HIM CALL me. I'd been thinking about my conversation with Reardon since I left his office, and now, sitting behind my desk drinking coffee, more thoughts, like gas bubbles in a tar pit, kept rising to the surface of my mind.

Could it be that Reardon wasn't quite as dumb as I'd thought while we talked? Everything could have been perfectly on the up and up, of course, but my gut—upon which I relied probably far more than I should—told me something wasn't quite right.

Friendship is friendship, but money is money. To hear Reardon tell it, Art volunteered to lend him the money—which, of course, might be true. But why would Manners have told Don Gleason he'd be managing the Male Call, while Reardon claimed he'd offered to have Art manage the Spike. If, as I suspected, Reardon couldn't have afforded to buy the Male Call on his own, that would mean Manners was probably going to put in most of the money, which in turn would have put him into the driver's seat in deciding which bar he was going to manage.

Yet again, to hear Reardon talk, it sounded as though he was still planning to buy Brewer out. While he hadn't said anything about there being a formal business arrangement between him and Manners, I wondered if they had one; I'd imagine a partnership would have been the most logical way to go. And if there was a legal agreement between them, I wondered if it contained any contingency for death of one partner.

While I could in a way understand Reardon's reluctance to turn in his friend after he learned that Art had killed Hysong, it struck me as odd that he hadn't come forward right after Manners died to get Jake off the hook—especially since he didn't seem particularly reluctant to tell a perfect stranger—me—that Manners had confessed to killing Hysong.

Well, I guess different people have different priorities. Nevertheless, and for whatever reason he might have had to tell me that Art killed Cal, the fact was that now he had told me, Glen had to know. It might be the key to stopping Jake's trial even before it started.

I rummaged around until I found Reardon's home number and dialed it. I knew I might be waking him up, but it was a chance I had to take.

I heard the phone being picked up, followed by "Hello?"

"Mr. Reardon, Dick Hardesty. Sorry to bother you again, but I should have asked you when we talked yesterday—would you be willing to tell Jake Jacobson's attorney what Art told you about having killed Hysong?"

"Why should I?"

"You said you'd come forward at trial if you had to, but we might be able to stop this whole thing before it ever gets that far. And if you don't, Jake may go to prison for a crime you know he didn't commit. I appreciate your loyalty to Art," I said, "but the fact is he's dead now. He can't be prosecuted for Hysong's murder. I can't imagine you'd want to see Jake tried for it."

"No, of course not." He paused, then said, "But you're asking a hell of a lot."

"I know that," I said. "But Art doesn't need your protection now. Jake does."

"Let me think about it."

"That's all I ask."

He hung up without saying goodbye, and I replaced the receiver on the cradle, my lips pursed.

I really wanted to call Jake and Jared right away to let them know that Reardon had confirmed Art Manning had killed Hysong, but Glen had specifically asked me to channel anything I found out about the case through him. Hard as it was to resist the temptation to let Jake and Jared know immediately, I understood.

I knew Glen could and would subpoena Reardon for the trial even if he couldn't get him as a voluntary witness for the defense. And I knew that even if he did cooperate, St. John would claim his testimony was hearsay and probably try to get it ruled as inadmissible. Shit! What did I know about how lawyers and DAs did their jobs? I shouldn't even have been speculating.

And why did I keep getting a mental picture of Reardon pushing his motorcycle backwards up the ramp? It must have been a bitch maneuvering the rear tire. Lowering it down the ramp rear tire first would be infinitely easier, I'd think.

And what the hell did that have to do with anything?

I knew that, whatever Reardon's decision, for me the bottom line was the case was solved. Art Manners had killed Cal Hysong. Jake was, as I'd known from the beginning, innocent. It was up to Glen to convince either the DA or a jury of that fact. I'd do whatever else I could to help, but I largely saw my job as done.

I did, but something in the back of my mind didn't.

I was glad I decided to eat lunch at my desk—I'd called down to the diner in the lobby to order a chili cheeseburger, two cartons of milk and salad, and when I ran down to pick it up I left my phone off the hook. I did that sometimes to avoid having someone leave a message when I knew I'd be right back.

I was just wiping a glob of chili off the edge of my desk when Glen called at twelve-thirty. I quickly sketched in what I'd learned from Reardon, and he asked if I could type up a detailed report of exactly what had been said and drop it by his office on my way home. Since he was on a lunch break from court, we didn't have much time for anything else.

I spent the next hour or so typing up as much of my conversation with Reardon as I could remember, including some of the questions it had engendered, then decided that rather than waiting until the end of the day, I'd take it over to Glen's office in case he might return early.

THE WEEKEND CAME AND WENT QUICKLY, AS WEEKENDS ARE WONT TO DO. THOUGH WE hadn't seen the gang in a while, we managed to talk with everyone at one point or another. All was well with Tim and Phil and Mario and Bob and we made the usual promises to get together soon. However, with Jake and Jared the casualness of the call was not quite the same.

I always find it fascinating to consider the little dances we all do to protect those we care about. I was, as always, particularly concerned about Jake and how all the stress he and Jared were under might affect his health. I didn't discuss this with Jonathan because I didn't want to upset him, which I knew it would. I didn't directly ask either Jake or Jared—I was sure they'd tell me if I did, but I didn't want to intrude upon what was a very private part of their lives.

So, aside from the obligatory "How are things?"-type questions, I had to rely on what information they might volunteer. From everything I could gather, Jake was doing very well. He was, Jared had told me, under the careful watch of his brother Stan and had been put on a regimen of medications that changed from time to time as new information on AIDS became known.

Again I took comfort in the fact that Jake had access to the very forefront of the fight against the disease, which was still bloating the obituary columns of the newspapers.

No matter how hard I tried to keep my mind off it and to tell myself my part of it was largely over, I kept going back to everything that had happened since Manners was killed. Something just wasn't right, and of course, I hadn't a clue as to what that something might be. It had to do with Reardon, though. I wished to hell I knew more about the details of their relationship. Just how much of a relationship was it, and on what levels? I doubted it would fit with my conceptions of a romantic one—I found it hard to picture the two of them sitting on a sofa in front of the TV holding hands—but I long ago learned that every person sees the world through his own eyes.

I found myself wondering again about their financial arrangements. Had they ever been finalized? Carl Brewer told me Reardon had made what he called a "half-assed" offer, but I didn't know if that had been before or after Art's money had entered the picture. I somehow suspected it was before. With Art's money, Reardon could have made a more solid bid—and I wondered if he might have, subsequently. I made a mental note to check with Brewer on Monday.

The fact Reardon was still talking about buying the Male Call even with Art now dead made me really curious about the current state of Reardon's finances, and I made another mental note to see if there were some way Glen could check into them.

If I weren't still working for Glen, I quite probably would have wanted to talk directly to Marty and Lieutenant Richman to see if the police might be able to step in on the basis of the information I'd been able to gather. But this was Glen's show, and I trusted him to know when to do what as far as bringing the police in.

Even while we were spending time with Joshua at the park on Sunday afternoon, my mind kept flitting from thought to thought. There was something Don Gleason had said about the relationship between Manners and Reardon. What was it? Not about their being fuck-buddies, but…

Damn! Probably wasn't important anyway, but I hate not being able to remember things, and I particularly hated wasting my time worrying about things that were now out of my hands.

I WANTED TO TALK TO BREWER BEFORE CALLING GLEN ON MONDAY BUT HELD OFF UNTIL I was pretty sure he'd be up. When I finally did call, around ten-forty-five, the phone was answered on the first ring.

"Brewer."

"Yeah, Mr. Brewer, this is Dick Hardesty. I've got a couple of questions for you."

"I guess that means you haven't caught the guy who killed Cal, then?"

I wasn't about to go into the details of Manners's culpability, so I merely said, "Afraid not, but we're getting there."

"So, what do you need from me?" he asked.

"I was wondering if you've had any more offers on the bar?"

"As a matter of fact, yeah. I got a pretty good offer from a guy and I almost took it until I found out he was a front for Pete Reardon, so I turned it down."

"How long ago was that?" I asked.

"Last week."

"After Manners was killed?"

"Yeah, I guess so. What's that got to do with it?"

Well, it was a pretty good clue that Manners's and Reardon's financial arrangement had gone through. The question now was exactly what the arrangement was, in that it apparently had not terminated with Manners's death.

"Nothing, really," I said, pulling myself back to reality. "I just was surprised Reardon would make an offer so soon after Manners's death, since I'd heard they were really close. Any idea how Reardon got the money to come up with the new offer?"

"Not a clue. Probably just blowing smoke out his ass as always. But you never know what he might have up his sleeve."

Like Manners's money? I wondered.

"Do you think Manners might have been behind the offer, somehow?"

"Well, I've got my suspicions," he said.

"Oh? Like what, if I can ask?"

"I wouldn't be surprised if Manners hadn't been shoring up Reardon financially for quite a while. It's pretty clear to me Reardon held the hoop and Manners jumped through it."

"Master/slave, you mean?" I asked. That had never occurred to me.

"No, I don't think it went that far, but I think Manners would do just about whatever Reardon told him to."

Like kill Cal Hysong? The thought came totally out of the blue and actually startled me. And I realized that's what I'd been trying to remember about what Gleason had said—that Manners would do anything for Reardon.

"Like I think I told you," Brewer continued, unaware of my thought processes, "I always suspected the only reason Manners came to the Male Call was to keep an eye on things for Reardon."

"Interesting," I said, and meant it.

I was curious about the most recent offer he'd received and why he'd turned it down, so I asked. Again, I wouldn't have been surprised if he'd refused to answer—it wasn't any of my business, really, but that never stopped me from asking a question.

"The offer came from a guy whose name I recognized from the Dog Collar days as being one of Reardon's cronies. I might have taken it if I hadn't realized what was going on."

"But aren't you obligated to take an offer if it meets your asking price?"

"If I was going through a realtor, yes, which is why I'm doing it myself. You can always come down on a deal, but you can't go up. By doing it myself, I've got control over who gets it. It's a hassle, but I'm deadly serious when I say it's not going to Reardon. I'll lock up the place and walk away first."

We wrapped up the conversation a minute or two later. I didn't even set the receiver back on the cradle before dialing Glen's office.

Transferred to Donna, I asked if she could have Glen call me as soon as was convenient.

"He'll be calling in momentarily," she said pleasantly—Donna is never anything but pleasant, "and I'll give him the message. Are you in your office?"

"Yes," I said. "I'll be here for awhile and will wait to hear from him."

Not five minutes later the phone rang.

"Hardesty Investigations."

"Dick, Glen. Are you free for lunch?"

"I can be, sure," I said. "Etheridge's?"

"No," he replied, "I'm taking a deposition near the Imperator. You want to meet me there at our usual time?"

"Sure," I said, glancing at my watch. I could just make it.

"Okay. See you there," and he hung up.

The Imperator? That place was way out of my league. I'd had dinner there once a long time ago—about the time of the Dog Collar fire and, as a matter of fact, while I was working on a case that involved it. Fantastic food, but at those prices it should be. Actually, I remembered, I had no idea what it cost—the menus had no prices and the tab went directly to the host, who fortunately wasn't me. But it's like Andrew Carnagie or some rich guy once said: "If you have to ask the price, you can't afford it."

Luckily, I kept a sport jacket and tie neatly folded in the bottom drawer of a file cabinet for just such contingencies. I hadn't had occasion to use them in a long time but was glad they were there.

XXIII

THE IMPERATOR WAS JUST AS I REMEMBERED IT—THE VERY DEFINITION OF THE WORD *elegance.* Lots of heavy, rich paneling—probably mahogany—ornately carved moldings, soft lighting, large potted plants, original art you knew didn't come from a Starving Artists' sale, thick burgundy carpets with a quiet blue pattern of some sort that muffled any sounds in the large room. I took a glance around looking for Glen; not seeing him, I stepped to the maitre d's podium.

"I'm meeting Mr. O'Banyon," I said—I had no doubt he'd know who I meant, "but assume he's not here yet?"

The maitre d', impeccably dressed, impeccably groomed and impeccably well-mannered, smiled and said, "Mr. O'Banyon is expected any moment. Let me show you to his table." He then led me to a corner of the room near the large windows looking out over a manicured courtyard.

"Your waiter will be here momentarily," he said, smiling, and turned to go back to his podium, where two crisply business-suited men awaited his attention.

I wondered briefly what there was about the very rich that their clothes never seemed to wrinkle.

A white-coated waiter appeared to ask if I would like a cocktail, and I told him I would wait. Smiling, he poured water into a stemmed goblet, carefully and expertly tonged a sliced wedge of lemon onto the rim and left.

As I waited I looked around the room a bit more closely. I'd realized after my first visit that the restaurant that had gotten its name and many of its decorative features from the old pre-WWI German ocean liner *Imperator,* which was confiscated by the British after the war and renamed the *Berengaria.* That fact accounted for the large marble bust of Kaiser Wilhelm at the entrance and the elegant glass domed ceiling, which had come from the

199

ship's banquet hall.

Glen arrived as I was closely following the movements of a busboy who was definitely not part of the original ship's crew.

Apparently having noticed where my attention was focused, Glen grinned as he sat down.

"Admiring the scenery?" he asked.

I grinned sheepishly. "Very much," I said.

"Well, the Imperator does provide the best in everything."

"Obviously," I agreed. "So, what's the occasion? The Imperator is a step or two above our usual meeting spots."

"No occasion, really. It's just that we all deserve a little self-indulgence from time to time. And since I was nearby…"

"Well, I certainly appreciate being included in this one," I said.

The waiter appeared with menus and to ask if we'd like a drink before lunch. When Glen said he'd like a vodka gimlet, I decided to step away from my usual Manhattan or Old Fashioned and try a martini, which I'd not had in I couldn't remember how long. I wasn't all that wild about martinis, but I liked the olives.

"You don't have to get back to your deposition?" I asked, and Glen shook his head, picking up the menu.

"Finished it. So, I thought I'd make it a double indulgence—lunch at the Imperator plus no rush to get back to the office. Glad you could join me. I can assuage my guilt by the fact we're talking about a case.

"I read your report over the weekend, and I've already arranged for Pete Reardon to come in so I can to depose him on Manners's confession. I guess I've got you to thank for convincing him to come forward. But I gather something else is new?"

"Well, I really don't know if this directly bears on the case, but I think it's important to let you know about it."

I then outlined my conversation with Carl Brewer, pausing only when the waiter brought our drinks. I was delighted to see two enormous cannonball olives skewered on the toothpick in my martini. I immediately ate one, putting the other, and the toothpick, on my bread plate.

"There's something about this whole buying-Brewer-out business that bothers me. The fact that Brewer said he'd been approached with an offer from somebody he thought was fronting for Reardon tells me that Manners's offer of financial support had gone further than just being an offer. If Reardon was, indeed, behind the latest offer on the Male Call, that means he had to have the money to have made it, and the only way he could have gotten it was through Manners. I'd like to know how that came about."

Glen looked at me and shrugged. "Interesting point, but I don't know how we could easily find out. I could subpoena Reardon's financial records, but I'd have to have some more solid basis for doing it than just curiosity."

I knew he was right, and I also wasn't quite sure what we could do with the information if we had it, or what it might mean.

We finished our drinks, and the waiter magically appeared to ask if we'd like another. We opted to order instead and did, both of us choosing the Veal Oscar and Glen urged me to try a small bowl of their world-famous—if the Imperator claimed it was world-famous, I believed them—Sweet Potato Bisque. More food than I needed, but how often did I get to eat at the Imperator?

"Well, it sounds like things are starting to look up for Jake," I said.

He gave me a small smile. "That depends on just how far off the deep end St. John happens to be. It makes no sense for him to insist on pursuing the case, but with the elections coming up, he probably feels he needs all the grandstanding he can get. He's skating on thin ice and he knows it, but I won't be surprised if his intention is to continue milking it until the election and drop it as soon as it's over. I just don't appreciate his continuing to put Jake through all this."

Our lunch arrived, and the conversation switched to more general and less stressful subjects. But even as we relaxed and concentrated on the food, something paced impatiently back and forth in the back of my mind like the sound of footsteps in the attic, but it was so nebulous at the moment I didn't want to bring it up.

BITS AND PIECES. THE MONEY. THE RELATIONSHIP. MANNERS'S MOTIVE FOR KILLING Hysong. The Male Call. The accident that killed Manners. That damned motorcycle. I kept worrying them like a dog with a bone all the way back to the office and was, as so often happens, more than a little pissed at myself for not being able to immediately see the connection, if there was one.

I found myself concentrating on Manners's motive for the killing. He had lost a friend—from what I'd heard he didn't have many—to AIDS and blamed Hysong for it. So had a lot of other guys. The humiliation of Hysong's having beaten him in a fight probably festered for someone who considered himself as butch as Manners did. He claimed he had never had sex with Hysong himself, but I wondered.

I made a mental note to call Tim after dinner, to see if he might be able to look at the coroner's records to see if, just by chance, Manners showed any signs of AIDS, which might indicate that not only had he had sex with Hysong at some point but that he believed Hysong had given it to him. That would strengthen his motive.

Once I started off on that path my mind began weaving a scenario made totally of speculation. Reardon had said Manners had been severely depressed before the ride. If Manners did have AIDS, when did he learn about it? And—reaching way out into left field—if he found out about it just before the ride, was there the possibility the accident that killed him had not been an accident but suicide?

Stretching, Hardesty, a mind voice said. *Really stretching.*

It was right, of course, but I suddenly wanted to take a look at the police report on the accident. I picked up the phone and dialed the City Annex, asking to speak to Detective Gresham. I was a little surprised to hear his voice when the phone was picked up.

"Detective Gresham."

"Marty, hi. It's Dick. Can I ask yet another favor of you?"

"Like what?" he asked.

"Can you get me a copy of the police report on Art Manners's death?"

There was only a slight pause before: "Yeah, I can do that. Any reason?"

"Just a hunch," I said.

"Okay. No problem. I'll leave it at the desk for you within the hour."

"Thanks, Marty," I said.

I LEFT WORK A LITTLE EARLY TO SWING BY THE CITY ANNEX TO PICK UP THE REPORT AND read it while walking back to my car in the Warman Park underground garage.

The semi driver reported he was rounding a curve in heavy rain when he saw two motorcycles coming toward him, fast. The one behind looked like it was trying to catch up to the first one and had pulled up almost beside it when they passed the semi's cab. The driver felt the impact of the wheels passing over the cycle and driver and came to an immediate halt, calling for help on his CB radio.

A nearby squad car was there within three minutes and an ambulance and another squad arrived fifteen minutes later. The report of the driver of the second motorcycle (Reardon) claimed he had still been some distance behind Manners when Manners's bike suddenly swerved and slid beneath the semi. Nothing was noted about the apparent discrepancy between the accounts of how close the two bikes had been, but given the traumatic circumstances of the accident and the different perspectives of Reardon and the driver, I didn't make too much of it.

Well, I'm not sure exactly what I was looking for, but whatever it was, I didn't find it. Still, the "sudden swerve" might have been due not to road conditions but to a deliberate act on Manners's part.

Still, if I were going to kill myself, I think I'd look for a way that didn't involve an eighteen-wheel semi truck.

Yeah, my mind countered, *but he was a biker doing what he loved to do. Maybe it wasn't such a bad choice. And obviously it was quick, if not painless.*

I CALLED TIM AFTER DINNER TO ASK IF HE COULD CHECK ON WHETHER MANNERS MIGHT have had AIDS. I was right in assuming Tim hadn't been involved in the examination of Manners's body, since the accident had happened on a Sunday, when he was off.

One of the things I most admired about Tim—and all my friends, now that I think of it—is that he never asked why I wanted to know whatever it was I asked of him. He just said he'd get back to me and we moved on to other subjects. He and Phil were planning an informal dinner gathering of the gang at their place the Friday before Jake's trial as a way of showing our collective support and maybe taking Jake and Jared's minds off the pressure for a few hours. I thought it was a great idea and accepted immediately.

When he heard me mention Tim's name, Joshua—who, I learned at length at dinner, had inexplicably been given some sort of good conduct award at daycare (I suspected either everyone else had gotten one, too, or he had somehow rigged the awards process)—insisted on sharing the information with Uncle Tim, after which Jonathan also got on the line for a few minutes.

STORY TIME CAME AND WENT—JOSHUA REQUESTED A RETELLING OF YET ANOTHER OF HIS many favorites, "The Ugly Duckling," and Jonathan did the honors—and after my watching a little TV while Jonathan studied for his horticulture class, we went to bed and at Jonathan's suggestion played a pleasantly exhausting game of "Tarzan and the Shipwrecked Sailor." I have no idea where he comes up with the titles for these games, but it sure was fun.

Normally, I'd be out like a light within four minutes, but instead I found myself wide awake, staring at the ceiling.

Manners had killed Hysong. Okay, I could accept that, especially if it turned out he had gotten AIDS from Hysong, which at the moment was purely speculation. The case was solved. So, why couldn't I just wrap the whole thing up and move on?

There doesn't have to be a link between everything, a mind-voice counseled wisely. All this other stuff about Reardon and the money and the Male Call didn't all have to be part of the same puzzle. Why was I trying to insist they were?

And then I was on a motorcycle in the rain and Joshua had just come home with a Nobel Prize and I was asleep.

TIM CALLED ME AT THE OFFICE DURING HIS COFFEE BREAK TUESDAY AFTERNOON TO LET ME know he'd checked Manners's autopsy results—though there was little doubt as to the cause of death—to report there was no evidence of AIDS, though he added the coroner's office did not yet have the facilities for doing AIDS blood tests. They'd known Hysong had it because of the lesions on his body; Manners had no such indications. Which, while it did not mean he did not have the virus, probably meant that if he did it hadn't yet manifested itself and Manners would not have been aware of it.

After hanging up, I could almost hear an ignition switch being turned in my head and my mental motor revving up.

So, why was Manners so depressed before the ride? There could have been any number of reasons, of course, but it was Reardon's mentioning it that had triggered my speculating that Manners might have found he had AIDS and killed himself. That theory was pretty much shot full of holes now.

But why would Reardon lead me to believe Manners was depressed if he wasn't? To plant exactly the seed that was planted about suicide? Was Reardon that smart? And why would he do it?

One of the biggest problems with being a private investigator, as I have said before, is that I find myself questioning everything—doubting everyone's word, looking for the cracks in every wall. And sometimes, reading things between the lines that simply weren't there. I've really never understood my mind, or how it works the way it does, or why it and my gut often know things I don't. I'd been hired to prove that Jake was innocent of killing Cal Hysong. I'd done that. Point A to Point B. What the hell was I doing roaming around F, P and X? The whole Male Call/Reardon/Manners thing was only peripheral to the fact that Art Manners had killed Cal Hysong and Jake was, indeed, innocent.

But I still sat at my desk, my mind idly rummaging through a large pile of guesses and pieces of information that had for some reason clung to me like static-charged lint. I'd gone over them all before, of course, but they were still there—the relationship between Reardon and Manners; their financial arrangement, if there had been one and if it had survived beyond Manners's death, which I suspected it had, since Brewer had gotten an offer on the Male Call after Manners had died. It was, of course, possible the money had come from somewhere else—maybe from the crony who made the offer.

Convoluted sentence, convoluted thoughts.

If the offer had come from someone fronting for Reardon, though, there were two possible explanations. One, Reardon knew Brewer would never take an offer he made directly, and two, Reardon was for some reason trying to cover up the fact that he might have had access to Manners's money. The first was the most logical, the second more typical of my line of thinking.

And there was that damned motorcycle again. Why had it been backed up the ramp? Maybe because there was something wrong with the side now closest to the wall? There was only one way to know—go back to the Spike and look.

But I had to do it in some way not to call Reardon's attention to what I was doing. Best to go at night, when there'd be enough other people around for me not to call attention to myself. It would still be tricky, though, since the front of the bike was facing the ramp, which would make it hard to get close to. It was also now close enough to the wall—another difference from the first time I'd seen it—to make it difficult to see the entire length of the bike between it and the wall, and another indication maybe there was something on that side Reardon didn't want seen. But what? And why?

SINCE IT WAS A TUESDAY—JONATHAN'S NIGHT FOR CHORUS PRACTICE—I DECIDED TO TAKE a quick run to the Spike when he got home. I was getting ready to change into an old pair of jeans and a white T-shirt and boots, which I hoped would be close enough to the bar's uniform of the day to keep me from standing out, when the phone rang. I didn't make it into the living room before Joshua had a chance to pick it up.

"Hello?...This is Joshua. Who are you?"

I'd reached him by that time, and he handed me the phone.

"Hello?" I said.

"Dick, it's Glen. I just wanted to let you know I'm deposing Pete Reardon tomorrow at my office at three-thirty. I was a little surprised at how willing he was to cooperate but am glad he is. I just wanted to let you know."

"I appreciate that, Glen," I said, and I did. He was under no obligation to let me know what was going on. It was me who was working for him, after all, not the other way around.

"Well, I know you have a stake in how this all progresses," he said. "If the deposition goes as I hope, I'll have it on St. John's desk before he leaves work tomorrow night. I don't hold out much hope it will convince him to drop the charge against Jake, but it will sure shoot another large hole in his case, which already has more holes than a chunk of Swiss cheese. All we can do is try."

I thanked him again, and we hung up.

If Reardon was being deposed at three-thirty, that meant if I got to the Spike when it opened at four Reardon would probably still be at Glen's. I doubted the bartender would remember me, and he wouldn't have much of a reason to say anything to Reardon even if he did.

Joshua and I played a game of "cards," then I got him ready for bed and Story Time. When he complained he'd read all his books and insisted on my telling him a story, I promised him the three of us would go make a weekend trip to the library and get him his very own library card—it would be in my name or Jonathan's, but as long as Joshua thought of it as being his...—so we could begin reading our way through the children's section. Joshua, of course, thought it was a great idea and wanted us to go the next day. I told him I'd think about it.

XXIV

A T FOUR WEDNESDAY AFTERNOON I PULLED UP IN FRONT OF THE SPIKE. I'D TAKEN THE jeans, boots and T-shirt I hadn't worn the night before to work and changed there. It wasn't that I wore anything fancy to work, but this outfit was a little *too* casual for the office.

There were three guys in the bar, plus the bartender, whom I fortunately didn't recognize: It seemed the Spike had as high a bartender turnover rate as the Male Call. I ordered a beer and then wandered over to the platform with Reardon's bike on it. He'd obviously cleaned it up since the ride; I could see myself in the fender. He'd even cleaned the tires. It looked as though it had just come off the dealer's showroom floor.

Pretending to look at the pictures, I went first to the back of the platform, where I was able to get close to the wall. I tried as casually as I could to look down the length of the bike. Everything appeared perfect. What the hell did I think I was looking for, anyway?

I then strolled casually around the platform, taking an occasional swig of beer. The ramp was the same width as the platform and extended probably five feet in front of it. In order for me to get close enough for a good look down the side of the bike from the front, I'd have to really lean forward and support myself with my arms. That might have looked a bit peculiar if anyone was watching, which I hoped they weren't. Awkward.

I got as close to the wall as I could at the base of the ramp and, again on the pretext of looking at the photos, tried to look down the front side of the bike. Nothing...or wait! It looked like there *was* something—the fender about a foot back from the very front edge. What the hell was it? Just...something— a definite irregularity on the almost liquid shine of the surface. Sort of like a ripple on a smooth pond.

I had to look closer. Glancing toward the bar to make sure no one was watching me, I took three steps up the ramp to where I could see better. It was definitely a dent maybe four inches long and two wide, where the paint looked just slightly different from the rest of the fender.

"Hey, buddy, no one's allowed up there," the bartender called.

I quickly stepped back. "Sorry," I said. "I was just admiring the bike. A real beauty."

He just nodded and went back to whatever he was doing. I returned to the bar and sat down to finish my beer.

The jumbled pile of unrelated facts and suspicions my mind had been accumulating began to sort themselves out without much conscious effort on my part, forming into a plausible scenario. The key was the relationship between Manners and Reardon. Both Carl Brewer and Don Gleason had told me Manners would do anything Reardon wanted. Obviously, what Reardon wanted was the Male Call. I had no doubt Manners might have acted as Reardon's eyes on what went on at the Male Call—Reardon was eager to spot any chink in Carl Brewer's armor, which the AIDS rumors and Cal Hysong provided.

Now came the really murky part of the picture. Might Reardon have gotten Manners to steal Jake's gun? Maybe even have used it *himself* to kill Hysong? Or had Manners acted completely independently? He definitely had ample motives that didn't involve Reardon.

But regardless of whether he or Reardon had killed Hysong, Manners himself was dead, now and the picture from this point suddenly became much clearer. That Reardon had made an offer for the Male Call through a surrogate—and I had no doubt that's what he'd done—meant he had somehow gotten the money from Manners before Manners's death. Money has motivated more than one murder. I had no idea how it had happened, but the idea that Manners would expect something in return was logical. And if Reardon didn't want to give it to him...

EVEN BEFORE I CHANGED BACK INTO MY REGULAR CLOTHES AT THE OFFICE, I CALLED THE City Annex and asked to speak to Detective Gresham. Once again I was in luck.

"Detective Gresham."

"Marty, it's Dick. Quick question—where would I find a motorcycle involved in a fatal accident?"

"Depends on where the accident took place," he said, then paused. "Are you talking about that AIDS ride accident?"

"Yes. I know it wasn't within the city limits, but I gather it was somewhere around the county line."

"Well, as I recall, it was on this side of the county line and the sheriff's office has an impound lot here in town. What's up?"

I quickly outlined my suspicions.

"Interesting," he said.

"Could you arrange for me to get in there and look at Manners's bike?"

"Well," he said, "if you're right, it'll be a police matter, so I wouldn't have any problem in getting in, but they might not let you in alone. I'd be willing to go with you, if you'd like."

"That'd be great!" I said. "When would be good for you?"

"Let me give them a call," he said, "and I'll get right back to you."

HE CALLED BACK WITHIN TEN MINUTES, GIVING ME THE ADDRESS OF THE SHERIFF'S impound lot and telling me he and Detective Couch would meet me there in an hour. Fast worker, that Marty, and much appreciated.

The lot was in a fairly new industrial park on the far east side, surrounded by a concrete block wall unbroken except for a small window and glass door next to a sliding metal gate. Parking was no problem, and since I was, as usual, early, I got out of the car and stood by the gate until an unmarked police car pulled up. I don't know who they think they're fooling by not marking them—I can usually spot them a mile away.

I joined them for handshakes as they got out of the car, and we walked to the office. A deputy behind a small metal desk looked up as Marty pressed a buzzer beside the door and, in turn, pressed a button somewhere just out of sight on the desk, letting us in. Marty made the brief introductions, and the deputy got up from his desk. He'd obviously been expecting us, since he said, "I'll show you where it is," and led us outside through a rear door.

The lot was relatively small, unlike the vast salvage yard to which the city sent wrecks from within its jurisdiction. There were maybe only a dozen or so vehicles in various stages of demolition—a couple of them were nearly unrecognizable as motor vehicles. At the end of the line was a twisted blob of yellow metal from which a pair of bent handlebars rose above a tire that looked like a Salvador Dali watch.

Pointing toward it, the deputy said, "If you need anything, holler," and turned back for the office.

The bike lay on its right side, which was the side I wanted to see. It took all three of us to lift the wreck, which still smelled of gasoline. It wouldn't stand on its own, so we lowered it back to the ground. I knelt to inspect the badly crumpled fender.

"There it is," I said, pointing to a deep fold in the metal. "It" was a three-inch scrape of bright blue.

Detective Couch leaned over for a closer look and nodded.

"I'll go get the camera," Marty said.

XXV

A ND THAT WAS IT.
Well, not really, of course, but for all intents and purposes, my part in the case was over. It was all in the hands of the police from that point on.

The blue paint on the right front fender of Manners's yellow bike came from the left front fender of Pete Reardon's when, the police speculated and on which I'd have bet a bundle, Reardon had deliberately swerved into Manners as the semi passed, sending him under the wheels and to his death. That the semi driver had seen Reardon moving up fast behind Manners as he passed was a pretty good indication Reardon had seen an opportunity and gone with it.

Reardon denied everything, of course, but the case the police were able to build against him was pretty ironclad. The fact he had tried to cover up the damage to his bike himself—tools and a small can of manufacturer's touch-up paint found in his garage verified that point—by pounding out the dent and repainting it and then replacing the bike on the platform—albeit facing in the wrong direction—was obviously to prevent anyone from noticing the damage.

In the confusion and emotion of the immediate aftermath of the accident, it was very unlikely anyone would have noticed it. Reardon was probably waiting until enough time had passed before taking it for a professional repair, or more likely, to replace the entire fender. The fact he had endangered his prize possession was an indication of how much he had wanted to get Manners out of the way.

That one of his reasons might have been because it was actually Reardon rather than Manners who had killed Hysong—Manners merely having stolen the gun at Reardon's request—remained an unprovable possibility, and no one but he would ever know the truth.

A look at Reardon's financial records revealed there had, indeed, been a partnership contract drawn up between him and Manners shortly after Hysong's death, with a clause giving everything to the survivor in case of one partner's death. I found it a little hard to imagine Manners could have been so gullible, but then I wasn't him, and still didn't know how deep the relationship between the two men went.

So, if Reardon had actually killed Hysong, getting rid of Manners would have prevented the possibility of his ever telling anyone else. Perhaps the fact Reardon agreed to have Manners as a full partner might have been an another indication Manners had something on him.

Unfortunately, with the elections rapidly approaching and the District Attorney slipping in the polls, he refused to drop the case against Jake rather than admit he was obviously trying to convict the wrong man. He obstinately held that Manners's supposed confession to Reardon was tainted by the fact Reardon was now accused of Manners's murder.

Jake's trial began the week of the election. Victor St. John was ousted from the DA's office and the new DA, at Glen O'Banyon's insistence, dropped all charges against Jake, who managed to come through all the stress in good spirits and with no further health problems, for which all his friends breathed a deep sigh of relief.

STORY TIME OVER, JOSHUA SAFELY ASLEEP AND JONATHAN AND I IN BED, I ONCE AGAIN speculated on how life is so not like a movie or a TV show. No white-knuckle car chases or sudden, adrenalin-filled exchanges of gunfire; no wrestling someone on a tightrope over a crocodile-filled moat, or long drum roll ending in a crash of cymbals and timpani. Just another case solved, another bad guy getting what he deserved. I could live with that.

END

ABOUT THE AUTHOR

DORIEN GREY started out as a pen name, nothing more, for a lifelong book and magazine editor who wanted to write his own novels as a bridge between the gay and straight communities. However, because he was living in a remote and time-warped area of the upper Midwest where gays still feel it necessary to keep a very low profile, he did not feel comfortable using his own name—a sad commentary on our society, he admits.

But as his first book, a detective novel, led to the second and then the third, he found Dorien slowly became much more than a pseudonym, evolving into an alter ego.

"It's reached the point," he says, "where all I have to do is sit down at the computer and let Dorien tell the story."

As for the Dorien's "real person," he's had a not-uninteresting life. Two years into college, he left to join the Naval Aviation Cadet program—he washed out and spent the rest of his brief military career on an aircraft carrier in the Mediterranean. The journal he kept of his time in the military, in the form of letters home, honed his writing skills and provided him with a wealth of experiences to draw from in his future writing.

Returning to college after service, he graduated with a BA in English and embarked on a series of jobs that led him into the editing field. While working for a Los Angeles publishing house, he was instrumental in establishing a division exclusively for the publication of gay paperbacks and magazines, of which he became editor. He moved on to edit a leading LA-based international gay men's magazine.

Tiring of earthquakes, brush fires, mudslides and riots, he returned to the Midwest, where Dorien emerged, full-blown, like Athena from the head of Zeus.

He—and Dorien, of course—recently moved to Chicago, and now devote their energies to writing. After having completed ten books in the popular Dick Hardesty Mystery series, and now Calico, a Western historical romantic suspense, they are currently working on a new mystery with a new protagonist, which may have the potential to become a series.

"Too early to tell," Dorien says. "But stay tuned."

But for a greater insight into the real person behind Dorien Grey, the curious are invited to read *The Poems of Dorien Grey*, an ebook available from GLB Publishers.

ABOUT THE ARTIST

MARTINE JARDIN has been an artist since she was very small. Her mother guarantees she was born holding a pencil, which for a while, as a toddler, she nicknamed "Zessie"

She won several art competitions with her drawings as a child, ventured into charcoal, watercolors and oils later in life and about 12 years ago started creating digital art.

Since then, she's created hundreds of book covers for Zumaya Publications and eXtasy Books, among others. She welcomes visitors to her website at www.martinejardin.com.

Printed in the United States
83284LV00004B/256-303/A